THE EXTRAORDINARY

DISAPPOINTMENTS OF

☐ MONO
☐ STEREO
☐ NR

☐ SP
☐ LP
☐ EP

LEOPOLD

BERRY

SUNDERWORLD V-01

□ MONO	THE EXTRAORDINARY	□ SP
□ STEREO	DISAPPOINTMENTS OF	□ LP
□ NR		□ EP

LEOPOLD
BERRY

RANSOM RIGGS

DUTTON BOOKS

DUTTON BOOKS
An imprint of Penguin Random House LLC,
1745 Broadway, New York, New York 10019

First published in the United States of America by Dutton Books,
an imprint of Penguin Random House LLC, 2024

Visit us online at PenguinRandomHouse.com.

Library of Congress Cataloging-in-Publication Data is available.

ISBN 9780593530931
1st Printing

Printed in the United States of America

LSCC

Design by Anna Booth
Text set in Minion Pro

For Tahereh

☐ MONO **THE EXTRAORDINARY** ☐ SP
☐ STEREO ☐ LP
☐ NR **DISAPPOINTMENTS OF** ☐ EP

LEOPOLD
BERRY

GOOD FOR ONE RIDE · GOOD FOR ONE RIDE · GOOD FOR ONE RIDE

Leopold Berry had been trying to ignore the raccoon in the tree out the window, but like so many things in his life, it seemed impossible. The raccoon was perched on a branch that aligned perfectly with the head of the man Leopold was supposed to be listening to—a man who'd just asked Leopold a question he hadn't really heard. It almost seemed like the raccoon was trying to distract him on purpose. Twice the creature had nearly fallen out of the tree, only to drag itself back onto the branch after a lot of clawing and flailing. Just now, its tail had burst into flames.

The natural thing to do, Leopold realized, would've been to direct the attention of his father and the interviewer to the animal-on-fire as explanation for why he'd been so distracted these past minutes. He couldn't, of course, because the raccoon's tail was not really on fire. The raccoon was not really there at all.

These things happened to Leopold sometimes.

When he was twelve, a therapist told him he had a hyperactive imagination—that he saw strange and impossible things at the moments he most wanted to escape from his life. He'd once been plagued by these dissociative episodes, but it had been years since the last one. Then, a week ago, Leopold had seen a single, small rain cloud trail a harried fruit vendor down a sidewalk in Hollywood.

The week before that, through the windshield of his traffic-stalled car, he'd watched a man pry a tooth from his mouth and insert it into a parking meter, prompting a fissure to open in the pavement. With a furtive glance behind him, the man had climbed into the cavity, disappearing just before it closed over his head. But these episodes had been brief, and each time Leopold had assured himself it was nothing to worry about. Who didn't occasionally fantasize while stuck in traffic?

But now the raccoon.

This episode had lasted longer than either the tooth man or the fruit vendor, which was disconcerting and, at the moment, extraordinarily inconvenient. He desperately wished the raccoon that was not really there anyway would just disappear.

Then, with a peevish flick of its flaming tail, it did.

The meeting had not been going well even prior to the raccoon. Leopold wasn't purposely trying to frustrate his interviewer, an avuncular older man in golf clothes who had started off smiling but now looked like he, too, wished he were somewhere else. Nor was he hoping to piss off Richter, his tall, barrel-chested father, who was growing quietly apoplectic in the chair beside Leopold. He really was doing his best, if only to appease Richter, but he couldn't focus. The gray suit Leopold had been forced to wear was loose in some places and tight in others. He was certain his pale skin had flushed bright red. He'd forgotten most of the canned responses his father had encouraged him to memorize, and the ones he did remember came out sounding forced. And now he'd allowed six seconds of excruciating silence to elapse as he stared out the window at a nonexistent raccoon.

Leopold directed his eyes back to the man behind the desk.

"Sorry, what was the question again?"

There was a creak of stiff leather as Leopold's father dug his fingers into the arms of his chair. "Larry's just tired," he said through peroxide-white teeth. "Poor kid was so excited about this meeting, he hardly slept last night."

Larry was a nickname Leopold had acquired in childhood and had never been able to shake. *Larry Berry*: It sounded like a punchline. The only person ever to call him by his given name, Leopold, had been his mother, and because it rang foreign on anyone else's tongue, he'd long ago resigned himself to Larry, a name that made him cringe whenever it was spoken aloud.

The man glanced at his watch. An electric guitar, signed by the members of some famous band, was displayed proudly on the wall. "No need to be nervous, Larry. We're just having a friendly conversation." He grinned in a way that was designed to put Leopold at ease. "I asked, what's your greatest strength? What do you feel you're best at?"

Leopold cleared his throat. He could feel his father's eyes drilling into him.

"Well, um, I guess . . ."

He tried to conjure one of the answers he'd rehearsed, something about leadership and problem-solving.

". . . I don't really know?"

"If you ask me, Mick," his father cut in, "Larry's problem is he has too many strengths. Makes it tough to decide where to focus his energy. Berry family curse!" He laughed like a sputtering engine.

The man chuckled politely. "Then I'll make this easier. How about you give me your top three."

Leopold's mind went blank. He saw something flick among the branches of the tree out the window but forced himself to ignore it. His palms began to itch.

"Larry," his father hissed. "No need to be modest."

3

"I'm not." Leopold shifted in his seat. "I'm just . . . not the best at anything."

His father made a strangled noise.

"Now, I'm sure that's not true," said the interviewer.

But it felt true. It was the truest-feeling thing Leopold had said aloud in a long time. What he excelled at were minor things his father thought categorically worthless: working on his old car, tinkering with small electrical objects, and making homemade movies set in the world of a certain fantasy TV show that had gone off the air before he was born. He was ashamed of these forgettable skills, so he never mentioned them.

The man winked. "Don't worry. I'm good at finding hidden talents."

"I certainly hope so," Larry's father muttered.

In Richter Berry's opinion, there were two types of people in the world: winners and losers. He'd argued as much in his first book, *Think Like a Winner*, the publication of which he'd parlayed into a career as a success coach, a profession that suited him perfectly because it involved, mainly, yelling at people. So long as he did it with a smile, a shocking number of seemingly well-adjusted people would submit to being berated, harangued, and belittled by Richter Berry in the name of self-improvement. Whole auditoriums of them, all paying for the privilege.

Richter was very proud of himself, and of his two stepsons, Hal and Drake. Hal, captain of his high school wrestling team, and Drake, going into his second year at USC's business school, were turning out to be killers in the barrel-chested mold of their stepfather. But Richter was worried—had been worried for years—that his biological son, a lean, dreamy, distractible boy with no discernible talent for, or interest in, anything practical at all, was growing up to become . . . *not* a winner.

But Richter was no quitter.

He couldn't abide a failure in the family; it simply didn't fit the brand. He'd given his son several perfectly good options for a future career: Larry could go to law school and become a lawyer (preferably corporate); go to business school and get on the executive track (Fortune 500, or what was the point); do a finance program that would lead to private equity or investment banking (Goldman, ideally, though the boy was hopeless with numbers, so that seemed the least likely of the three). All Larry had to do was choose one, and like magic he'd have the inestimable blessing of his father's support. Richter, self-made son of a pig farmer from a hardscrabble town in the Midwest, would've killed for such an opportunity at seventeen. But the boy was like a cat: strange, lazy, and nearly impossible to train. His mother had been far too easy on him, so now, to compensate, Richter had to be hard; Larry had made it abundantly clear that he would never be hard on himself, that if given half the chance he'd spend the rest of his life with his head in the clouds and accomplish absolutely nothing. So when, after innumerable lectures and tirades, Larry had still not chosen one path over another, Richter had engaged the (very expensive) services of the best private college admissions counselor in Los Angeles, a man who had miracled C students with no legacy credentials into Harvard, and felonious delinquents from nothing families into Stanford. It was amazing he'd even found the time to slot them in for a meeting. And now, probably just to spite him, his son was flushing a golden opportunity down the toilet.

"What about the aptitude test?" Richter asked.

The interviewer's bulletproof smile faltered. "Wasn't too helpful, I'm afraid."

The raccoon was back on its branch, one leg extended skyward, earnestly licking its privates.

"Larry's results were a bit . . . inconclusive. His grades don't reveal any special aptitude for one path over another, though that's not especially uncommon. As for the test, Larry scored the perfect average on every metric." He almost looked impressed. "Never seen that before."

"You mean to say," Leopold's father huffed, "he's perfectly average."

The counselor hesitated. "I think results like this reveal the limitations of testing, not of your son. Which is exactly why we bring potential clients in for these little heart-to-hearts." The word *potential* seemed to hang in the air. "I can help you, Larry. But first you have to be honest with me."

Stop calling me Larry, Leopold thought.

The counselor steepled his fingers beneath his chin. "Let's forget colleges and careers altogether for a minute. Here's the most important question: What do you love? What's your passion?"

Leopold's instinct was to give a canned answer, but there was an attentiveness in the man's eyes that caught him off guard. He actually seemed to be listening. Leopold couldn't remember the last time an adult had done that. And so he was compelled to do something he almost never did in front of his father: tell something like the truth.

"Well, I think I might be good at editing movies," Leopold ventured. He hadn't quite found the courage to say *directing* movies, and editing sounded like a more achievable but still respectable career prospect.

The man leaned forward, head bobbing.

"I was wondering, maybe, about . . . film school."

His father wafted a hand through the air. "Four year jerk-off."

"Actually, this could be perfect," said the counselor. "This, I can work with."

Leopold felt a small hope spark in his chest. Like maybe his whole life was about to change, and a door was opening he'd never known was there. And then the man said, "You should consider entertainment law. Some of the best-paid lawyers I know work for movie studios," and as he began to describe the impressive house in Malibu owned by one such lawyer, a ringing filled Leopold's head, and he saw something out the window he could no longer ignore: The raccoon, now fully engulfed in flames and leaping from branch to branch, had caught the tree on fire. As the blaze spread quickly through the canopy, a flock of small birds, also on fire, shuddered out of the leaves and scattered into the air.

Leopold went rigid, suppressing a sudden urge to panic. Not because the tree was on fire—he knew it wasn't—but because there was no denying it now.

It's happening again, he thought.

He was Seeing into Sunder.

TWO

"Drugs. He actually asked me if you were on drugs."

That was all Richter Berry said to his son during the long march back to the parking structure, after which he fell into a boiling silence broken only by the sound of his angry breathing, a labored whistle that issued from his nose as he stared vacantly ahead, trying to calm down enough to start yelling.

Richter was silent during the interminable elevator ride down into the parking structure's muggy bowels. Silent during the whole drunken elephant ballet that was getting out of the congested garage—a procedure made more difficult by the awkward length of Leopold's ancient Volvo station wagon and its lack of parking sensors, backup cameras, or any other modern conveniences. Silent as Leopold struggled to click his frayed seat belt into place. That Richter hadn't even made a comment about the Volvo, a family embarrassment which he consented to ride in only when his Porsche was in the shop—as it was today—meant he was well and truly about to explode.

They reached the pay booth without incident, only to discover that three seventy-five was owed even though Leopold had gotten their parking stub validated, that the garage only accepted cash, and that aside from an old movie ticket stub and his driver's license,

Leopold's wallet was empty. He knew better than to ask his father for the money, or he'd get the You're Never Prepared lecture on top of whatever tirade was already in store for him. In a panic, he ran his hands through the cup holder, the side-door pocket, and the never-used ashtray, which netted him a grand total of three fifty, still a quarter short. As a car honked somewhere in the line forming behind them, Leopold apologized to the old lady attending the booth, unbuckled his safety belt, and jammed his arm down into the crack of the cloth seat. That earned him a cut on his finger, a smear of belt actuator lubricant on his wrist, and two sticky dimes. He gathered the coins and wadded bills and held them out in cupped hands.

Accepting them with a lugubrious sigh, the attendant began to tally the change. She was of young grandma age, just elderly enough that Leopold wondered what had gone wrong in her life that she had to work a job like this, forced to make change all day in the lightless belly of a Beverly Hills office building. She wore a rumpled green vest with the words *Underground Parking Corp* stitched above a name badge that read *Rochelle*.

Another horn bellowed in the rumbling gloom. Sweat trickled down Leopold's collar. Rochelle finished her leisurely count and looked up at him, expressionless. "You owe me a nickel."

"I know. I'm really sorry. That's all I have." Leopold prayed she would just shrug and wave him through, but she only stared.

Leopold tried again. "Could I come back with it later?"

Richter sighed, leaned roughly across Leopold, and thrust a hundred-dollar bill at the woman. This meant the You're Never Prepared lecture was now unavoidable. The attendant pursed her lips and pointed to a sign that read NO BILLS OVER $20. Richter Berry retracted his hand with imperial slowness before folding the money carefully into his crocodile-leather wallet. He preferred cash and never carried anything smaller than a hundred, on principle. A principle covered in chapter four of *Think Like a Winner*.

"You have five days to pay via mail," the attendant monotoned, "or your debt will be turned over to a collections agency. I'll give you the address."

Even in the dark, Leopold could sense his father turning purple.

The attendant swiveled on her stool to grab a slip of paper, and that was when it came to Leopold's attention that she had a pair of wings sprouting through the back of her vest. They were dull gray, about the size of a backpack, and lay folded against her shoulder blades, the feathers a bit rumpled from long hours of sitting.

Leopold sat blinking, his face going tingly.

He seemed to lose a bit of time: One moment he was staring at the wings and wondering how she'd gotten her clothes on over them, and the next he was jolted by another car horn, the attendant having swiveled back to face him. She gave him a strange look while waving the slip of paper in his direction.

He reached out to take it, his eyes fixed on her vest. He was sure the words stitched above her name badge had changed. With the addition of a single letter, they now read SUNDERGROUND PARKING CORP.

He whispered the word aloud, his lips forming it involuntarily. *Sunder.*

The woman snatched his outstretched wrist. Her hand was icy, and the strength in her arthritic fingers was unbelievable, like talons digging into his skin. She leaned toward him and whispered in a voice that was low and raspy and slightly threatening:

"It ain't polite to stare."

The ghost of a smile touched her lips, then vanished just as quickly.

She let him go. He reeled back into his seat. The barrier arm swung upward as another car blasted its horn.

"Drive!" Richter snapped, looking up from something he'd been typing on his phone. "What's wrong with you?"

Leopold eased the car forward, watching the woman's reflection shrink in his mirror until sunlight blasted the windshield, erasing her. As Richter wondered aloud whether his son might really be on drugs, Leopold waited for a break in traffic, gripping the wheel tightly so his father wouldn't see his hands shaking.

THREE

Mercifully, Richter hadn't seemed to notice Leopold's bizarre interaction with the parking garage attendant, nor had he seen the wings—because, of course, they hadn't been there.

Leopold knew from experience that his episodes tended to cluster in threes. The raccoon had been the first; what happened in the garage, the second. Given what usually triggered them—and how badly he wanted to be anywhere other than trapped in the car with his father in steadily thickening traffic—it seemed reasonable to expect that a third would be along anytime now.

He couldn't let it happen.

Not while he was behind the wheel of a moving car, especially with Richter riding shotgun. Telling his dad what was happening to him was not an option, so Leopold focused on the road ahead and pretended Richter wasn't there, nodding occasionally to simulate listening. Maybe this way he would make it home without seeing any more flame-engulfed fauna or parking-garage angels. Maybe this way he wouldn't blank out for thirty seconds and crash the car.

"Damn it, Larry, I said take Fountain!"

Richter's sudden bellow pulled Leopold from his reverie and back into La Cienega Boulevard's rightmost lane, where he'd just missed a crucial turn. This sparked the Always Take Fountain speech, which he endured with little nods and apologies.

He'd learned early in life that there was no arguing with his dad. That would only prolong the lecture and raise its emotional temperature a few notches on the Richter Scale. You just had to endure, and eventually he'd wear himself out. The lectures could be cool-tempered speeches or angry tirades, but they always fell into one of a few categories, so predictable Leopold had given them names. After they'd left the garage and become enmeshed in traffic, Richter had launched into an impassioned delivery of I've Never Been So Embarrassed in My Life, an old favorite. He then veered into You've Got No Ambition, downshifted into Aren't You Ashamed of Yourself, and pirouetted with virtuosic flair into a weirdly self-pitying version of It's My Fault for Spoiling You—all interspersed with highlights from Larry's a Shitty Driver, a classic Leopold could've recited from memory.

At a red light he felt the Volvo stutter and threaten to stall. He shifted into neutral and feathered the gas so it wouldn't die in the middle of the road, which would almost certainly trigger a high-volume rendition of I Should Sell This Shitheap for Scrap—which, of all his father's lectures, was the one Leopold hated most.

The Volvo—Bessie—was Leopold's dearest possession. She was egg-yolk yellow and speckled with rust and had belonged to his mother. Richter regularly threatened to get rid of it because it was unreliable and ugly and didn't fit the Berry brand. That he never followed through on his threats seemed a rare proof of kindness in his father, as well as a quiet admission that he, too, missed Leopold's mom, though they never spoke about it. It was also, Leopold assumed, the only reason Richter allowed the Volvo to remain in their driveway.

Leopold glanced at the trip odometer.

7,261 miles.

It hadn't been zeroed since she died. Leopold couldn't bring himself to hit the button, because he marked her death with miles rather than years. Five and a half years ago sounded infinite, an unbridgeable vastness. Somehow, 7,261 miles ago felt closer. That was just a long plane trip.

Sometimes Leopold rode his bike or took the bus because he couldn't bear to watch the number creep any higher. Sometimes, when he could no longer stand being in his father's house but had nowhere else to go, he'd slip out and sit in the car for hours, just reading or listening to music. When things got really unbearable, he'd sneak out at night and sleep in the back seat.

Green light.

He shifted into first and the Volvo jerked into motion. At some point the lecture had morphed into a recounting of Leopold's recent failures, Richter totting them up on his fingers. *Cut from the baseball team. Rejected from that internship. Only summer job you could find was in some lousy coffee shop. And now this—*

The steady drumbeat of *loser, loser, loser* threatened to suffocate him.

He willed himself to think of nothing. Instead, watching the odometer tick over another mile, Leopold thought of his mother—and then of Sunder.

One often begat the other.

FOUR

Shortly after his twelfth birthday, in the unseasonable heat of a Los Angeles December, Leopold's mother had died. It was cancer, rare and aggressive and swift. Before it took her, Monica Berry had insisted on celebrating her son's birthday despite the circumstances, and in the grim period following her death, he was haunted by the image of a forgotten balloon slowly deflating in the corner of her hospital room.

That summer, in the gloom of a sunless June, the episodes had begun.

He came to think of them as Seeing into Sunder.

Sunder was a fictional realm from a 1990s fantasy TV series called *Max's Adventures in Sunderworld*, which had aired, and gone off the air, over a decade before Leopold was born. It was in the blurry weeks after his mother's burial, amidst the hectic move from their bungalow in Venice to Richter's house in Brentwood, that he'd found the seven VHS tapes of its one and only season in a cardboard box bound for the trash. He'd never seen the tapes before and had never heard of the show; he assumed it was one of the many projects his mother had worked on during a youthful stint as a film and TV assistant.

He rescued the tapes and a battered old VCR. It was a few weeks before he bothered figuring out how to hook the VCR up to a TV, and another few before, late at night in his cold new room in Richter's house, he got around to popping in the first tape.

He engaged with only mild interest at first, because *Sunderworld* was kind of campy and cheap-looking: wooden acting, flimsy sets, cinematography that sometimes wasn't even in focus. It followed the adventures of a seemingly unremarkable boy named Max who meets a talking, half-mechanical coyote in the desiccated field behind his apartment complex. The coyote, harried and short on details, gives Max an ornate key before vanishing in a puff of flame. Max locates the corresponding door beneath a freeway overpass, discovers a pleasantly cliché-ridden magical society hidden in the nooks and crannies of Los Angeles, then further discovers he's not only a spark—as the magically inclined citizens of Sunder are known—but a once-in-a-generation channeler, gifted with great power and tasked with protecting Sunder against Noxum, monstrous invaders from the Ninth Realm. Max learns to wield an Aether focuser and spends the rest of the season kicking Noxum ass up and down the streets of Sunder in ways that were highly creative—and surprisingly gory—for what was ostensibly a kids' show.

Leopold was aware of *Sunderworld*'s surface-level crappiness even at age twelve, and yet there was something about the show and its weird LA fantasy world that captured his heart.

It wasn't long before he was properly obsessed.

He watched *Sunderworld* so many times his ancient VCR started eating the tapes, unwinding them into tangled black nests that could be extracted from the machine only with chopsticks and surgical precision. Having committed every episode to memory and hungry for more of what was clearly an unfinished story, Leopold set out to make new episodes himself. He wrote scripts longhand on legal pads, assembled costumes and props from thrift store junk, and recruited neighborhood kids as actors. He cast his best friend, Emmet Worthington, as Max, and in rec rooms and backyards across LA they spun out the continuing adventures of Max and his magical companions. They spent weekends shooting and long nights creating mangle-faced monsters that spouted fountains of corn syrup blood. They never finished a single episode, but it didn't matter. Through the bleakest time he had ever known, Leopold was happy only when immersed in Sunder.

"Forget Fountain," his father said with a rough sigh. "Take Sunset instead. I need to check on the new billboard."

Leopold, who'd been trying to circle back to Fountain via a series of painful left-hand turns, felt a loosening in his chest as he signaled and made a comparatively easy right. The emotional temperature in the car began to drop. His father's publisher had taken out an actual, physical, in-person ad to promote his latest book, *Only Losers Don't Win*, and the prospect of seeing his own face, fifty feet wide and glowering across Sunset Boulevard, seemed to improve Richter's mood almost instantly.

Leopold merged carefully into the six-lane circus that was Sunset at rush hour. Now all he had to do was pilot them home without Seeing into Sunder again.

The first time it happened, over that long-ago summer following his mother's death, Leopold had been scouting locations for a shoot near the Tar Pits. It was down an alley between Gardner and Detroit, ringed by overflowing dumpsters, that he'd seen a pair of rust fiends feasting on a pile of old computers. They'd looked up, keyboards impaled on their blunt tusks, and spat a volley of steaming green bile in Leopold's direction.

Terrified, he'd fled straight home.

Leopold assumed it had been some kind of waking dream. Then, a week later, it happened again. He'd been in Hollywood with Emmet and a couple of other friends, waiting on the sidewalk for Emmet's mom to pick them up after a matinee at the El Capitan. The paladin woman was unmistakable in her long leather coat and boots, a heavy glass Aether focuser dangling from a holster on her belt. She could've been another Hollywood impersonator trolling for tips, except that *Sunderworld* was completely unknown outside his small circle of friends—and because her head had been engulfed by a bright blue glow.

No one else had even noticed her.

By the time Leopold had collected his wits and followed her into the laundromat next door, she was gone. But this time he wasn't terrified.

Leopold was elated.

In the show, Max had also seen things that didn't seem to align with reality. They were pre-coyote peeks into Sunder—before he got his key—designed to prepare Max's mind for what would otherwise be an unalloyed trauma. Naturally, Leopold came to believe his episodes were preparing him for his own adventures, and that soon he'd be meeting a half-mechanical harbinger of his own, getting his own key, finding his own door. He'd felt more certain of this than about anything since his mother died.

Still, Leopold told no one, not even Emmet.

He marked the date on his calendar: Keys were usually granted at the summer solstice. But when the solstice of his twelfth year came and went without a visit from a key-bearing coyote, Leopold was crestfallen. With the rug pulled, the enormity of his mother's death threatened to crush him. His father, rather than help Leopold mourn the woman from whom he'd been acrimoniously divorced, shuffled Leopold off to a series of grief counselors. The boy sank into a dark place and drifted away from most of his friends.

When another year came and went without a key, Leopold began to wonder if it was because he'd moved away from the house where he'd lived for so long with his mom, and some Sunderian functionary had simply failed to inform the coyote of Leopold's forwarding address. So he spent the solstice day of his fourteenth year camped out on the sidewalk in front of their old house in Venice, where strangers now lived.

No key was delivered.

He'd gotten badly sunburned from sitting outside for hours, but no coyote had come.

And so at fourteen he'd finally stopped hoping, stopped believing, stopped seeing sparks and magical creatures. With the help of a therapist, Leopold realized he'd been seeing those things only because he'd needed the fantasy to move through the darkest depths of his grief.

In that way, Sunder had saved him, even though it was just a crappy old TV show. He was grateful for that, at least.

He'd thrown away his props and buried the tapes in a closet. These days, Sunder rarely crossed his mind. Unloved and obscure, *Sunderworld* had never been released on DVD or Blu-ray; no one had even bothered uploading it to YouTube. It had been three years since he'd seen so much as a snippet of it. Three years since he'd Seen into Sunder, too, though he didn't think of his episodes that way anymore.

Now there'd been two in a day.

And then Richter exploded, and there was another.

FIVE

It was the billboard that set him off. Perched on the hill above Carney's—on the north side of the street across from the Sunset Tower hotel—it loomed into view and sent Richter into an instant rage.

The printers had misspelled the name of his website.

Leopold's adrenaline spiked as his father ranted about suing the printer, demanding that his son look, *look* at the incompetence he was forced to deal with—

Leopold glanced at the billboard for only a moment, then returned his eyes to the road to discover a red blur filling the better part of the windshield. Some kind of streetcar was crossing in front of them, careening through the intersection—and they were about to slam straight into it.

Leopold shouted and hit the brakes.

Their seat belts locked as a tide of trash from the back seat broke over them, the Volvo fishtailing while cars swerved and honked. The unhinged screaming began even before they'd come to a full stop.

"Are you trying to kill us?! What the hell is wrong with you?"

"We were going to hit that—that red trolley thing—"

"What trolley? What are you talking about? Are you out of your goddamn mind?"

Leopold looked again.

There was no streetcar climbing the hill to their left. No trolley tracks in the pavement.

"I should take away your license!" Richer plucked a crumpled hamburger wrapper from his lap and flung it at his son. "This shitheap is getting scrapped first thing tomorrow. And this time I mean it."

His father got out, slammed the door, and flipped off his own giant face. Then he started speed-walking down Sunset, leaving Leopold to sort out the mess on his own.

Leopold's hands were shaking and itching. He tried to start the Volvo. It had stalled, of course, and now it refused to start again.

He screamed in pure blind rage, then slammed his hands against the wheel as hard as he could—and a Roman candle's worth of bright red sparks came flaring out of them, blinding him briefly while filling the car with amber-hued smoke. It was several seconds before it dissipated, leaving ghostly whorls of whitish vapor curling in the air.

Leopold sat there, stunned, as the last traces evaporated. He couldn't hear the horns anymore, or Sunset Boulevard at all—only the blood pounding in his ears.

He turned his hands over and stared at them. They throbbed a little, but aside from the old, faintly ridged line of moon-shaped calluses that cut across the center of both palms, his hands looked normal.

Only they didn't itch anymore.

SIX

The city's din filtered back into his ears: honks, brakes, shout-ing. He was blocking two lanes of Sunset Boulevard at rush hour. He tried to forget what had happened with his hands. Reality was more pressing now: If he didn't get his car moving soon, it was only a matter of time before he got towed, rear-ended, or shot.

He turned the key, though he knew it was useless; the engine only sputtered. Leopold sighed and banged his head against the steering wheel, a familiar sensation of failure enveloping him. When he raised his head again, the first thing he saw was his father's giant face looming against the sky, radiating disappointment. And then he read the line below the new book's title about how the last one had been an "instant bestseller," and he pictured the corner of their garage that was filled almost to the ceiling with unopened boxes of the book his father had bought himself, and something inside Leopold turned to hot metal.

He yanked the hood release, threw open his door, and got out of the car without waiting for a break in traffic. Ignoring the honks from passing motorists, he circled the Volvo, opened the hood, and tugged apart a bundle of wires beside the inlet manifold. The oxygen sensor cable had rattled loose from its harness again. He reseated the wire and wrapped it with fresh electrical tape from the roll he kept on hand for such occasions. A new sensor was expensive, one of several chronic maintenance issues that would've cost more to fix than the Volvo was worth; this summer he'd already poured most of what he'd earned slinging lattes at his coffee shop job into keeping her running. His dad was certainly not interested in throwing money at a car that left oil stains on his pristine driveway. Richter had even tried to bribe him with a less elderly and mechanically superior BMW if Leopold would only let the Volvo go, but Leopold had refused, and Richter, assuming the cost and trouble of fixing the Volvo would eventually break his son's will, had let the matter drop. Instead, Leopold had learned how to deal with all but the most complex of the car's issues himself, and in the past year had become an expert in the seemingly endless mechanical quirks of 1991 Volvo 240 station wagons.

This was surprising to Richter only because he didn't pay much attention to his son. Leopold had always been stubborn and proud, and he liked doing fussy, technical work with his hands. It had started with learning to repair the janky old VCR, back when he was watching *Sunderworld* ten hours a day. Lately he'd been coaxing the coffee shop's temperamental fifty-year-old espresso machine back to life whenever it broke. Leopold found the close attention such tasks demanded of him centering; they distracted him from the mental quicksand of anxiety and self-doubt. At the moment, reseating the detached oxygen sensor cable was distracting him from the question of whether he might be losing his mind. As vehicles whipped dangerously around him on both sides, he wondered if he'd crossed the line from stubbornness to stupidity. He was now risking his life for an old car. Maybe it really was time to let her go.

He'd just finished wrapping the new connection when a great boom sounded, rattling the ground and startling Leopold so badly he cracked his head on the underside of the hood. He emerged, rubbing the back of his skull, to find that the sky—which a minute ago had been its usual smog-stained tan—was now crowded with thunderclouds.

All at once, it began pouring rain. He closed the hood and dove back into the car, though not quickly enough to avoid getting soaked. He sat for a moment, gazing at his still-throbbing hands, then out at the rain.

A small, quiet voice in the back of his mind whispered, *Did I do that?*

He chased away the thought, then turned the key in the ignition. The Volvo started.

Rain transformed the windshield into a weeping smear of re-fracted neon. He turned on the wipers, but only the one on the passenger's side worked. The other had been wrenched off by a vandal back in March—the last time it had rained in LA—and he hadn't yet bothered to replace it. He leaned his body all the way across the center console so that he could see through the windshield's unsmeared half and drove with one stretched leg and one pointed toe working the pedals.

He joined the halting flow of early evening traffic. After a few blocks it occurred to him that he had no intention of going home. He didn't want to face his father, couldn't stomach another lecture, and wasn't about to deliver Bessie back to a place where a tow truck might be waiting to haul her away. If anyone was getting rid of the Volvo, it would be Leopold himself, on his own terms and in his own time. So for a few minutes he just drove, the touristy glitz of Sunset giving way to the gritty strip malls of Hollywood, and he tried to make sense of what had happened to him.

It all seemed obvious enough, in retrospect.

The flaming raccoon, the winged woman, the red streetcar: episodes, all in his head. And the red sparks? Could his mind really have manufactured such an intensely real-seeming thing, just inches from his eyes?

He folded the fingers of his right hand inward to trace the scarred ridge along his palm. It was a self-inflicted wound from years ago, when he used to clench his fists so hard the fingernails bit indelible half-moons into his flesh. The itching and heat could be some new phase of the healing process, he supposed. He'd read that certain scars could take a decade to mend.

But the rain: He hadn't imagined that.

The city was in the grip of a monthslong drought, so dire that wildfires had been erupting in the foothills. No rain had been forecast; even a drizzle would've been news. Suddenly, he couldn't seem to get enough air into his lungs.

Of course you didn't make it rain.

Just entertaining the idea made him feel like he was losing his grip on reality. It had been a coincidence, obviously, and making anything more of it was dangerous. If he let himself believe he could control the weather, who knew what he'd let himself believe tomorrow—and then he'd be off the deep end completely, back to the days he'd spent waiting for talking coyotes to deliver magical keys. No, no, it was all in his mind—old, undigested traumas being regurgitated. He just prayed the episodes would stop. It was one thing for a fragile twelve-year-old who'd lost a parent to have psychotic breaks—call it what it was—and quite another for an almost-eighteen-year-old who was supposed to be applying to top-tier colleges to endure them.

The rain worsened, grinding traffic to a crawl. It was hard to see even through the wipered section of windshield. Bessie inched along a block of sagging courtyard motels, their signs boasting amenities like "Electric Heat." At a standstill he collected the fast-food wrappers and parking receipts that had cascaded forward during the near-crash, tossing them into a Ralphs bag. He was nearly finished when, beneath it all, he uncovered something that gave him pause.

A flimsy book, one that had been wedged tight under the passenger seat. It was his mother's old Thomas Guide, a spiral-bound street atlas of Los Angeles with a bleached photo of downtown's stubby skyline on its cover. Though Leopold hadn't looked at it in years, he'd never forgotten it was there.

The Guide was long, long out of date. It had been ancient even 7,261 miles ago, but his mother had refused to drive anywhere without it. *Just in case*, she always said, although she'd never said in case of what. One day, after he'd finally gotten his license, he'd cracked it open and found a note inside the front cover, inscribed to him, in his mother's handwriting.

To Leopold. Just in case.

He'd shoved it back under the seat like it was radioactive, and there it had stayed.

Now he shoved it back again. A truck horn blared and Leopold's head snapped up as if he'd been caught doing something he shouldn't have. He stomped the pedal and Bessie lurched forward, his heart racing inexplicably—and then, spotting a rain-bleared figure through the passenger window, Leopold's mind produced a word he hadn't thought of in years.

Shiggoth.

Leopold relaxed. A shiggoth was a lizard-like monster from *Sunderworld*; this was just a woman shielding herself from the rain with a fold of sopping cardboard, her stringy hair like a wet mop. She ran toward one of the glarey neon motels, taking shelter under a ragged awning. The Fade Inn was the grungiest on the block, with barred windows and a faulty sign that blinked irregularly.

The woman seemed to be staring at Leopold, her head turning as the Volvo passed at a walking pace. Then she opened her mouth and a long, narrow tongue shot out, snatched something from the air, and reeled back again.

Leopold thought: *Nope.*

That would be his mantra.

Nope. Not today.

The woman took a moment to savor whatever it was she'd caught before tossing away her cardboard umbrella and scurrying inside the motel.

Nope, nope, nope, not happening, Leopold repeated to himself, and then traffic unclenched its grip, and he began to move forward.

Now his heart was pounding. He was starting to get scared. Not of the visions, but of his own unraveling. He swore and swore, a long, angry litany of foulness directed at himself and his traitorous brain.

He knew he should've parked the car and called an Uber, but he was too stubborn to pay twenty bucks to get somewhere he could've driven blindfolded. In fact, his hands had already made the right turn onto Las Palmas, because they seemed to have figured out what he needed even before his brain had.

He needed to talk to Emmet.

Emmet Worthington, Leopold's best friend since the fourth grade, was the only person in the world with whom Leopold could imagine having a conversation about whether he might be losing his sanity. Just as this occurred to him, his phone started vibrating. With some effort he wedged it out of his pants pocket.

Mind meld. It was Emmet.

"Are you almost here?" Emmet said, half shouting over noise in the background. "I don't see you."

"Almost where?" Leopold asked, but then he remembered, and his stomach sank.

"The Stench. Mika's show." He was annoyed. "Her band plays in half an hour."

Mika was Emmet's girlfriend, and Emmet was nothing if not a dutiful partner. In all the craziness of the past few hours, Leopold had completely forgotten that he'd promised to be there. Which meant it was going to be very hard to talk to Emmet alone.

"Shit, I totally spaced. I'm sorry. It's been . . . a day."

"But you're coming?"

"Yeah. Yes. And hey, at some point tonight, I need to talk to you."

"What happened? Your dad's head finally explode?"

"Something like that."

There was a slight pause. "You okay, Mister Berry?"

They'd addressed each other with a formal *mister* since age nine. A joke that stuck.

"I'm fine, Mister Worthington. See you in twenty."

"Take Fountain. Traffic's shit."

"Always," replied Leopold.

SEVEN

Leopold sat parked across from The Stench, the rain slacken-
ing to mist, his heart slowing as Bessie's hot engine ticked. A painterly
twilight had settled over the city, magical and portentous, lending
this soot-stained slice of downtown an otherworldly splendor. The
dead-eyed windows of old warehouses lining the street had come
briefly alive, reflecting the bruised violet of the sky, and the razor wire
that snaked everywhere across their roofs glinted like tinsel. Even the
grim little dive bar at the end of the block looked halfway inviting
now, draped in the kind light of dusk.

There had been no more episodes since the woman outside the
motel. Leopold's mind was beginning to settle, his chest to unclench.
Still, he needed to calm down a bit more before he could face The
Stench and its regulars.

A few teenagers smoked outside an iron-barred door. The Stench
had no proper sign, just a graffiti wall where the name was sometimes
painted and sometimes not. It was an old punk club that had gone
belly-up in the early 2000s and been reclaimed by straight-edge vegans,
who'd turned it into an art and music space that only served juice and
funky mushroom-tasting coffee, so people as young as fifteen could
get in. It had been adopted as the hangout spot of choice by seemingly
half the weird art kids in the city—who'd all started unlistenable noise

bands that performed here—and by a smaller population of nerds, who dominated the upstairs loft space with tabletop role-playing games. The two groups tolerated each other but rarely mixed, though detachments of nerds would occasionally wander downstairs, eyes glazed from long dragon battles, to watch a noise band with bemused curiosity. Leopold didn't care much for noise bands or role-playing games or mushroomy coffee, but he did care for Emmet, who loved it all, so he ended up spending a lot of time at The Stench.

Regarding himself in the rearview mirror, Leopold found the sight so comically discouraging he almost laughed. His suit jacket was soggy, his neck ringed with red marks from his tight collar. He unbuttoned it and tossed his tie into the footwell. Wet, rust-brown hair hung limply over his hazel eyes. He raked the strands aside with his fingers, inadvertently drawing a third eyebrow of engine grease across his pale forehead. As a boy his mom had often held his face in her hands, promising him he'd grow up to be a handsome young man—but she hadn't lived long enough to judge the results. At the moment, in Leopold's humble opinion, he resembled a traveling salesman who'd slept in a bus station.

With a resigned sigh, he reached behind his seat and dragged out The Club, a heavy steel bar with a U-hook at each end. Not that anyone would want to steal Bessie. Still, he couldn't bear the thought of her being joyridden or dismembered for parts, so he wedged The Club's hooks through his steering wheel and locked it, then got out and ran across the street. Maybe if he hurried, he could still catch Emmet before Mika's set began.

The smoking kids ignored him. So did the bouncer, engrossed in his phone. Leopold hurried down a dim hallway papered in peeling posters, following an amplified whine that might've been Mika's band tuning their instruments—or might've been a song.

He emerged into the main room to discover Mika posing with her bandmates under the spotlights of the little stage. A few dozen art kids congregated in cliquey knots. A respectable turnout. If the audience outnumbered the band on a random weeknight, the gig could be considered a success.

Leopold threaded the crowd and found Emmet at the front. They'd met on the first day of fourth grade, when Emmet, one of the few Black kids in his class, had shown up wearing an *Evil Dead* T-shirt three sizes too big for him. Recognizing a kindred spirit, Leopold had walked right up to him and shaken his hand like a bona-fide adult, and Emmet had been calling him Mister Berry ever since.

"You okay?" Emmet said by way of hello, shouting over the noise.

"Yeah," Leopold shouted back, which at the moment was honest enough.

Just being in his friend's presence was making him feel better than he had all day. Emmet nodded—*good*—held up a finger—*talk in a minute*—then turned his attention back to the Broken Typewriters, who were, as it happened, in the middle of a song.

Leopold did his best to feign interest.

All four members wore white painters' jumpsuits. A girl in giant lensless grandma glasses was playing a saw with a violin bow, bending it to produce a noise that sounded uncannily like weeping. A hollow-cheeked goth boy tore pages from a phone book while kicking a drawer full of silverware in 4/4 rhythm. Mika herself, who Leopold supposed was the singer, held a microphone up to an old tape deck that played a warbly recording of Mika's eight-year-old sister singing "Earth Died Screaming" by Tom Waits. The band was originally conceived as a Waits cover act but had diverged at some point during the first rehearsal. Talent-wise, the Typewriters were on par with most bands that played at The Stench, all of which were locked in a self-defeating war to out-weird one another. Legend had it a crowd once gathered to watch a janitor vacuum the stage and applauded when he'd finished, to which the janitor had reacted with confusion, then disgust.

Mika's band abruptly stopped.

After an uncertain quiet there came a smattering of applause from the crowd, then wild cheering from Emmet and an older Japanese couple. Mika announced they were taking a break. She jumped down from the stage, gave Emmet a deep kiss, said hi to Leopold, and slouched off to talk to her parents. Mr. and Mrs. Yamamoto, also in the front row, were Broken Typewriters superfans.

Emmet turned to face him. "So?"

There were people everywhere.

"Roof," Leopold said, and they headed to the stairs.

Nerds crowded the second-floor landing, a gangly, blue-haired one buttonholing Emmet as they tried to pass. "Em, you playing tonight? Jeremiah's got a killer campaign plotted out." Through an open doorway Leopold counted ten or twelve people in cosplay regalia pulling chairs up to a long table covered with papers and figurines.

Emmet demurred. "Rain check."

Emmet was the rare social chameleon who was popular with the athletes, the art kids, and the nerds—and who paid no social price for his association with any of them. Leopold, who seemed to fit nowhere in particular, had always floated at the margins.

"Larry? What about you?"

Blue-hair was throwing him a bone. Leopold tossed it back. "Not tonight."

"Your loss."

Leopold followed Emmet up another set of stairs, through a metal fire door, onto the hallowed rectangle of open space that was the roof:

tar-paper shingles underfoot, a loose confederacy of wet lawn chairs, sagging Christmas lights strung along a chest-high barrier.

For the moment they had it to themselves.

They stepped around a puddle of drowned band flyers, leaned against the barrier, and looked out at the skyline, such as it was: pockets of dark interspersed with neon, downtown's distant high-rises shrouded in mist, the whirling lights of an ambulance tracking through the maze at right angles like Pac-Man pursued by ghosts. Emmet had worn a white painter's jumpsuit in solidarity with the band, and standing there surveying the city he looked like a super-hero awaiting his call to action. His height and athletic build helped the effect. Emmet Worthington was many things Leopold was not: levelheaded, socially adept, well-liked. He was a shoo-in for either Stanford or Caltech, where his parents were professors. He was also loyal, and even as he'd graduated from outcast-adjacent to something like cool in the ninth grade, he'd never made Leopold feel extraneous. Emmet wasn't Leopold's only friend, but he was, in many ways, the only one who mattered.

"Have you ever heard of it raining like this in August?" Emmet said. "I bet there's actual water in the LA River right now, not just dead bodies and old shopping carts."

"So weird," Leopold agreed, his anxiety rising at the mention of rain. *Which he'd had nothing to do with.*

Emmet took out a vape pen and held it to his lips. It glowed brightly; a moment later he blew a cloud of apricot-flavored smoke toward the high-rises.

Leopold shot him a look. "Seriously? I thought you quit."

"I did. Then I un-quit."

"Well, re-quit. That's disgusting."

Emmet sighed. "Tomorrow. Don't tell Mika, okay?"

"I won't tell Mika. I'll tell your mom."

"Wow." Emmet raised an eyebrow, then took another drag. "I think it's been too long since the last time I kicked your ass."

Leopold cracked a smile. "I'm serious. It's not cool to smoke anymore. It's celery juice or die."

Emmet poked him in the chest. "*Beep*. Next track."

"I'm concerned. You can't just *next track* me—"

"I'm the one who should be concerned. You sounded freaked out on the phone. And that *suit*—" Emmet winced as he appraised Leopold.

"It was Richter's idea. For the interview."

"Right, that was today," said Emmet, nodding. "I'm guessing it didn't go well?"

It couldn't have gone worse if Leopold had ripped down his pants and evacuated his bowels onto the floor, but there was no need to belabor the point, so he just said no.

"Did you finally pick a career from Herr Richter's Wheel of Futures?"

"Not yet," said Leopold. "I may have mentioned film school."

"Jesus take the wheel." Emmet exhaled another curl of vapor. "So Richter finally lost it. What happened?"

Leopold only shook his head.

"What? He kick you out? Slash Bessie's tires?" Emmet raised his eyebrows. "Threaten you with community college?"

When Leopold didn't laugh, Emmet looked genuinely concerned. "All right, talk. You're starting to scare me."

For an hour he'd been dying to tell Emmet about the episodes, but now he found himself hesitating. What did he want from his friend? Reassurance he wasn't going crazy? He didn't know if Emmet could give him that. He only knew he needed to tell someone he trusted what had happened. Feeling like he was about to dive into a pool of icy water, Leopold said quietly, "I started seeing things again."

Emmet took a beat, his expression carefully neutral. "Like what?"

"Sunder things."

Emmet turned his head and blew out another jet of smoke. "Haven't heard that word in a while. When did it start?"

"A few weeks ago. Just a little at first. Then, today, a lot."

"What's a lot?"

"Three or four times?"

Emmet swore softly.

Leopold hazarded a glance at him, but in his friend's narrowed eyes he saw only concern. So Leopold laid out the whole strange story, beginning weeks ago with the fruit vendor chased by a rain cloud and ending with the lizard-tongued woman outside the motel. He found himself downplaying the terror of some moments, like when he thought they were about to collide with a streetcar, because he didn't want to worry Emmet more than necessary. But he left nothing out.

"And then you drove straight here?"

"Yeah," Leopold said.

The whine of a musical saw echoed faintly through the propped fire door. Mika's band had started again, but Emmet made no move to go inside.

"Why'd you wait so long to tell me?"

"I didn't think it was a big deal."

Emmet's eyes flashed. "Your first episode in years and you didn't think it was a big deal? Come on, Larry."

"I figured it was a one-time thing."

"You mean you hoped it was."

"And I guess I was embarrassed."

That was only half the truth. The other half was that he'd been afraid it would push Emmet away, as it had when they were younger. When Leopold's episodes had persisted even after his first major no-key, no-coyote disappointment, he'd finally confessed to Emmet that he was seeing rust fiends in alleys and so on—and Emmet had gone along, assuming it was all part of some elaborate game. Eventually, Emmet made the mistake of mentioning Sunder in front of his parents, and something in the way he'd talked about it, with nearly as much conviction as Leopold, spooked them so much they told Emmet he couldn't hang out with Leopold for a while, and to make certain of it, they'd packed Emmet off to summer camp.

When Emmet finally returned, Leopold pretended he'd never believed Sunder was real in the first place, and slowly their friendship revived. It wasn't until they were sixteen, long after Leopold really had stopped believing Sunder was real, that he was brave enough to admit how long the episodes had persisted.

"You *should* be embarrassed," Emmet said dryly. "We both know a shiggoth will shrivel up if it's out of water for more than twenty minutes, so unless she was living in that motel's pool, those were some really low-rent hallucinations. If you're going to bug out, can you at least do it in a way that respects canon?"

"It was raining," Leopold said, flipping him off.

"All right, listen." Emmet's grin vanished. "You've been going through some shit with your dad and it's been triggering you. Seeing Sunder is one of the ways your brain deals with that. Right?"

"Right." Leopold pushed a hand through his damp hair. "I hate my brain."

"No. We're not doing that." Emmet pointed at him with the vape pen. "I know your brain, and it's a perfectly good one. But when things like this happen, you have to talk about it or they only get worse. So next time, tell me. Right away. Middle of the night, whatever. Okay?"

"Okay," Leopold said, exhaling. He felt a sudden rush of gratitude for Emmet and resisted the urge to give him a giant, back-slapping hug. He was trying to affect the air of someone who wasn't on the verge of a breakdown, and it was hard work keeping up the show. "Thanks, man."

"Anytime." Emmet watched him carefully. "You good?"

"I'm good." For the first time in too long, the words felt almost true.

There was a beat of companionable quiet between them. The band's wheezing music drifted up the stairs. "You should come out with us after the show," Emmet said. "I know you don't love Mika's friends, but—"

"What's not to love?" Leopold cut him off. "The last time we hung out, Jessica told me I had *the potential to be hot but no hope of being memorable.*"

"Damn." Emmet's eyes dimmed, then brightened. "She said you had potential, though?"

Leopold was smiling as he said, "Dickhead."

"Potential in a three-piece suit!" Emmet nodded at Leopold's still-damp clothes. "You're looking dapper as a rich murder victim, Mister Berry."

Leopold laughed despite himself. "All right, whatever, I'll come. I'm not ready to go home and deal with Richter yet, anyway."

"Yes." Emmet fist-pumped as they headed for the exit. "It'll be the best night of your life, I promise."

"We're going to eat shitty diner food and talk about noise bands, aren't we?"

Emmet briefly looked back. "Like I said."

EIGHT

The Typewriters cranked out some more noise, then finished with a funereal rendition of Britney Spears's "Toxic," the lyrics sung in Latin. It wasn't quite nine o'clock. Leopold's phone had been buzzing with angry messages from his father—*Get your ass home*, and so on—until finally he'd just silenced it.

As the small crowd cleared out, Leopold and Emmet clustered by the juice bar to pick a restaurant. Joining them were Mika and two of her bandmates, Clark and the aforementioned Jessica—the phone book ripper and musical saw player, respectively. Leopold had lifted his hand in limp hellos, and though Clark acknowledged him with an uncertain look, Jessica had tucked her platinum-blond hair behind her ears and said, without cruelty, "Have we met before?"

The Typewriters had shed their white jumpsuits and were now dressed like standard art kids in band shirts and shapeless light-wash mom jeans, except for Mika, who'd paired her band shirt (*WEIRDO RIPPERS*) with tan canvas pants and ugly-on-purpose Teva sandals from the nineties. The pants, Mika never tired of explaining, were from a store in Panorama City called Pants Town, which sold unironic workwear in bulk and had been experiencing a recent and baffling influx of teenagers. Leopold thought she looked good despite her clothes, but because he tried not to dwell on Mika's attractiveness—she being Emmet's girlfriend and everything—he pretended to study the juice bar menu and turned his thoughts to food. He hadn't eaten since breakfast and was suddenly ravenous.

"Clifton's," Emmet suggested, now dressed in the white tee and black jeans he'd been wearing under his jumpsuit.

"The Perch," Clark countered.

Jessica wrinkled her nose. "Too expensive."

"You have a trust fund," Clark pointed out.

"Not until I'm twenty-five."

"So, Clifton's," Emmet insisted.

Clark looked defeated. "It's so *old.*"

Leopold just watched, amused. He knew where this was heading.

"Z Café," Mika suggested, then waved her hand and said "Never mind" before anyone could respond. "Too avocado toast."

"I thought you liked avocado toast," Clark said.

"Do you know how water intensive avocado farming is?"

"Do you hear me giving you shit about all those almonds you eat?"

"I don't know why we go through this when we always end up at either The Pantry or Clifton's," Jessica whined.

"No Pantry," said Mika, crossing her arms. "There's meat in every-thing and I'm vegan this month."

"Clifton's it is!" Emmet crowed.

NINE

Clifton's was twenty blocks from The Stench, at the foot of Bun-
ker Hill below the high-rises, wedged between a liquidator of second-
hand mannequins and an old theater that hadn't shown a movie since
Charlie Chaplin was starring in them. Clifton's was nearly as ancient,
which for Emmet was half the attraction. He was an aficionado of
LA history and, by extension, a connoisseur of quirky old LA diners.
His favorites looked like somewhere a 1930s hobo would cough up
his last dime for a ham sandwich and a cup of coffee. Clifton's food
was barely a notch above school cafeteria fare and the menu hadn't
changed in half a century, but neither, it seemed, had its prices. For
that reason alone, it usually won out.

Leopold found parking down the block, Clubbed his wheel, noted
the new number on Bessie's odometer (7,274 miles), then met Emmet
and the Typewriters in front of the restaurant. They were doing a
postmortem on the show, which Leopold tuned out as he pushed
open the heavy log-cabin door and held it for the others.

Stepping inside Clifton's was like entering a magical forest—albeit
one that had been neglected for years. There were fake shrubs everywhere, fake streams that flowed with heavily chlorinated water, fake
woodland creatures that peeped out from the branches of fake trees.
The place was nearly empty but for a few tipsy thirtysomethings and

a man in a heavy coat who appeared to be asleep at his table. Clifton's was the rare survivor from an era when every third restaurant in LA was like a miniature Disneyland without the rides. Its theme was "enchanted redwoods," and though at one time it might really have felt magical, it was now faded and sort of depressing. Leopold figured it would fold in a year or two and give way to some avocado toast place. It was the way of things.

A yawning hostess escorted them to their usual table, a curved brown booth built into the hollow of a giant plaster tree. Its trunk rose halfway up the wall before melding into a painted mural of a redwood grove. A waiter with a graying comb-over brought menus and took drink orders. Leopold asked for black coffee.

For a while Mika and Co. talked about noise bands, which allowed Leopold to zone out and sip his coffee, but then the conversation turned to college applications. It seemed like everyone already had it figured out, their whole unimaginable life in all its snaking turns—or the next few bends of it, anyway. Jessica would be premed at one of the better UCs. Clark was a legacy at some private liberal arts school in the Midwest, and Mika was taking a gap year to backpack around Europe, having convinced her parents that she needed to "study her soul" before deciding what to study in college. Emmet was almost certainly going to either Stanford or Caltech, and it was easy to imagine him becoming a rocket scientist like his parents.

Leopold, meanwhile, was trying to figure out what to say about his own murky future when the waiter came back to take their food orders and he was granted a stay of execution.

"I think I'll have the salmon," Jessica said after a cursory look at the giant, laminated menu. "Is it wild or farmed?"

The waiter scowled. "Microwaved."

Emmet nudged Leopold. "You know what you want?"

"Not yet," he said quietly.

Sometimes, when his eyes popped open and his heart set to racing at three in the morning, Leopold knew exactly what he wanted: for his mother to come back to life. It was a notion so impossible, even his disordered middle-of-the-night mind knew it to be absurd—and yet it sometimes occurred to him, in clearer moments, that his troubling visions of Sunder had been birthed in retaliation to this fact; that if he couldn't live in a world where his mother was alive, perhaps he could live in another world altogether. It was childish and stupid and embarrassing, the fantasy of Sunder every bit as fake as the tree whose plaster trunk they were sitting inside, but he couldn't figure out how to let it go.

He lowered his head, turning a page in the menu. Mika, too, was taking forever to decide. Everyone was giving her advice.

"The chicken-fried steak is excellent," Emmet said, then reversed himself after Mika made a face. "Right, you're vegan."

"Greek salad?" Jessica suggested.

"That's on page *six*." Clark looked horrified. "Geriatric diner rule number one: Never order anything after page four. Past that, you're taking your life into your own hands."

Inexplicably, a strange sensation had begun to steal over Leopold. A leadenness in his limbs and a lightness in his head. He blinked at his dinner options, trying to affect outward calm, and noticed that someone had defaced his menu. In blue ballpoint, above the list of appetizers, was a doodle of a man with a big nose peering over the top of a wall.

Kilroy.

Leopold's face felt warm. Suddenly, he was nine years old again. Ten. Eleven. The big-nosed man had been a wink shared between him and his mother. Only later had Leopold learned its origins, as a bit of inside joke graffiti left behind by Allied soldiers during World War II, often accompanied by the words *Kilroy was here*. For Leopold and his mother, it had begun when she created a word search for him on the back of a restaurant menu with Kilroy drawn at the top. He'd solved it quickly and requested another, and they'd sat there at Shakey's Pizza for two hours after their meal was done, passing paper menus back and forth, the little man at the top of each one. Word searches evolved into cipher puzzles and eventually weekend-long scavenger hunts that led him all over their neighborhood.

Often she wouldn't even tell him there *was* a puzzle to solve—that became part of the game—but Kilroy, chalked on some unmissable square of sidewalk outside their house or drawn on a Post-it tucked inside a book she knew he'd open at school, was always her signal that something was afoot. It meant, essentially, *pay attention*. Leopold had never considered himself some kind of puzzle genius—or any kind of genius—but when his mother asked him to pay attention, he did.

A sudden movement drew his gaze upward.

Above Clifton's main floor was a second-floor atrium, roped off and rarely used. It was crowded with more tables and faux greenery, and Leopold thought he'd seen a trembling in the bushes there.

The bush moved a second time. His head tingled as his eyes fixed on it.

A furry, ring-eyed face popped out from behind a limb and peered down at him.

No. Nope.

The goddamn raccoon again. It pressed its little hands against the glass fall barrier, eyes pleading. Leopold clenched his jaw and willed it to disappear.

"*Fuck off*," Leopold hissed under his breath. "You're not real."

"Excuse me?" Clark said, turning to face him.

Leopold quickly lowered his head. "The crab cakes," he said, pretending to study the menu. "They've got to be fake, right?"

"Uh, I guess." Clark gave him a strange look, then returned to the conversation he'd been having with Jessica.

When Leopold glanced up again, the raccoon was gone.

He remembered, with a rush of relief, Emmet once telling him that most of the fake woodland creatures in Clifton's were animatronic; at some point in the restaurant's history they'd all been functional, so that as you walked around, you might see a tin gopher poke its head out of a hole or a wooden woodpecker tap on a tree. That would account for the raccoon; maybe a few of them still worked.

"And for you?"

It was his turn to order. Leopold scanned his open menu for anything that didn't sound overtly poisonous. His gaze snagged on an item in red, sandwiched between the liver and onions and the shepherd's pie:

24. Go upstairs, Leopold *$6.95*

He squeezed his eyes shut, opened them again.

It was still there.

He slapped the menu closed and handed it back to the waiter. "I'm not hungry."

Emmet frowned. "You said you were starving."

"Must've been the coffee. Appetite suppressant."

Aware that he'd hardly touched it, he picked up the mug and took a long, bitter sip, then excused himself to the bathroom. Leopold could feel Emmet's gaze following him as he walked away, but he didn't look back. It was time to finish this.

Leopold headed for the stairs.

TEN

The stairs that led to the second floor were carved to look like fallen logs. A red rope was stretched across the landing. Leopold checked over his shoulder to make sure no one was watching, ducked under the rope, and hurried quietly up the rest of the steps. At the top was a closed door and a STAFF ONLY sign.

He didn't know what he was doing, only that he was tired of doing nothing. The powerlessness he felt in the face of his own mental deterioration had become a tightening coil of anxiety around his throat, and if he didn't do something to take control of it now, he feared he might do something far more destructive later, like go home and punch Richter in the face. By comparison, opening a door in a musty diner seemed downright sensible.

He ignored the sign and turned the handle.

Inside was the atrium he'd seen from below. A thicket of plastic bushes stretched along a balcony to his left. Across a carpeted aisle, amber-tinted bulbs cast an eerie, irradiated glow over dusty red booths. He walked along, peering into the tangle of greenery.

There was no woodland creature, animatronic or otherwise, in sight. As usual, it had all been in his head. He dragged his hands down his face and cursed himself.

Then something darted out into the aisle.

That damn raccoon stood in the middle of the carpet, staring at him. *Taunting* him. Clasped in its forepaws was something small and glinting.

Leopold hesitated, then took a step forward. The raccoon turned, scampered toward a row of replica pines along the back wall, and dove into their branches.

Aware he'd officially lost his mind, Leopold chased after it anyway. When he reached the pines, he searched around, thinking he might find a small hole in the wall or in the floor. Instead, as he parted the branches, he discovered a doorway.

Wedging himself awkwardly through a blind of pipe cleaner needles, Leopold emerged into a room-sized diorama of a pine forest. There were no tables or chairs, just artificial bushes, trees, rocks, and animals. A glass-eyed deer stood eternally frozen beside a dry stream. A beaver lay toppled beside a dam of sticks and branches. Birds perched here and there, and the walls were painted, in the style of Hollywood sets, to look like woods that continued endlessly into the distance. At the far end of the room, a small window looked out onto the street, an odd intrusion of reality.

Leopold turned slowly, scanning the scene. He'd nearly come full circle without finding the raccoon when he saw, right at eye level, a thin velvet rope that dangled from the ceiling. Attached to the bottom was a dainty, gilt-lettered sign that read PULL FOR SHOW.

Without stopping to question his choices, Leopold wrapped his hand around the cord and gave it a tug.

He heard a muffled metallic whir from somewhere out of sight, and through hidden speakers came the distinctive pop and scratch of a record needle dropping onto vinyl. As a string orchestra began to play a warbling tune, a peppy male narrator intoned, "Ah, the majesty of nature! It has the power to soothe, to heal, to rejuvenate even the most harried denizens of the modern metropolis." Birds turned and twittered in the trees. The deer lowered its head with a rusty squeak to drink from the dry stream. To the sound of recorded breeze, a few branches moved up and down as if shifting in the wind.

Leopold stood in the center of it all, so fascinated he nearly forgot about the raccoon.

"And for the patient observer," the narrator went on, "for the acute of vision, something more awaits. For the camper, the hiker, the explorer, the adventurer, here is a ticket to another world . . ."

Across the room, the leaves of a small bush began to shiver. A moment later, the raccoon poked out its head.

"So come, weary traveler! Join us!"

Leopold moved cautiously toward the animal.

The raccoon's head jerked from side to side. It didn't run. It didn't seem to be aware of him at all. It was the same raccoon he'd been seeing all day, with the same distinctive markings, but now, up close, it appeared to be animatronic.

Leopold crossed the room until, finally, he found himself standing right in front of it.

His heart was drumming. The raccoon's head swiveled toward him. Its paws stuttered upward, cupped in offering.

They held a silver coin.

With some trepidation, Leopold reached down and took the coin from the raccoon's stiff paws, then studied it in the reddish light.

On one side was written: *Good for One Ride.*

On the other: *Angels Flight Railway.*

He stared at it for another long moment, then slowly raised his head. The room's only window was just a few feet away, framing a view of Eighth Street and the steep rise of Bunker Hill, stippled with palms and sad apartment buildings. A narrow metal track ran straight up the middle, and stalled on the tracks, not far from the bottom, was a solitary red trolley car.

Leopold had the sudden, weightless feeling of having left his body. He'd seen this image many times before: this hill, those buildings, that trolley.

It was a shot from the opening credits of *Sunderworld.*

He became aware, gradually at first, of a cool breeze across his skin. A kiss of fresh night air. *Forest* air. The pine bough beside the window had resumed its rustling, but the sound it made was gentler than before—a whisper, not a creak. Looking closely he saw that it was made not from plaster and pipe cleaners but real wood and real needles and real, dripping sap redolent of the outdoors. And then he looked at the raccoon, which lowered its paws and scratched itself without a trace of jerky awkwardness. He was about to speak to it when his name rang out.

"Larry?"

It was Emmet. He burst through the door in the wall of pines behind him, and the spell was broken. "What the hell is going on?"

There was an abrupt, grating screech from within the walls and a noise like gears stripping. The trees and animals around him began to shudder and shake, demonstrably mechanical again. The raccoon emitted a shrill whine that made Leopold wince, and then an electrical spark arced through the wiring behind its eyes.

It caught fire.

"Holy shit!" Emmet cried.

Flames erupted from the raccoon's eye sockets, then quickly spread to its bristle-brush fur. Leopold tried to stomp it out and instead sent the thing tumbling stiffly into a bush. The fire roared, engulfing the fake shrubbery. Leopold tore off his suit jacket and threw it on a rill of flame that was spreading toward the pines, which were nothing but ninety-year-old kindling. He and Emmet both stomped on it, but then the jacket itself began to burn. Leopold had just decided to run for help when their waiter suddenly appeared in the doorway with a fire extinguisher.

"Out of the way!" he bellowed, and sprayed white foam until the extinguisher ran dry. In a few seconds it was over, and the air was filled with smoke and char and the stink of chemicals.

The waiter rounded on them, his face flushed, his comb-over flopping down the wrong side of his head. "What were you doing in here?" he cried. "No one's allowed in here!"

They ran.

Emmet and Leopold raced down the fallen-log stairs and
through the ground floor of the restaurant. Leopold's head was a war-
ring clangor of mortification, adrenaline, and a growing conviction
that something bizarre but important had just happened. Somewhere
behind him he heard Emmet bark "Get the check and meet me outside" at their table, and Leopold pushed through the main door to
find himself briefly alone on the sidewalk.

He stood catching his breath in an eddying cloud of smoke from a
taco cart, then held the coin up to a shaft of streetlight.

Good for One Ride.

He hadn't imagined it.

A hand grasped his shoulder and spun him around. "What the
hell happened back there?" It was Emmet, winded and puffing. "What
were you doing upstairs? You almost burned the place down!"

The token still clutched in his hand, Leopold saw the exasperation
on his friend's face and knew, in his gut, that the best course of action
was to lie.

Instead, he told Emmet the truth.

The story poured out in a jumble: the raccoon; #24 on the menu;
the hidden room and the scene that had come to life; the coin; and
then Angels Flight, framed through the window in a nearly perfect
re-creation of one of *Sunderworld*'s opening shots.

"Let me see the coin," Emmet said when the story was over. He held out his palm, dubious.

Leopold handed it over. After a few seconds of inspection, Emmet's expression mellowed from anger to bemused fascination. "There's a simple explanation for this."

Leopold attempted a smile. "I just got invited to Sunder?"

Emmet's eyes narrowed. He gave back the coin. "The raccoon was obviously animatronic. And this token was part of some old promotional deal Clifton's used to have with the trolley operator, like you got a free ride up the hill if you ate at the restaurant and a free cup of coffee at Clifton's if you bought a trolley ride. Also, there used to be this little park with real redwood trees near the top of the hill, which explains the connection between the *escape into the majesty of nature* stuff and the trolley."

"Wait—Angels Flight is a real thing? I thought it was invented for the show."

"C'mon, man, it's a classic piece of LA history." Emmet rolled his eyes, tension leaving his body. "The shortest and steepest railway in the country and the gateway to Bunker Hill—which used to be the fanciest neighborhood in Los Angeles. I'm honestly embarrassed for you that you don't know this. You still haven't read that book I gave you for your birthday?"

"It was five hundred pages!"

"Whatever. It had pictures." Emmet turned to face a darkened lot across the street, then pointed. Beyond a chain link fence, stalled on its track a short distance from the bottom of the hill, was the red trolley. "You've really never noticed it before? We walk past this trash heap every time we come to Clifton's."

"Oh." Leopold felt stupid.

"Yeah."

"Damn."

"Exactly."

Leopold frowned. From their vantage point at street level, the trolley was slightly obscured by palms. "I guess I don't look up enough."

"There's a metaphor in there somewhere."

Leopold sighed. "So. It's a real thing."

"It *was* a real thing. But it hasn't worked in forever."

"I had another episode," he said, almost trying to convince himself. "It was all in my head."

"Yeah." Emmet still looked a little angry. He tossed a look over his shoulder. "And we'll be lucky if they don't call the cops."

Leopold felt himself losing this fight, his earlier adrenaline replaced by cold mortification. He hadn't realized until that moment just how much he'd been hoping the token would mean something. That all of it would *finally* mean something. "But what about the trolley I thought I saw when I was driving with my dad?"

"Didn't you say that happened by Carney's?"

"Yeah."

"Carney's *is* an old streetcar, just like the Formosa Café and the Pacific Dining Car and like three other restaurants around town. You did see one; it just wasn't flying across the Sunset Strip."

"But the raccoon upstairs catching fire," Leopold said, trying again. "It was almost identical to the one I saw this morning—"

Emmet was shaking his head. "Tonight was probably the first time that whole Disneyland-on-acid scene had been switched on in years. That wasn't Sunder trying to tap you on the shoulder; Thumper and Bambi would've caught fire no matter who pulled the rope in the ceiling."

"Okay," Leopold said, nodding because it was the expected thing to do, the sane thing to do. But inside, he was spiraling.

Emmet raised his eyebrows. "You need me to point out any more flaws in your logic?"

They were pacing now, passing in and out of the taco cart's ghostly smoke.

"No. Yes. *Wait*—the raccoon handed me an entry token," Leopold said in a rush, "and then, like the scene where the coyote gives Max a key to Sunder, it—"

"Vanishes in a puff of flame," Emmet finished for him.

"I thought it was a shower of sparks."

"No, it was definitely a puff of flame," Emmet insisted. "We re-created that scene shot for shot, remember? With a red smoke bomb from the Army-Navy store and everything."

"Okay—a puff of flame," Leopold said, his mind working. "And you don't think it's strange that the same exact thing happened in front of me five minutes ago?" He held up the coin. "An entry token is a kind of key."

"Look." Emmet sighed, deflating. "You had an intense day. When you're already on edge, small coincidences can feel bigger than they really are."

"I wouldn't call them small—"

"*It's not a key,*" Emmet said slowly, emphasizing each word.

"Can we at least acknowledge that this has been weird? A little uncanny? Slightly out-of-the-fucking-ordinary?"

"No." Emmet halted and turned to face him. "I'm not going to encourage this. It isn't healthy. You just had a serious episode—and instead of asking for help, you ran off after some malfunctioning raccoon and almost burned down my favorite restaurant."

"I know, I'm sorry—I just—I think we should recognize that something strange is happening—"

"In your head? Yes. Something strange is happening in your head."

Leopold flinched. "C'mon, man."

"Listen, I'm sorry." Emmet sighed. The anger seemed to leave him, but not the intensity. "I'm not trying to be an asshole, I swear. But I'm not a therapist. Everything I know I learned from the internet, or from listening to Mika talk about things her own therapist taught her. I don't know how to help you with this anymore, and I think—Larry, I think you need to talk to Richter about seeing a professional again. I'm worried about you."

Leopold nodded, trying to look calm, but he felt like he'd been punched in the chest. Emmet was literally taking a step back from him, and the worst part was that Leopold understood why. He knew how he must've seemed. He knew magic wasn't real and he knew—deep down—that Sunder wasn't, either. But it was the very fact that he could recognize this cognitive dissonance in himself that gave him pause—because how could he be logical and illogical at the same time?

Leopold shoved his trembling hands into his pockets, the metal token biting into his closed fist. If he wasn't careful, he was going to lose Emmet, which somehow felt worse than losing his mind. He took a centering breath and stared across the street at Angels Flight: the lot below it heaped with trash, its tracks overgrown with weeds, a congregation of grimy palms standing sentinel around its base. The trolley clearly hadn't been operational in years, and it certainly wasn't about to transport him anywhere tonight, token or no token.

"You're right," Leopold said finally. "You're right about all of it. I got wound up today and instead of resisting the shitstorm, I leaned into it. Old habits. Bad habits." He shook his head. "And I'm sorry I didn't say anything before. If it happens again, I will. I promise."

"You promised before."

"I mean it this time." Leopold held out his hand with the pinkie up.

Emmet glowered at it. "What's that supposed to be?"

"It's a fucking pinkie promise."

Emmet stared at him a moment. Then he slapped Leopold's hand out of the way and pulled him in for a quick, crushing hug.

Soon they were both smiling.

"You're really okay?" Emmet asked, gaze narrowing.

"Yeah. I think I just needed to talk through this stuff out loud."

Emmet held up his hands. "In that case, I hereby acknowledge a *small, totally coincidental* amount of uncanny weirdness. Now, your turn." He nodded at the token still clutched in Leopold's hand. "Repeat after me: This is not a key."

Leopold rolled his eyes. "This is not a key."

Emmet pointed to Angels Flight. "That is not an entrance to Sunder."

"That is not an entrance to Sunder."

He poked Leopold in the chest. "*I, Leopold Berry, am not going to try to ride Angels Flight.*"

"I, Leopold Berry, am not going to try to ride Angels Flight."

"It doesn't work anyway. Probably a total death trap."

"I said I'm not going to."

"Plus, you'd break an ankle trying to hop that fence—"

"I'm not going to ride it!"

"Good." Emmet clapped him on the arm. "We good?"

Leopold nodded. "Sorry I probably got us banned from Clifton's."

"Oh, you *definitely* got us banned. It's for the best, though. Their food was going to kill us eventually."

Leopold rubbed his face, suddenly exhausted. When he looked up, the fake-log door to Clifton's had swung open, and Mika and her friends were trailing out onto the sidewalk holding to-go boxes.

"What's going on with you two?" Mika called out, leading the others toward them at a leisurely pace.

"Leopold was about to hook up with a red flag," said Emmet, grinning. "I had to stop him."

Mika raised a skeptical brow at Leopold and his bedraggled appearance. He was still wearing the remnants of his ill-fitting three-piece suit; the jacket had been sacrificed to the fire, but his vest, white shirt, and slacks—all wrinkled and soot-stained—continued to do him no favors. She laughed, but in a confused way. "Um. Okay."

"If that's true," said Clark, "then why was the waiter so freaked out? He kept asking if you were going to sue—"

"Sue?" Leopold raised his eyebrows. "Is that why they didn't call the—*oof*—"

Emmet had elbowed him in the gut.

"Yeah," Jessica went on, "he said something about faulty wiring upstairs."

"Right, exactly," said Emmet, improvising. "I told Larry it was a bad idea to take a girl up there. Zero atmosphere. Wasn't even sanitary—"

Now Mika looked disgusted, and Leopold—whose book of romantic history contained no more than two uneventful chapters—was beginning to worry this story was taking a wrong turn. Cheeks flushing, he shot Emmet a warning look and said, "All right, that's enough—"

"You're a good friend," Jessica said to Emmet, before turning a sympathetic gaze on Leopold. She was objectively beautiful, so it made sense that she could never remember him. "Bad hookups can't fix a bad day. And you"—she looked him up and down—"you look like you've had a really bad day."

"Uh." Leopold frowned. "Yeah."

"You know, you could be hot if you made an effort," she said, tilting her head at him. "You've got great hair. What's your name again?"

"All right, I'm going home," Leopold announced, turning away from Jessica.

Emmet looked disappointed. "You sure? You could crash at my place tonight. We'll do breakfast at Jerry's. We're going to need a new shitty diner."

Leopold shook his head. He knew Richter would blow a gasket when he finally showed his face at home, but he needed to start dealing with his problems instead of running from them. Avoiding the reality of his mom's death was what had started him down the path to this bleak moment, and Leopold was determined to stop repeating the same mistakes. He sure as hell wasn't going to let Richter break his mind.

Leopold Berry might've been perfectly average, but he wasn't a fucking coward.

TWELVE

Leopold crossed the street and hurried toward his Volvo. A sol-
itary car hissed by, passing in and out of streetlights as it splashed
through the remnants of the afternoon's rain. He was relieved to find
Bessie just where he'd left her, windows unbroken.

He got in and unlocked The Club from his wheel. A lonely siren
wailed somewhere in the distance. Drawing in a deep breath, he
counted to five, then slowly exhaled.

Today had been shit. Tomorrow he would start over.

As he pulled his keys from his pocket, he noticed a dark smudge
on the vinyl that wrapped the steering column. He frowned and
turned on the dome light. There was a second blackened mark below
the door handle. Both had been imprinted upon the places his hands
had come to rest after they'd emitted—*he'd imagined*—a shower of
red sparks. He rubbed his knuckle along one of the marks, and it
smeared.

Soot.

He felt his face getting hot. His scalp began to tingle.

No. Nope. Not again.

Never again.

He clenched his teeth, fumbling the key into the ignition just as someone rapped hard on his window, startling Leopold so badly he hit his head against the ceiling.

It was Emmet.

Leopold cranked down the window, his pulse suddenly racing. Streetlight cast a harsh glare across Emmet's shoulders. There was a strange, intense look on his face.

"Mister Berry," he said, his voice grave. "We have a problem."

THIRTEEN

They stood on the sidewalk, hands cupped around their eyes, peering through the chain link fence. Above them loomed Angels Flight, beyond which they could make out the shadowy, weed-fringed rise of Bunker Hill.

Leopold broke the silence. "We've been standing here a full minute. Are you going to explain why you dragged me back here?"

"Just look," Emmet said anxiously, pointing into the gloom. "Halfway up, right side. What do you see?"

Leopold squinted. "Crappy apartment buildings."

"And there." Emmet's arm shifted higher and to the left. "What about over there?"

"I don't know, man, it's pretty dark—"

"How about a huge building with what looks like a crown on top? The US Bank Tower."

"No."

"Do you see any tall buildings at *all*?" He was gesturing toward the crest of the hill now, cloaked in a fine shroud of mist. "There should be a bunch of skyscrapers."

"Yeah." Leopold hesitated, then frowned. "I mean—no. I don't see any of that."

"That's what I'm saying. Where the hell did they go?"

Leopold blinked at Emmet. "What do you mean?"

"What do you mean, *what do I mean*?" He was getting frustrated. "They're gone."

Leopold turned to face his friend. Emmet's eyes were wide, his expression bordering on panic. Emmet was freaking out—and Emmet never freaked out.

"Buildings don't just disappear," Leopold said slowly.

"Great. Yeah. Let's make a list of other obvious facts." Emmet shot him a stony look before returning his eyes to the hill. "First: Buildings don't just disappear. Second: I know what the downtown LA skyline is supposed to look like—and that's not it."

"What are you trying to say? A minute ago you were giving me this big speech about how all this weirdness was just coincidental. Now you're making me think my episodes are contagious."

Emmet was shaking his head. "I realize I just spent hours telling you that what you've been seeing isn't real. But I'm not seeing, like, half-human monsters outside motels. This feels like a cosmic problem. I was born and raised in this beautiful, disgusting city, and it's never looked like *that*." He nodded toward the hill again, then took a deep breath. "There might be more than just a tiny bit of uncanny weirdness happening right now. And I need to know why."

A snap of silent lightning split the night sky. They turned at the same time to gaze at Angels Flight.

Inside the trolley, dimly, a light was burning. For a moment, neither boy drew breath.

"Holy shit," Leopold said softly.

Emmet turned to him. "You still have that token, right?"

FOURTEEN

Neither of them spoke as they jumped the flimsy fence, the sound of metal jangling as they landed on the filthy ground. They navigated a maze of garbage, then ran up fifty feet of steep, rutted track to the back of Angels Flight. They stood together on its rear step, winded and grasping a rusted rail as they peered through its door, open to the elements.

They exchanged a look before ducking inside, Emmet leading the way.

A single bulb in a wire cage cast weak light from the ceiling. Two rows of scarred wooden benches faced off across a long aisle of stairs, rising from one end of the car to the other at a forty-five-degree angle. Trash lay in scattered heaps. Crumpled newspapers, piles of clothing, empty cans. Graffiti crawled across the cracked windows.

At the high end of the car, beside the operator's seat, was a panel of levers and switches.

"Here," Emmet called, jogging up the steps, Leopold close behind him. "There's gotta be a place to drop the token somewhere."

"Wait." Leopold hesitated, gazing at the token in his hand. The bulb above them flickered. Moonlight slanted through the trolley, illuminating movement among the trash: a rat, skittering across the aisle. "This doesn't feel right."

Emmet turned back to face him. "What do you mean?"

Leopold swayed, briefly, before catching himself against one of the hard benches. Something slick smeared his sleeve and a slither of revulsion shuddered through him. He stared again at the token. This was everything he'd wanted for so long. Emmet was all but admitting that Sunder might be real. That they might be on the precipice of discovering a world he'd dreamed about for years.

But it wasn't supposed to happen like this.

Max—of *Max's Adventures in Sunderworld*—had ridden Angels Flight, yes, but he hadn't been forced to jump a chain link fence and tear a hole through his shirt to reach it. He hadn't waded through piles of filth or described the ride to Sunder as smelling vaguely of dried vomit and urine. The door beneath the overpass had led straight to a clean, orderly trolley station, where a friendly conductor had been waiting to escort him onto Angels Flight.

"You okay?" Emmet prompted. "You ready?"

Where was the friendly conductor? The welcome delegation? Then again, when would Leopold have another chance like this—a moment where he and Emmet were aligned, both of them ready to take a risk on Sunder at the same time?

"Yeah," Leopold said, his chest constricting. "Yeah, okay, I'm ready."

They crowded around the switch panel. There it was, beside a big brass lever: a coin slot. Pale blue light pulsed dimly within.

Leopold refused to overthink it. Steadying the slight tremor in his hand, he lifted the token to the slot and let it drop.

He heard Emmet's breath catch just as the ceiling light went out, and they were plunged, all at once, into darkness.

Immediately the floorboards began to vibrate and a series of loud, startling clanks resounded beneath their feet. Before either of them could speak, the trolley shuddered violently into motion. They stumbled and fell onto the benches behind them, so that they were facing one another across the aisle. A sharp crackle issued from ancient speakers in the ceiling, followed by a tinny recorded voice: "Welcome aboard Angels Flight. We're glad you could join us. To ensure your safety, please ensure all hands, arms, limbs, and other appendages remain fully inside the conveyance." Leopold could've sworn it was the same even-toned voice that had narrated the scene upstairs in Clifton's. With another bone-rattling jolt they were grinding up the hill, the trolley tilting precariously to one side as it picked up speed.

"Find something to hang on to," Emmet said urgently, his eyes tracking the darkened windows.

Leopold grabbed one of the handrails, his palms slick and clammy. "Emmet—when you said this thing was a death trap—you were exaggerating, right?"

Emmet shook his head. "A few years ago the trolley fell off its tracks and killed a bunch of tourists."

A knot of dread was expanding in Leopold's chest. "Did they fix it?"

"Does it look like they fixed it? Why do you think it was fenced off?"

The tram was fairly rocketing up the hill now, squealing and clattering as it went, wheels barely clinging to the weed-choked scribble of track. Leopold searched frantically for an emergency brake in the dark. There was a sudden, dramatic pressure change, a sharp pain building in Leopold's ears before they finally popped, then a stomach-churning moment of weightlessness—it felt, briefly, like the trolley had lifted off the ground—and Leopold, who never got motion sickness, thought he might throw up.

Through the windows he could make out a passing impression of shadowy buildings and what seemed to be a grove of tall, thick-trunked trees—and then with a jolt they were slowing, only their tight grip on the handrails preventing them from being thrown to the floor. There was a dissonant chorus of brakes, and with a long shriek of protest, they came to a stop.

Finally, it was quiet.

FIFTEEN

Leopold rose unsteadily to his feet. From the trolley's cracked windows he could see, through settling coils of dust, a small platform that extended to white tiled walls.

They were in some kind of station.

The speakers in the ceiling crackled, and a door to one side of the operator's seat folded open with a sudden slap. "Thank you for riding Angels Flight. Please take a moment to collect your belongings before disembarking, and don't forget to—"

The last few words were garbled, and then the speakers fell silent.

Leopold and Emmet stumbled off the trolley in a daze, their shoes kicking bits of trash from the steps as they descended onto the platform.

The station was pungent and dilapidated. The floor was layered with grime. A row of broken benches lay tipped in a corner. The high ceiling was arched with curving wooden beams skinned in dust and cobwebs, through which the few glass-domed lights still working cast a hesitant, greenish glow. This desolate place would've been the worst kind of disappointment except for two words, faintly illuminated on the wall in front of them, rendered in blocky blue tile:

SUNDER HILL

"*Bro,*" Emmet said quietly, his eyes fixed on the sign as he back-handed Leopold in the chest.

Leopold absorbed the blow, blinking hard. He tapped the floor with his foot. It felt solid; the sound echoed. He was pretty sure he wasn't dreaming. "What the hell," he whispered.

They heard a distant car horn and turned toward the sound. It had come from a corridor blocked by a turnstile, from which other city noises murmured faintly.

Emmet cocked his head toward the corridor, and Leopold nodded.

Wordlessly they crossed the station, their shoes leaving tracks in the dust. Emmet pushed through the turnstile, its metal teeth revolving with a sharp cla-*clack.* As Leopold took his turn, he saw a small analog counter in the stanchion flip from one unreadable, runic-looking character to another. He reached out and slid a hand along the wall tiles as they went, feeling their coolness. The corridor ramped upward, and as they followed its gently spiraling path, a golden-pink light became visible ahead. The city sounds grew louder. Another horn. A siren rose and quickly faded, its odd, songlike wail strangely familiar.

They came to a halt at an arched doorway; just beyond were a city street and a strip of sky.

Pink sky.

The boys traded a heavy, loaded look.

Emmet took the first step out into the unknown, and after a moment, Leopold followed.

SIXTEEN

They couldn't stop staring at the sky.

When they'd boarded Angels Flight, it had been fully dark; here, the sky was a dusky pinkish gold. Above the flats of downtown—from which they'd recently arrived—the heavens were a black canvas brushed with moonlit clouds. If he squinted, Leopold could see the outlines of squat buildings gleaming down there in the night, distant constellations of windows lit from within. But up here, at this eerie trolley station atop the hill, an island of cottony pink luster hovered overhead, bathing the palm-fringed streets around them in a soft, shadowless glow.

Leopold realized, with a sudden jolt and a subsequent shiver, that he'd seen this phenomenon before.

He'd seen it in an episode of *Sunderworld.*

Drawing a tight breath, he turned to stare at a three-story apartment building directly across the street, all stained glass and curving turquoise tilework. This, too, he recognized.

"You seeing what I'm seeing?" Emmet asked, his voice faint.

Leopold's face was tingling as he croaked, "Yeah."

It was an art deco masterpiece floating thirty feet off the ground, pipes and wires dangling from the foundation. A few elderly cars were parked in a gravel lot underneath it, their owners apparently unconcerned about their vehicles being crushed.

ALTA VISTA HOTEL, read the large electric sign in front. COME FOR THE VALUE, STAY FOR THE VIEWS.

Emmet laughed nervously.

Leopold pivoted, only to find that his friend was already yards away, turning in circles to take it all in. Along the street, the salmon-hued clouds merged with a block-long riot of color and light: flashing marquees, glaring billboards, and glimmering shop windows all competing for their overtaxed attention. An enormous, long-finned car from another era whooshed by, but there didn't seem to be anyone at the wheel. Leopold's eyes darted from one shiny thing to another: a window sign that read ACCOUNTING, TAX PREPARATION, DIVINATION beside a neon crystal ball; a store called Best Quality Magic Doors and Portal Repair, Inc.; a shaggy-haired man in sunglasses whistling as he passed them, taking what appeared to be a bush for a walk on a leash.

Leopold tripped along after Emmet, absorbing the scene with dizzy wonder.

There was a café filled with water, chairs and tables bobbing like pool toys near the ceiling, rivulets escaping under the door and running across the sidewalk. THE SEVEN SEAS, read the gilt-etched window. CLOSED FOR MAINTENANCE.

A woman in a high-collared coat brushed past, pursued by three shopping bags.

It felt like he'd stumbled into an old recurring dream, dizzyingly strange but uncannily familiar, too, the edges and details gone fuzzy. He was certain he'd never been here before, yet the many bizarre sights bombarding him didn't feel entirely alien.

A shop window across the street caught his eye.

"*Emmet*," he practically shouted, pointing at its neon sign. "Is that Norm's MagiPawn?"

Emmet jogged over in stunned slow motion, his eyes wide as he turned to look. "Shut the hell up."

Spotlighted in the window was a mannequin holding what looked like a sagging shadow over its shoulder. The sign beside it read: PORTABLE HOLE. GENTLY USED. ASK ABOUT FINANCING!

Emmet pressed his nose against the window. "I always wanted one of those," he said, breath fogging the glass.

A wild-haired man in a huge brown cardigan came suddenly into view. "We're closed!" he shouted from inside, rapping sharply on the window. "Come back tomorrow!"

Emmet jumped back so quickly he nearly sprained an ankle. When he'd recovered his balance, the two boys bolted down the sidewalk. After a brief sprint they collapsed against another building. Leopold felt an inappropriate giggle building in his chest. He covered his mouth, but it couldn't be contained.

"Larry," Emmet said, his tone a warning. "Pull yourself together."

"I can't." Leopold shook his head, a high-pitched laugh escaping. "I'm freaking out. *I'm freaking out—*"

"Me too."

Leopold made an effort to calm himself, but he couldn't stop shaking his head. "You don't understand. I promised myself I would move past this—that I wouldn't lean into the visions anymore—"

Emmet picked up a discarded soda can from the ground, then turned the label for Leopold to see. AETHERBLAST was printed on it in bold letters. "You think this is a vision?" He squinted at the fine print. "*'Extends casting effectiveness up to three hours.'* You're telling me this is fake?"

"Yes?"

Emmet tossed the can away. It rattled across the pavement. "I'm the logical one, Larry." He poked himself in the chest. "And logically speaking, two people can't hallucinate the same thing at the same time."

"We're in LA!" Leopold tossed up his hands, sounding a little desperate even to himself. "What's more likely, that we're in Sunder—that magic is real and my childhood fantasy has come true—or that we're on some weird, elaborate studio backlot?"

"I don't know." Emmet's gaze had fixed on a nearby storefront. On its roof stood a massive, lighted *T*. The letter by itself made no sense, but the jaunty neon sign on the door was simple enough to understand: INFORMATION. "But there's one way to find out."

═══ SEVENTEEN

The place was small, just a short counter fanned with colorful pamphlets, a few posters on the wall. *Experience the Sunderhoods of SoCal. Take a Trip via Tumbleport.* A gentle thrumming sound emanated from a short corridor at the back.

There didn't seem to be anyone around.

Leopold noticed a desk bell on the counter and gave it a tap; it let out a surprisingly loud, resonant *ding*. After a moment they heard what sounded like footsteps approaching—not from the corridor, but underground.

From the center of the room came the loud clack of a bolt sliding. A door in the floor swung open on a squeaking hinge, and then the top few rungs of a ladder rose up as if on a spring.

"What," Emmet said, pointing, but that was all he could manage before a hand appeared on the ladder, followed by a red-sleeved arm and a head with a matching red cap atop it. Then a whole person was climbing out of the floor—a young man in what appeared to be a bellhop's uniform.

"Keep the coffee hot!" he called down the ladder. He dumped an armload of pamphlets into a box under the counter, shoved the ladder back down with one foot, and kicked the door shut with a bang. With all this accomplished he pulled his jacket straight, nudging the cap on his head to a slight angle, and turned to face them with a chipper smile.

"Sorry to keep you folks waiting! You caught me on my two-minute break." He laughed to show it was no big deal. "Name's Art," he said, tapping the name tag on his jacket, "and you've just arrived, if I'm not mistaken?"

Emmet balked. "How'd you know?"

"I can always tell," Art said with a wink. "Something in the eyes— stunned by the majesty of it all. Or the noise and the smog, depending on where you're in from. Where *are* you in from, if you don't mind me asking?"

"In from?" echoed Leopold.

"Which sunder, I mean to say."

Emmet began, "We're just from regular old—"

"Iowa," Leopold interjected, instinct advising him to lie. "The . . . Iowa one?"

Art squinted, then snapped his fingers. "Right—Dubuque! Sometimes I forget we have sunders out in flyover country, no offense meant and none taken, I hope. Not a big spark community, Dubuque. Though I suppose none are, compared to good old Los Angeles"—he pronounced it *angle-eez*—"biggest and best in the whole US! Though I'm biased, of course. Either of you been to Sunder Hill before?"

They both shook their heads.

"Well, on behalf of the Department of Inter-Sunder Cooperation and Commerce, welcome in. You caught us short-staffed today, but I'm happy to give you the nickel tour, so if you've got any questions . . ." He pointed to a button on his jacket that read ASK ME!

Leopold cleared his throat. "Well"—he cleared his throat again—"I guess, um, just to be clear? We're definitely in, like"—he laughed nervously—"Sunderworld right now?"

Art frowned. "You mean Sunder Hill."

"Yeah." Emmet shot Leopold a look. "Sunder Hill. That's what we meant."

Art peered curiously at the boys, as if sensing something was off. "Yes, this is—"

He was interrupted by a loud bang, which drew Leopold's attention down the short rear corridor, where he glimpsed a few large, industrial-looking washers and dryers in an adjacent room.

"There's a laundromat back there?" said Leopold. "I thought this was an information post."

"Information-post-slash-tumbleport-station," Art corrected. "Not technically a laundromat, though there was enough confusion on the matter that we decided to offer the option. Washers and dryers down that aisle, tumbleports over there." He nodded toward the connecting room.

Leopold craned his neck to get a better look. Tumbleports had figured briefly in an episode of *Sunderworld*. An old lady dozed beside one in a plastic chair, the curls of her blue perm vibrating against the whirring machine.

"Now, pardon my confusion," Art went on, his brow furrowed. "But if you came all the way from Dubuque and didn't arrive via tumbleport"—he nodded again at the machines—"then how did you—"

Leopold startled as one of the tumbleports flew open, releasing a cloud of gray smoke. A middle-aged man in a suit crawled out, coughing and swearing. "Damn thing's defective!"

Art rushed over to help him, Leopold and Emmet shifting for a better view of the commotion. The man was covered in mud and cobwebs. He stood up, furiously trying to brush off his clothes while Art fussed over him.

"Let me help you, sir—"

"Get off me, you imbecile! I had an important meeting in Poughkeepsie—ended up in Madagascar! Six hours in the jungle, missed the whole conference, ruined my best traveling suit!"

"I'm very sorry, sir!"

"Do you know how big the insects are in Madagascar?" he cried.

Art wrung his hands. "I don't, sir, but I'm sure the Department of Transportation will pay for your suit to be cleaned—"

"Lot of good that'll do me, I already missed the meeting! And that's not the worst of it. Look at my focuser!" He reached into the machine and pulled out what looked like a smashed camera lens. "This was a *Leica*!"

Leopold stared. He'd dreamed his whole young life of owning a focuser like that. He and Emmet had made countless prop versions from old magnifying glasses and broken thrift store telescopes.

"I'm sure you'll be compensated, sir—"

"I want this problem fixed! Do you think I have time to cross the country on a damned airplane?" He was scraping clumps of mud from his clothes and tossing them at Art's feet. "I suppose they'll blame it on the Aether drought, like everything else. Well, I'm sick of it. Don't I pay my taxes? This place is falling apart!"

With that, he stormed toward the exit without so much as a glance at Leopold and Emmet, slamming the door so hard a banner fell off the wall. Leopold read it before it folded over on itself:

KEEP LA MAGICAL. BE AETHER-WISE!

Aether, even a casual fan of *Sunderworld* knew, was the fuel without which spells could not be cast and magical objects could not function. It occurred naturally in trace amounts in the air, the rain, certain foods, and the bodies of sparks, but the most potent variety was drilled from deposits buried deep in the earth.

Art turned to face them, looking sheepish. "I'm terribly sorry you had to witness that." He produced a small sign from his jacket that read OUT OF AETHER and went to set it on the broken machine.

Leopold and Emmet traded nervous looks. They didn't know anything about an Aether drought, but it was clear they needed to leave before Art started asking more questions they couldn't answer.

"Well, we better get out of your way," Leopold said. "I'm sure you've got a lot to do—"

"Now, wait a second," said Art. "We didn't finish the tour—"

Emmet was shaking his head as they backed toward the door. "Sorry, we're meeting friends for, um, dinner—"

"Oh," Art said, straightening. "I see." He studied the boys, a trace of suspicion still lingering in his eyes. Then, glancing once more at the smoking tumbleport, he seemed to make a decision, and herded them out the door and onto the sidewalk without further interrogation.

"Well, uh, thanks," said Leopold. "For the information."

Art nodded, pasted on a thin smile, and shoved a plastic bag into Leopold's hands. "I can't let you leave without your welcome kit. Inside you'll find one token each for Angels Flight—it hasn't worked in years but it's a Sunder Hill tradition, so consider them souvenirs— and a coupon for a complimentary meal at the Brite Spot." He gestured to a diner down the block, its neon sign glowing orange against the dusky sky. "Try the pie, steer clear of the soup, and tell 'em Art sent you. Any more questions, or if you need anything at all, my card's in there, too . . . Reach out anytime, living or dead. I mean, day or night!" He seemed in a hurry to get back inside. "And if a survey ghoul visits you, I hope you'll rate me five out of five stars. Have a great night! Enjoy your time in Sunder!"

≡ EIGHTEEN

Leopold and Emmet stood in front of the Brite Spot, a warm but weathered greasy spoon that exuded coziness. ANYTHING SERVED ANYTIME was chalked on a sign in its curtained window, through which they could see people snugged into booths and clustered around tables. They only stared, neither of them saying a word.

At the sound of a bell, the glass door swung open. An older gentleman in a precariously tall hat emerged and nodded in their direction.

"Coming in?"

With a glance at his friend, Leopold seemed to emerge from a trance, then moved slowly toward the entrance. He mumbled a thanks to the stranger, then held the door for Emmet, who took another beat to thaw.

Once inside, Leopold was enveloped by the smell of frying eggs.

The place presented, in many ways, like a hundred diners he'd patronized in LA: the aroma of overbrewed coffee, the warm hum of conversation, the clink of silverware. Snug red booths lined the walls. A long counter bisected the room, waitresses in uniform bustling back and forth behind it, balancing plates of food. And yet—there was something distinctly unique about this place. A sign on the wall read NO SLACK DEVICES ALLOWED. A man in a Western jacket dug into a plate of food as he scanned a newspaper that hovered before him, the pages turning on their own. A waitress stopped to warm up his coffee, and as she poured it, a scintillating puff of silver sparks shot up from his mug.

"This place is amazing," Emmet whispered.

Leopold nodded in mute agreement. Then, feeling like his limbs had gone numb, he wobbled over to a booth and collapsed into it, his bones having taken on the consistency of jelly.

Emmet, still fully in possession of his bones, sat down normally, then stared across the table at Leopold. "Okay," he said quietly.

"Okay what?"

"Okay." Emmet leaned forward, his elbows splayed across the chipped brown Formica. "You were right."

"I was right?" That strange thing was still happening to Leopold's extremities, his limbs going heavy and his skin prickling.

"About everything."

"I'm never right about everything."

"Larry. Look at me."

Leopold couldn't. He was staring down at the menus, the two tomes as fat as dictionaries, then up at the ceiling, where bumpy, yellowing tiles were silently rearranging themselves for no obvious reason. A young couple at the next booth sat shoulder to shoulder, chuckling as they watched images dance in the lens of a shared Aether focuser.

For a moment, Leopold wasn't even sure whether he *wanted* this to be real.

"Larry." Emmet snapped his fingers in front of Leopold's face. "Don't freak out on me again."

Leopold shook his head. "I won't. I'm not."

"Listen. This changes *everything*—"

"Hi there!" came a cheerful voice. A waitress with horn-rimmed glasses and bobbed brown hair stood at their booth, chewing gum like she was mad at it. Her name tag read *Kaye*. "Sorry to keep you guys waiting—the kitchen's a hot mess tonight." She snapped her gum and took an order pad from her apron. "The transatomiser is on the fritz, so if you came in hankering for double-broiled char, you'll have to go to Izzy's. You're not here for the char, are you?"

Leopold hesitated. "I don't even know what that is."

She laughed out loud, snorting a little, then swatted his arm playfully. "You're hilarious." She smacked her gum again. "All right, what'll it be?"

Emmet and Leopold looked at their unopened menus. The cover pictured a smiling man in a chef's hat holding a focuser in one hand and a wooden ladle in the other.

"How long is this?" Emmet said, struggling to peel open the pages; they were stuck together with a smear of something that was either strawberry jam or blood.

Leopold managed to pry his apart, and the book fell open with a heavy thud.

"Thirty-seven chapters," Kaye said. "Of course, that's just our late-night menu. If you want the full monty, come back for lunch. So, what'll you have?"

Leopold turned a page, then closed the book. His head was too full; he couldn't decide. Remembering Art's recommendation, he said, "Uh, how about a slice of pie?"

She smiled. "What kind? We've got seventeen—"

"Anything is fine."

"Oh, that's my favorite," said Kaye.

Emmet frowned. "What's your favorite?"

"Anything," she said, cocking a hip. "So. One for each of you, or are you going to share?"

Emmet looked offended. "I don't share food."

"Two slices. No problem. That all?"

"Um, no," said Leopold hesitantly. "Could we get two cups of coffee?"

"You got it. Back in a few." She flipped her notepad shut and, with another crack of her gum and a friendly smile at Leopold, she sauntered off.

Emmet was the first to speak. "Okay, that was weird."

"This whole place is weird."

"No—I mean, why'd she keep smiling at you like that?"

"I don't know."

"Apparently, you're hilarious." Emmet seemed to consider this. "*Are* you hilarious?"

"I'd say my hit rate is like forty-nine percent."

"That seems generous," Emmet said impassively. He returned his attention to the menu, open to a page showing a Jell-O mold in which something resembling eyeballs was suspended.

Leopold exhaled sharply. "Hey."

Emmet looked up. "Yeah?"

"Why the hell aren't you freaking out?" Leopold looked around, then lowered his voice. "This is *crazy*."

Emmet closed his menu. "No," he said calmly. "This is *awesome*. Sunder is real. You had the visions, then you got the key."

"The token."

"The token, whatever. The point is, this is *fate*. You're supposed to be here, Larry—"

"Yeah, but what if I'm not?" he said quietly. "What if this was all some big mistake?"

Emmet hesitated. "What are you talking about?"

From the moment they'd stepped onto Angels Flight, the idea that this had all been an accident had occupied a small but increasingly loud corner of Leopold's thoughts. There'd been no gloss, no fuss, no finesse to his arrival. Everything had been dark and grimy and difficult—like he'd been pushing through a barred door.

It was hard to reconcile: His dreams were coming true, but they weren't happening the way he'd dreamed.

There hadn't been a key, but a token. There had been no magical door, just an unmanned, half-broken trolley car. There had been no welcome, no acknowledgment of his arrival. Instead, his every move had been trailed by literal garbage. Even now he was skulking around in Sunder—hiding his identity for reasons that felt important but unclear.

"What if it turns out they don't actually want us here?" said Leopold. "What if this was all a screw-up at the head office or something? What if the raccoon got its depressed teenagers mixed up?"

"No chance." Emmet was shaking his head. "That raccoon did not get its teenagers mixed up. If anyone's supposed to be here, it's you." He pointed at Leopold. "*This* depressed teenager. Sunder has always been your dream."

Leopold forced a laugh. "She never even mentioned it, you know."

"Who?"

"My mom." Leopold took a breath. "The videotapes were hers—but she never gave them to me. I found them in her stuff, after she died."

He'd been over it a million times in his head. Searched his memory again and again. If his mom had so much as breathed a word to him about Sunder, or about the tapes, it would've been seared into his mind. In his more desperate, younger years, Leopold had convinced himself she'd left the tapes behind on purpose—that she'd wanted him to find them, and to find Sunder—but eventually he'd resigned himself to the disappointing fact that he'd probably never know for sure.

Now he was here, in Sunder, grasping for meaning again.

Grasping for his mother.

"Look," said Emmet. "The only thing we know for sure is that we're here. You're *here*." He shrugged. "And yeah, maybe it's a little grittier than we imagined it would be—but it's real. You really want to know whether we're supposed to be here?" He pointed out the window. "Let's fuck around and find out."

Leopold sank back into his pleather seat, suddenly short of breath. Heat was building behind his eyes. Years of agony were unknotting in his chest, a lifetime of self-doubt being undone in minutes. It was almost too much to bear.

"Hey," Emmet said quietly. "You're not crazy, Larry. And you never were."

NINETEEN

Kaye slid two overfull cups of black coffee toward them,
dumped a handful of creamers onto the table, then set two chipped
plates down with a clatter. Emmet mopped up some spilled coffee
as Leopold stared in awe at the large, golden-crusted wedges of pie.
Oozing from the crust was a jammy indigo filling.

"Enjoy!" she said, before swishing off to another table.

Once Kaye was safely out of earshot, Emmet asked, "What kind of
pie do you think it is?"

"Blueberry?" Leopold guessed.

An aged busboy paused beside their booth to readjust the tub of
dishes he was carrying, then glowered into it. Something in the bottom was snarling. "Oh, shut up in there," he growled, using his free
hand to slap the dishes with a dirty rag.

Emmet and Leopold looked at one another uncertainly, and then,
more uncertainly, at the pie.

"We have to take at least a couple of bites," Leopold said.

"It'd be rude not to," Emmet agreed.

Leopold leaned down and gave his slice a sniff. Seemed safe. He
picked up his fork and cut a small bite. The texture was convincingly
pie-like.

Slowly, he chewed. And then he nearly fell out of the booth. "Oh my God."

"What?" Emmet said, alarmed. "Is it disgusting?"

"No," said Leopold, taking another bite. "It's *amafing*."

"I hope you mean *amazing*."

Leopold nodded eagerly, too distracted by the bright flavors going off like fireworks on his tongue. The first bite had started out tasting like perfectly ripe, sweet raspberries, but before he'd swallowed had become the best apple pie he'd ever had. The second bite began as pumpkin, then transformed to cherry cola spiced with something incongruously savory but delicious, which left a pleasant fizzing sensation in his mouth.

Emmet leaned in. "What does it taste like?"

"Lots of things—I can't describe it," Leopold said while cutting a third bite, "but it might be the single best thing I've eaten in my entire life."

"Seriously?" Emmet picked up his fork and took a huge bite, his eyes widening as he chewed. "Holy shit," he said with his mouth full. "Are we eating *magic* right now?"

"Yeah." A thrill laddered down Leopold's back. "I'm pretty sure we are."

As Emmet redoubled his efforts, something drew Leopold's attention to a corner of the diner. Alone in a dim booth sat a girl about his age. She wore a dark green cloak that matched the mossy green of her eyes, its hood pooling around her shoulders, her dark hair pulled into a tight ponytail. She was beautiful. He couldn't help but register this as she stared at him—with a look bordering on suspicion—until he met her gaze straight on and she ducked behind one of the Brite Spot's voluminous menus.

How long had she been watching? Were other people? Leopold worried that he and Emmet had been talking too loudly and did not sound at all like magically abled tourists from Iowa.

"Larry." Emmet was snapping his fingers at Leopold. "Where'd you go?"

"Sorry. This girl was staring at me."

Emmet looked skeptical. "Where?"

"Wait—*don't look*—"

Emmet turned and sat up in his seat, obvious as a fire alarm. "The one in the booth by the bathrooms?"

Leopold scowled. "Idiot. I told you not to look."

Emmet dropped back into his seat. "Okay, is there something about this place that makes you irresistible to women?"

Leopold's face went hot. "Shut up."

The girl was still pretending to read her menu.

"Oh shit," Emmet hissed. "Is that really what time it is?" He was gaping at a clock on the wall. It was well after midnight. "I told my parents I'd be home by eleven thirty." He dug out his phone. "I have to text them to at least let them know I'm . . . What the hell?"

He turned the screen toward Leopold. It was black, with a message in red across the middle:

Slack Tech Disallowed

Leopold raised his eyebrows, took out his own phone, and tapped its screen. He got the same message.

Slack was the pejorative Sundarian term for people with no magical ability, and though Leopold was increasingly sure he wasn't one, his phone apparently qualified as "slack tech."

"All right, time to go," Emmet said, gathering his things. "I mean, at this point your dad's going to straight-up kill you when you get home, right? You don't want to be late for your own murder."

Leopold didn't laugh. A sudden apprehension had gripped him. "Wait—we can't just leave."

"Why not?"

"How will we get back in again?"

"Art gave us two tokens for Angels Flight, remember? And I'm sure we could get more just by asking. He was super casual about it."

"Right," Leopold said, relaxing. He fished the coins from the welcome bag and held them gingerly in his hand. After years of waiting for his key to Sunder, the idea that he could come and go as he pleased was so profound he felt lightheaded just thinking about it. Why Angels Flight had been retired and abandoned was a question for another time. But that was the point: They had time.

"Take both," Emmet said generously. "There's no way I'm coming here without you, anyway."

Leopold took a bracing breath. "Thanks, man," he said. "I appreciate that."

He dropped the coins back into the small bag and placed it on the table. He'd go home tonight to face his father, who'd rage at him for at least an hour, but the idea didn't fill him with the same dread it usually did. Just knowing this world would be waiting for him—and that the tokens were safely in his possession—was like wearing a suit of armor, one Richter could do nothing to pierce.

"Check, please!"

Emmet signaled to Kaye while Leopold searched the welcome bag for their meal coupon. Along with a few brochures, a bright green card fluttered out. It was about the size of a dollar bill and printed on heavy paper.

Leopold read it, reread it, then slid the card across the table. "Hey, look at this."

Emmet snatched up the card. "It's a gift certificate," he said, his eyes widening as he scanned the text. "For *spells.*"

They looked at each other.

"Mister Worthington," Leopold said evenly. "I'm of the opinion that it would be completely irresponsible of us to leave here tonight without first doing some magic."

Emmet nodded seriously. "Stupid, even."

Kaye arrived with the check. "You guys have a coupon, is that right?"

Emmet handed it over, then held up the green certificate. "You wouldn't happen to know where we could use this, would you?"

She squinted at it, then glanced out the darkened window. "To-night?"

"Tonight," the boys said at the same time.

Kaye pursed her lips, thinking. "At this hour, only one place will be open."

TWENTY

The blindingly bright sign on the roof read 99 Spells . . . and More!
The magic store stood between a hamburger joint and a print
shop, both closed for the night. Despite the late hour, Sunder Hill's
eternal dusk still cast its pinkish glow over everything, but the streets
were increasingly deserted and a chill had sharpened the air. Leopold,
arms folded tight across his chest as they crossed the small parking
lot, wished he still had his jacket.

It looked like the kind of chain drug emporium that anchored
every strip mall in LA, its windows allowing a glimpse of neat aisles
and carpeted floors within. The automatic doors whooshed open.
They walked into a blast of garish white light and overzealous air-
conditioning.

At the front, a young man in a purple vest was passing a woman's
purchases over a beeping scanner. A lone shopper meandered with
a basket. Signs above each aisle announced categories like Cleaning Prod. & Household Charms; Cold Remedies; Glamours
& Bladder Control.

The in-store speakers were playing an old, cheesy pop song,
which was quickly interrupted by a PA announcement. "Jorge, customer assistance in Beauty and Life Extension. Jorge, Beauty and
Life Extension."

The store was a mishmash of the magical and the mundane. There were shelves of items that didn't seem magical at all mingled with things that clearly were. Leopold grabbed a plastic-handled basket from a stack by the door, then joined Emmet, who was already browsing.

"Okay, this isn't magical," Emmet said, turning over a stick of deodorant in his hand. "I use this brand. And here"—he picked up a box of toothpaste—"they carry this at CVS."

"Well, CVS sure as hell doesn't carry *this*." Leopold studied a small black bottle. "Nev-r Stink. Says it makes you 'odorless forever.' In fact"—he squinted at the fine print—"if you take enough, you even become 'odor absorbent.' Whatever that means."

Emmet crossed to the other side of the aisle. *"No way,"* he said, his voice hushed with wonder. "Doppel-Buddies!"

"What, seriously?" Leopold turned to look. A stack of dusty boxes lined a shelf, each containing one naked, sexless, blank-faced action figure. The stock color was gray, but the label promised the figures would adapt to any skin tone.

Grow a New You! read the display.

Leopold grabbed a box, turning it reverently in his hands. "Remember the episode when Max makes a copy of himself?"

"Yeah—so it would impersonate him at school while he was battling Noxum in Sunder."

Leopold dropped a Buddy into their basket. "But then it turns violent in episode six or seven, and he has to hunt it down and—"

"Hold up," Emmet said. "Why doesn't anything here have a price tag?"

"Maybe everything's the same price?" Leopold said doubtfully. He took the gift certificate from his pocket and studied the back. "Wait, this says it's redeemable for only one item." He peered at a line of smaller type. *"Of low value."*

Emmet muttered, "Art, you cheap bastard."

"Shit. Okay. If we can only get one thing, what should it be?"

They looked at each other.

"A focuser," they said in unison.

TWENTY-ONE

Emmet flagged down the only clerk on shift: a grumpy, gray-bearded man who'd been stocking supplies in the Divination aisle. The name tag on his red polo shirt read *Jorge*, and when Leopold and Emmet explained what they wanted, Jorge set down his price-tagging gun, cut them off with a single, tired look, and slouched off toward the Aether focusers.

With unsubtle irritation, he unlocked the doors of a glass cabinet. "All right, what'll it be?"

Arranged upon the cabinet's felt-lined shelves were all manner of focusers—which looked like gleaming camera lenses housed in sleek, circular bodies. For a moment they were all Leopold could see, as if a spotlight from heaven were illuminating the dingy cabinet, throwing all else into darkness. The Aether focuser was Sunder's answer to the magic wand, its lens designed to strengthen and concentrate a spark's magical energy in a particular direction. Spells cast without them were messy, unpredictable, weak—*unfocused*—and, with rare exceptions, illegal.

Leopold fought a powerful urge to grab one off the shelf without asking.

"We need your best model," Emmet said confidently, and Leopold nodded.

Jorge rolled his eyes. "Good ones with primo glass are up top. Contax, Rolleiflex, Hasselblad. They auto-calibrate to your ability level. The lenses open up to $f/1.2$ for maximum spell extraction and are built like Sherman tanks. You could drop one from an airplane and probably still get a decent cast out of it." Then, with a sidelong glance: "You planning on dropping yours out of an airplane?"

"No." Leopold laughed nervously.

"Then I'd recommend one of these." He pointed to a lower shelf, stocked with focusers that were more compact but still sturdy-looking.

Emmet took out the gift certificate. "Which one will this get us?"

Scanning it, Jorge's irritation blossomed into unveiled anger. He studied Leopold and Emmet a beat, then stalked away, muttering, "Goddamn teenagers. Always wasting my time."

"Wait—" Emmet called after him. "We're serious customers! Do you take regular-world credit cards?"

Quietly, Leopold said, "You have a credit card?"

"It's my mom's," Emmet answered under his breath. "For emergencies."

Jorge's only response was to scowl and point at a massive sign by the entrance, which read:

CASH ONLY

Undaunted, Leopold and Emmet rushed toward the register, where Jorge was trying to slip out a door marked EMPLOYEE EXIT.

"Is there anywhere around here we can get some Sunder money?" Leopold called after him. "An ATM or something?"

Jorge finally turned around, incredulous. "What the hell is *Sunder money*?"

Emmet and Leopold traded a glance.

"You know, I can't remember Max actually *buying* anything on the show," Leopold whispered. "I just assumed—"

"I've got cash!" Emmet exclaimed triumphantly, pulling a few bills from his wallet. "Ten—no, twenty. Twenty bucks. You take American dollars?"

"Are you kids stoned?" the clerk said flatly.

"No, sir," Leopold said, straightening to his full height.

Jorge considered them for a moment, then took the money from Emmet's outstretched hand. "All right, whatever," he said, nodding toward the cabinet. "I might have something for you."

TWENTY-TWO

What he had for them was a piece of shit.

The focuser in Leopold's hand was made of plastic, small enough to slip into his pocket, its fraying wrist strap printed with cartoon images of cats and ice cream cones.

FUNCAST was stamped on the back.

Jorge had thrown in a couple of disposable pre-cast spells: circular, semi-opaque filters that fit over the tiny lens, which was so badly scratched it looked like someone had tried to sand wood with it.

But it was a focuser. And it was theirs.

They stood in the alley outside 99 Spells, Emmet tilting the precasts up to a slant of streetlight so he could make out the writing around their edges. "We've got one called Lil' Levitator and one called Make It Snow," he said. "Seems pretty self-explanatory." He held them out to Leopold. "You pick."

Leopold chose the Lil' Levitator, then slipped his wrist through the focuser's strap. Cigarette butts and discarded pre-casts were scattered nearby; clearly, they weren't the first people to hang out here, casting cheap spells.

Suddenly, his throat went dry.

It was happening.

He was about to do magic. Real magic, on purpose. This night had been so surreal that he'd hardly stopped to process it all, to feel the weight of the moment. Years of dreaming—of doubting—had all come to this.

"Don't be in your head right now." Emmet nodded at the focuser in Leopold's hand. "Nike."

Leopold frowned. "What?"

"Just do it, Larry."

"Dumbass," Leopold said, cracking a grin, and Emmet smiled to match.

There was no one at either end of the alley. No one watching. Leopold was hardly even aware of the cold. He fit the pre-cast levitation spell over the focuser's lens and snapped it into place with a satisfying click. The Funcast's only movable parts were its flimsy aperture ring and a single CAST button on the side. His finger hovered over the button.

"Well. Here goes nothing."

He triggered the button and the lens flashed dimly. There was a robotic whisper at the edge of hearing—the auto-incantation—and then he was flung into the air and flipped upside down. Leopold cried out as his stomach did a somersault and his car keys dropped from his pocket. Emmet shouted in alarm and made a swipe for Leopold, but he was too late. Graffitied bricks blurred past as Leopold soared feetfirst toward the clouds, but his panic proved unnecessary. About twenty feet off the ground he came to a sudden halt, still upside down.

"You okay?" Emmet called out anxiously.

"I'm okay," Leopold said, his heart racing. "I think I aimed too high." Blood rushing to his head, he took hold of the focuser again and, this time, pointed it at the ground.

He pushed the button and flipped upright, the pavement and the pink sky trading places. His confidence slowly building, Leopold twisted the plastic aperture ring and descended a few feet. He twisted it the other way and rose again, bouncing to a stop a little higher than before.

"I think you're getting it!" Emmet shouted.

Leopold aimed the focuser at a nearby wall, pushed the cast button, and was yanked sideways until his feet met brick. He stood then at a ninety-degree angle to the wall, casting a huge shadow across the alley below. It was dizzying and surreal.

With his head gently spinning, he took a few exploratory steps. His shoes stuck like they were glued in place until the moment he lifted them, when they came away with easy *pops*.

From this vantage he could see the rooftops of Sunder Hill. He lingered a moment, gazing out across Sunder's dazzling main street, where a few night owls were leaving a beautiful art deco theater, the movie titles on its marquee sign spelled out in runic Sunderese. A few streets away, the top floor of the fortresslike Sunder Bank and Trust was encircled with angry, swirling mist—some sort of defense mechanism, Leopold reckoned, against thieves or something worse. Standing proud at the edge of it all, the tallest building in Sunder Hill was a towering pyramid of glass. Leopold recognized this as the headquarters of the Department, where Sunder's governing bureaucrats and decision-makers had their offices. Reflecting the sky, its mirrored surfaces were a beacon of gold and pink that stood in stark contrast to the dim, unmagical neighborhoods that rolled out endlessly beyond it.

It was all here, all knowable. All finally within Leopold's grasp.

There was a jangle below as Emmet scooped up Leopold's fallen keys. "You good?" he called up to Leopold.

"Yeah." Leopold could feel something strange coursing through him. A stinging behind his eyes, a fullness in his chest.

It was, he realized, happiness.

TWENTY-THREE

"I still don't understand why it didn't work for you," said Leopold. They were walking back toward Angels Flight, passing the Brite Spot, its windows now dark. "It was probably that crappy focuser. Or maybe that snow pre-cast was expired—"

"Seriously, it's not a big deal," Emmet replied, his eyes on a service station at the corner, where a lone man stood gassing an old, boatlike sedan. There was a wistful quality to his voice when he spoke. "I don't really care that much whether or not I can do magic."

Three times Emmet had tried and failed to get the Funcast to work, to no avail. Finally, he'd insisted that getting home before dawn was more important, and Leopold had begrudgingly relented.

Still, he couldn't deny the glaring differences between their experiences.

In Emmet's hands the focuser had seemed clumsy, alien. But to Leopold casting had felt natural, like something he'd done a thousand times before, the hum of power in his hands as he held the focuser a sensation embedded in cell memory. Somewhere in his marrow the feeling *fit*, and he allowed himself, for the space of a breath, to picture more: him, Leopold Berry, among the most powerful sparks in Sunder, entrusted with protecting the magical world from shambling, snarling night-realm beasts. Learning colossal spells. Wielding some fat-lensed focuser to blast a Noxum with a bolt of death magic, then dragging its body into a black, bubbling containment pit.

The fantasy was so grand, he was almost embarrassed for himself.

Leopold cleared his throat, cleared his mind, then returned his eyes to Emmet. "You sure you don't want to try again before we leave?"

"I'm sure," Emmet said, shifting his gaze skyward. "Sunder was always your dream, man, not mine. I was happy to be along for the ride then—and I'm happy to be along for the ride now."

Leopold nodded, ever grateful for his friend's even temper. They walked for a while in affable quiet, taking in the final blocks of Sunder Hill's dreamy, pink-hued cityscape before the Angels Flight station. They passed a travel agency, its window advertising trips to sunders around the country—there was a flash sale on tumbleport tours to Muncie—and then a grand hotel, this one firmly secured to the ground, with a tuxedoed valet standing outside a lobby gleaming with chandeliers. Nearby, a garbage man was tossing trash bags into a portable hole he dragged along behind him; the clatter the bags made when they finally hit bottom, several seconds later, was an almost inaudible *tink*.

"You know what's weird?" said Emmet, his eyes shifting to Leopold. "In the show, there were outer-realm creatures walking around in Sunder. Orax, perishers, the occasional well-behaved rust fiend—but can you remember seeing any tonight?"

Leopold paused, trying to recall, then shrugged. "In the show, Max rode a flying horse," he pointed out. "I don't think whoever made *Sunderworld* was super concerned with accuracy."

It occurred to him that the show might've fudged or exaggerated some details to make Sunder appear less real. The more artificial the fantasy seemed, the less likely some overly curious slack would go looking for an entrance. The same theory might also explain the show's bargain-basement production values. Leopold was about to suggest this to Emmet when he realized Emmet was no longer beside him, but had darted off to examine a nearby statue.

"Check this out," he said, beckoning to Leopold as he bent to study a plaque at its base. Emmet could never resist a good informational plaque. "It says this guy founded Sunder. Charles Vigdor."

Leopold joined him at the foot of the statue. "Sunder had a founder?" He gazed up at a stocky man cast in twenty feet of bronze, clad in bronze cowboy boots, a bronze ten-gallon hat, and a giant, bronze mustache that covered half his face.

"This says he drilled the world's first Aether well, right here in Sunder Hill, in 1909." Emmet began to read aloud. "'Striking what's known as The Vein, Mr. Vigdor tapped into a seemingly limitless deposit of Aether that attracted sparks from around the world to Los Angeles. Thanks to his discovery, magical technology has progressed more in the past hundred years than in the previous thousand—'"

The pink clouds flickered without warning, popping on and off like a faulty bulb.

"What the hell," Emmet said, looking up from words he could no longer read.

The sky went completely dark. Down the street someone shouted, "Oh, *come on!*"

"Aether outage?" Leopold guessed, remembering the angry guy from the tumbleport station.

"Whatever it is, it can't be good," Emmet said.

Just then they heard the distant, eerie wail of an emergency siren.

TWENTY-FOUR

The siren pitched slowly up and down. Pale moonlight shone across rooftops all along the block, but otherwise everything was enveloped in shadow and gloom. Even the streetlamps and lighted shop windows had gone dark. And then a voice rang out from every direction, issuing as if from loudspeakers. It was the same male announcer they'd heard several times before.

"This is the emergency warning system. Please proceed to the nearest refuge point to await further instructions."

"Refuge point?" Emmet repeated, sounding a little worried now. He pulled out his phone to use as a light, only to be reminded it didn't work. "Yeah, it's definitely time to go home."

Leopold stayed rooted to the spot.

His pulse was racing. There was an unease in the air—the promise of danger—and yet Leopold felt no compulsion to flee. In fact, he was experiencing an overwhelming surge of protectiveness for this absurd, magical place.

Something was wrong, and he wanted to know what it was. More than that, he realized: He wanted to help. Life had changed irrevocably for him tonight.

Hell, he'd done *magic* tonight.

Leopold knew he couldn't stay here forever—he knew he'd have to go home and deal with his normal life eventually—but he wanted to make sure that Sunder would still be here when he came back.

Because he was definitely coming back.

"Larry?"

"Proceed directly to the nearest refuge point," the announcement repeated. "And comply with all instructions given by paladins or peace officers."

At the word *paladins* Leopold straightened.

"Damn," Emmet said with a sigh. "Did he just say *paladins*?"

Leopold was fighting a smile. "Yeah."

"We have to stay now, don't we?"

"I think we do, Mister Worthington."

"After Richter kills you, my parents are going to kill me. Double homicide."

"Worth it, though, right?"

"Hell yeah," Emmet said, almost laughing. Then he turned and shouted into the empty air, "Does anyone know the way to the refuge point?"

"Thisaway!"

The voice had come from the sidewalk across the street, where a group of people were moving through a shaft of moonlight. They all appeared to be heading in the same direction, though they didn't seem to be in much of a hurry.

Leopold and Emmet jogged over to them. Emmet asked what was going on.

"Noxum alarm," said an older man in a coat too heavy for the weather. "Nothing to worry about. Probably just a drill."

Noxum were the most feared monsters in Sunder. While they ranged widely in size and lethality—minor Noxum could usually be dispatched without calling in the paladins—major Noxum were terrifying creatures of another order altogether and, in the show, were known for murderous rampages that claimed dozens of lives before they could be put down.

"Does this happen a lot?" asked Leopold, a thrill going down his spine.

"Once or twice a month," said someone whose voice they recognized. It was Jorge from 99 Spells. He turned on a flashlight and the beam bobbled ahead of them.

"First time they've cut the Aether, though," said a yawning lady. She sounded more tired than worried. "I was just about to cast myself to sleep."

In fact, none of them seemed worried. They had the slouching pace of high school kids during a routine fire drill.

"Larry." Emmet's elbow dug into his ribs. "Look."

Out of the shadows came a small troop of uniformed young men and women. They strode down the middle of the street, shoulder to shoulder in tailored green paladin uniforms and tall brown boots. Bandoliers studded with vials of Aether crossed their chests, and they carried serious-looking focusers, the lenses' thick glass glinting in the moonlight.

"Thank you for your service," Jorge called out.

Leopold and Emmet had once made paladin uniforms for themselves, repurposed from old Boy Scout stuff—costumes for their homespun version of *Sunderworld*. Most young sparks were required to serve for a time in the Paladin Corps, widely respected as Sunder's first and best line of defense against the Noxum. Max's mentor had been a paladin commander, battle-scarred from the last Noxum War.

They hadn't yet reached the refuge point when the siren began to wind down. A new announcement echoed and their group came to a sudden halt.

"This has been a test of the emergency warning system. You may return to your homes. Thank you for your cooperation."

There were murmurs of irritation, several people muttering choice words for the inconveniences they'd endured.

"Do you think the lights will come back on?" Leopold whispered to Emmet.

Before Emmet could respond, a pyramid of boxy televisions blared to life in the window of a nearby electronics shop, the jarring light and loud sound cracking the silence. A dozen flickering screens showed the same footage: a woman with cropped white hair and black-rimmed glasses fielding questions from a podium. A chyron across the bottom read:

Executive Angela Ramirez's news conference, earlier today

Her voice boomed. Leopold winced even as he pushed closer to the screens. "I want to assure you," the woman was saying, "that we are making every effort to ensure the Aether supply remains uninterrupted. I know these outages have been inconvenient for everyone, but the situation is temporary."

"They're showing this again?" Jorge complained.

The woman in the bathrobe shushed him.

Executive was an honorific reserved for the elected leader of Sunder, the head of its small but powerful governing body. In *Sunderworld* the Executive had been portrayed by an older male actor who'd given the character a sarcastic edge and a quick temper.

As he watched the genuine article speak, Leopold had a dreamlike moment. He was both exhausted and exhilarated, his mind running on fumes and adrenaline. The garish blue glare of the TVs contrasted against the dark around him, making the cold night feel milky and soft. After so many years of telling himself Sunder was fake, now he had to keep reminding himself it was real—that right now, he was standing in the middle of a Sunder street watching the Sunder Executive field questions.

It was not only real, but *surreal*.

"*Bro,*" said Emmet quietly.

Leopold smiled. "I know."

Off-screen a reporter asked, "Executive, is there any connection between the Aether shortages and the recent uptick in Noxum attacks?"

"None at all," she said firmly. "The shortages are due to unusually extreme seasonal fluctuations in our Aether wells and should resolve themselves before long. The attacks were isolated incidents and nothing our brave paladins couldn't handle. Even so, I would like to remind everyone to take basic anti-Noxum precautions, and to conserve Aether whenever possible."

Another reporter: "And what about the search for a channeler? Couldn't that offer relief on both fronts?"

Leopold felt a sudden shock at the word *channeler*, a wire pulling taut within him.

Chan·nel·er | ˈChan(ə)l ər | noun: the most powerful magical being on the planet

More specifically: an extremely rare spark that came along only once a generation or so, who could kill Noxum with little effort and summon vast amounts of Aether from the air, enabling them to cast substantial spells without a focuser. On the show, Max had discovered he was a channeler and spent much of the first season honing his untapped abilities.

"Are you hearing this?" Emmet hissed.

Leopold nodded numbly.

Emmet hit him in the arm. "That's gotta be you."

Leopold tensed, apprehension radiating through him. He turned sharply to Emmet. "Don't even joke about that."

"I'm not—"

"Will you two hush?" said Bathrobe Lady.

Several reporters were asking about the channeler search now, all talking over one another, and Executive Ramirez had to raise her hand for quiet. She adjusted her glasses and continued. "The search is ongoing," she said with a brittle smile. "That's all I have time for today. Thank you." With a respectful nod she turned and walked away while the camera held on the empty podium.

The sky came alight with pink clouds again, though dimmer than before, and the streetlights with it, jolts of static crackling the air as they snapped on. The process was staggered so that the lamps and neon signs at the end of the block lit up first, then rolled toward them until they were awash in color. A billboard advertising the services of a magical injury lawyer flickered on across the street, and the group of irritable stragglers slowly dispersed, leaving Emmet and Leopold alone.

The pair stood frozen, still watching the blaring televisions, as if hypnotized.

"That was Executive Angela Ramirez, earlier today." On the dozen screens, the camera had cut to a pair of news anchors inside a studio. "As always, if you think you know someone who might be a channeler, contact the Department right away."

A phone number flashed across the screen.

They both stared at it.

"Larry," Emmet whispered.

Leopold couldn't move.

"Mister Berry." Emmet turned to face him. "We need to find a phone."

"No," Leopold said sharply.

There was a sudden electrical pop from the street behind them. Emmet turned to look. When he turned back, he grasped Leopold by the shoulders and spun him around.

Across the street, lit from the inside and shining brightly, was a phone booth.

TWENTY-FIVE

Leopold and Emmet crammed into the small booth, Leopold wrestling the rusted accordion door shut behind them. Ivy had snaked its way inside the poorly sealed space, the interior half-devoured by vines that Emmet forcibly tore away from the heavy black receiver. Finally, he lifted the phone from its cradle, pressing it into Leopold's hands as if it were his firstborn child.

"*Call.*"

"This is crazy." Leopold gazed at the scuffed phone, shaking his head. A dial tone buzzed insistently. "I can't be the channeler."

"Why the hell not?"

"Are you kidding? Maybe because I've only ever cast one spell, like, twenty minutes ago—"

"So what?" Emmet countered. "Did Max start off casting tons of spells right away? That doesn't mean anything."

"If I'm the channeler, why was it so hard to get here? And why'd it take so long to get my token? And—"

"Who knows? You probably weren't ready yet." Emmet tried to gesture out the window, and in the process nearly slapped Leopold in the face. "Isn't it obvious?"

Leopold flinched. "Isn't what obvious?"

"All of it. The tapes, the show. The last six years of your life. There's a reason you were obsessed with *Sunderworld*. There's a reason you kept Seeing into Sunder. It wasn't random, and it wasn't just because your mom died. You found those tapes because you were supposed to." Emmet pointed toward the pyramid of TVs across the street, and this time he really did hit Leopold in the face.

"Ow," muttered Leopold. "What the hell!"

"Pay attention. They're running out of Aether. The Noxum situation is worse than they want to admit. They're overdue for a channeler." Emmet looked at him seriously. "What are the odds that everything you've been through—all these years—was some big coincidence?"

Leopold tensed. He'd always felt, deep down, that there had been more at work behind the scenes of his life than chance and randomness. That there had to be some meaning, some purpose in all he'd experienced. Emmet was only saying something he'd thought himself a thousand times.

Leopold was too practical to lie, and the truth was, he didn't want to. He remembered casting the spell in the alley—how natural the focuser had felt in his hands, how quickly and easily he'd mastered the basic technique.

"Larry," Emmet tried again. "These people need you."

Leopold's arms prickled with goosebumps. With one last look at the TV screens across the street, he raised the phone to his ear and began to dial.

TWENTY-SIX

"This is Executive Angela Ramirez."

Leopold nearly dropped the phone. "You answer this line yourself?"

"When it's of importance." Her tone was clipped and businesslike, but not unkind. "Is it?"

"Yes. I, uh"—he glanced desperately at Emmet, who flipped him off—"I saw you on TV, and um—the thing is—I think I might be the channeler."

Emmet did a silent fist pump.

There was a brief pause before the Executive replied, during which anxiety began to knot in Leopold's chest. He heard papers rustling in the background.

"That's a bold claim." She sounded vaguely amused. "Who am I speaking with?"

"Uh, my name's Larry. Larry Berry."

He could almost hear her smirk. "All right, Larry Berry. What makes you think you might be the greatest magical talent in recent history?"

"I don't," he said automatically. "I mean—I don't know—"

"You don't know."

Emmet frowned at Leopold, shaking his head as if to say, *What the hell are you doing?*

Leopold took a steadying breath. "I just—I have a really strong feeling about it. I mean, I know that's not, like, *evidence*, and I know you're probably super busy, and I'm sure you can't give a channeler test to every person who calls you up claiming to have a strong feeling, but—"

"Strong feelings are occasionally admissible as evidence, Larry, but I'd prefer something less hypothetical. Have you had any violent encounters with Noxum or other outer-realm creatures?" She sounded like a slightly bored doctor checking off symptoms. "Have you been stalked by any? Killed one, perhaps?"

"Um, no, but I think I might've made it rain? In Los Angeles, during a drought? And all day this flaming raccoon—well, sometimes it was on fire, sometimes it wasn't—has been following me around—"

The Executive *mm-hmm*ed, her tone inscrutably neutral, and Leopold knew he was losing her. He racked his brain for more. The shiggoth woman outside the motel. His near-collision with the trolley. "Tonight I did magic behind 99 Spells. It was just a pre-cast, but it went pretty well for my first try, I think . . ."

"The videos!" Emmet stage-whispered. "Tell her about the videos!"

Leopold waved him off. If the flaming raccoon and sudden rainstorm he'd conjured hadn't convinced her, why would his videotape collection?

"Your first try?" the Executive said curiously. "You mean, before tonight, you'd never used a focuser?"

"No." Leopold felt out of breath.

"Larry."

"Yeah? I mean, yes?"

"You're claiming you made it rain in LA without a focuser?"

"I—I think maybe—"

"When?"

He paused. "Uh, this afternoon?"

Another rustle of papers. "There was no rain forecast for today."

"No, ma'am."

After a moment she said, "The brief downpour earlier—that was your work?"

"Um, I think so." Emmet hit him, and Leopold yelped. "I mean, yes. It was."

The Executive sighed.

Leopold waited, his heart beating out of his chest. His eyes came to rest on a lost-pet flyer pasted to the wall, the strange, furry thing pictured resembling no species he'd ever seen before. Emmet whispered, *"Did she say yes?"* and Leopold backhanded him in the arm.

Finally, the Executive spoke. "Are you at liberty now?"

Leopold blinked. "At liberty?"

"To come and meet me. I realize it's late."

"You want to meet," he echoed, feeling dazed. Emmet's eyes widened, a grin spreading across his face.

"You sound a little unsure of yourself, if I'm being honest. But it's always better to be humble than arrogant. You're less likely to get killed that way. Also, I don't get as many calls from would-be channelers as you might imagine," she said, "and I'm obligated to take each one seriously. So, are you at liberty?"

Leopold looked at Emmet, who was shadowboxing the air.

"Can I bring a friend?"

TWENTY-SEVEN

Golden elevator doors slid open to reveal an expansive, glass-walled office, moodily lit and modern.

"Welcome, welcome," said the Executive, peeling off black-rimmed glasses as she rose from her desk. "Come right in." She was shorter than Leopold had expected. In and of itself this wasn't unusual—most people were shorter than Leopold—but in this instance he was surprised, given her intimidating presence on television.

Cautiously, Leopold crossed the polished floor to shake her outstretched hand. The last few minutes had been a blur: the long, driverless limousine that had arrived moments after he'd hung up the phone; being whisked through the neon chaos of Sunder Hill and into the tall, pyramid-shaped Department headquarters building; the dizzyingly fast elevator ride to the thirty-second floor; and now this, meeting the Executive herself.

Angela Ramirez had a remarkably firm handshake.

"Should I assume," she said, eyes crinkling as she flashed a friendly smile, "that you're the Larry Berry I spoke with on the phone?" She turned to Emmet. "Or perhaps—"

"I'm Emmet Worthington, ma'am." He stepped forward to shake her hand. "Not magical. Just along for the ride."

"Ah, well, that's all right," she said generously, then looked them up and down. "You're both kind of a mess, aren't you?"

"It's been a long night," Leopold conceded. He decided he already liked her: She had an easy elegance and radiated gentle power unmarred by insecurity.

"Should I pull some clean clothes from wardrobe?" said the man who'd accompanied them from the lobby. Leopold had nearly forgotten he was still in the room. The man in the baggy suit had introduced himself as Keeves. He had a shuffling gait and a wide, blotchy face, and there was something about his darting eyes and the way they studied Leopold that made him uneasy.

"I'm sure the furniture will survive, Keeves. That's all for now."

"Yes, ma'am." He flashed the saccharine smile of a first-class lickspittle and went out.

The Executive ushered the boys forward. Leopold hadn't spent much time imagining what the office of a Sunderian Executive might look like, but he would've expected it to contain a dripping candelabra or two and, at minimum, a stock of magical ingredients bubbling in a corner somewhere. Instead, it felt as if they were walking into the pages of some architectural magazine.

"Not very magical, I know," said the Executive, seeming to read his thoughts. She followed his gaze around the room. "But our designer is obsessed with the midcentury thing. We'll probably circle back to cast iron and cauldrons next year."

"Right." Leopold laughed nervously.

They approached the windows, pausing to admire the Executive's dizzying view of Los Angeles. Sunder Hill's island of pink cloud stretched toward the horizon before petering out into wisps of fog. Distantly, smaller patches of golden-pink cloud glowed here and there in the dark; Leopold realized they probably lighted the streets of other sunderhoods, scattered like pearls across the tapestry of the city. He couldn't help but wonder where the hell it had all come from—sparks, sunders, Aether, magic itself—but he told himself that he'd get all the answers he needed once he'd passed the test.

"Wow," he said. "You get to look at this every day?"

"Beautiful, isn't it?" the Executive remarked. "The magical and unmagical overlapping—"

Just then the pink clouds across the whole city flickered, and her smile disappeared.

"The color used to be brighter, of course," she said, "but increasingly we lack the resources to keep things going the way we once did. Though you know that already." She cast a sidelong glance at Leopold. "In fact, it's why you're here."

Leopold nodded as if this had been his plan all along, and more than twenty minutes old.

"Make yourselves comfortable." She gestured to a set of sleek, modern chairs. "Can I get you anything to drink? Green juice? Herbal tea? Coffee?"

"We had coffee earlier, thanks," Emmet said, settling into a chair beside Leopold. "At the Brite Spot?"

She laughed. "Then you'll be in no danger of falling asleep. Strongest brew in Sunder. When I was doing my finals at the Lyceum, I'd stay up for days on just one cup. Tends to give you strange dreams, though." She took a notepad and pen from the coffee table and sat down facing them. "Anyhow, it's late, so let's get to it. Now that I can look you in the eyes, Larry Berry, I have just one question." She leaned forward slightly. "What did you have for breakfast this morning?"

Leopold went rigid. "What?"

The Executive repeated the question, this time slowly: "What did you have for breakfast this morning?"

His mind blanked. The ease he'd felt in her presence a moment ago had vanished. What did it matter, what he had for breakfast? "Is this some kind of trick question?" he asked.

She only tilted her head at him in response.

His panic escalating, Leopold glanced at Emmet, who only shook his head, looking slightly lost. Leopold returned his eyes to the Executive. What could she possibly intuit from his answer? Was there a specific food only a channeler would eat? Rice Krispies? Toast with jam? What *kind* of jam? If he said sausage, would that mean he was a heartless animal-killer? If he said cereal, would that make him sound childish and silly? What the hell did this have to do with magic, or channeler-ness, or *anything*?

His head felt warm. He was overthinking it, already messing up a question he hadn't even answered yet. Finally, he said the first thing that came to mind, which happened to be the truth: "Yogurt. The kind you stir that has fruit on the bottom. And a banana. Well, half of one."

The Executive jotted something on her notepad, then looked up at him. "I see."

"And coffee. No milk. I usually take it black—"

"That's sufficient, thank you."

Leopold was pretty sure he was sweating. "Yeah, um—you're welcome."

Her face was a study in neutrality, neither pleased nor disappointed. "That completes the mental portion of your evaluation. The physical portion will begin in just a moment."

TWENTY-EIGHT

"Wait—what evaluation? Did the channeler test start already? I didn't realize there was a mental part—"

The Executive was hurrying them toward the elevators, notepad under her arm as her heels clicked across the floor. "It's a necessary assessment for any would-be channeler. You didn't think we'd just take your word for it, did you?"

"No—I mean, of course not, it's just—"

The elevator doors opened. "Your test consists of two parts," she said as they stepped inside. She pressed the button for floor seven. "The first, which you just completed, was a quick mental examination, purely pro forma. The second will be a more intense ordeal."

The doors closed and they began to descend, the gravity so strong it made Leopold lightheaded. A lump had already formed in his throat. He was pretty sure he knew what she meant by *a more intense ordeal.*

"He has to fight a Noxum, doesn't he?" Emmet asked breathlessly. "Just like Max in episode four."

"Episode four?" The Executive hesitated. "That's Star Wars, right?"

"No," Emmet and Leopold said together.

"Episode four," Leopold repeated, confusion briefly displacing his nerves. "Of *Max's Adventures in Sunderworld*—"

"You mean Sunder Hill."

"World," Emmet corrected her.

Leopold frowned, adding, "It's a TV show."

"That must've been before my time," she said, a note of impatience coloring her voice. "Now, as you mentioned on the phone, you've never encountered a Noxum in person—"

"I can't believe she doesn't know about Max," Emmet said under his breath.

"Me neither," Leopold whispered back, "but right now I'm a little more concerned that I might be about to die."

"Fair."

"Which means you'll be limited to whatever you have with you, provided it isn't too powerful."

"Wait, I'm sorry—I didn't catch that—"

Before Leopold could finish his sentence, the elevator came to a stop and dinged, its doors opening onto a bustling hallway. Sparks in dark-hued jumpsuits crossed back and forth, pushing heavy carts laden with equipment.

They stepped off the elevator, and the Executive turned sharply to face Leopold. "You have your focuser with you?"

"My focuser?" He patted his pockets, discovering with a mixture of relief and dismay that he still had the Funcast. "Yeah. Yes, I have it."

"But you're going to give him a real one, right?" Emmet said. "Like a Contax or a Leica? High-quality glass?"

The Executive's earlier impatience was turning into irritation. "A true channeler, sufficiently trained, doesn't need a focuser to cast spells at all."

"But his is just a cheap piece of garbage!"

"Nor," she added sharply, "does he need someone else to advocate for him."

"Emmet—"

"Larry."

"She's right," Leopold said, his jaw tensing. "Whatever happens, I'm going to have to do it on my own."

TWENTY-NINE

"Welcome to the Department of Cinemagical Production. Touch nothing."

The Executive was leading them past signs that read STAGES THIS WAY and NO CASTING IN HALL. A woman shouted, *"Hot points!"* as they dodged a cart piled with light stands and what appeared to be several flaming spears.

"I don't understand," Leopold said as he took it all in. "You're putting me in a movie?"

"No, just appropriating one of the old soundstages."

They had to hurry to keep pace with the Executive. "This is where we produce all our filmed entertainment," she was explaining. "A lot of the Sunderwood classics were filmed here—*'Til Death Don't Us Part*; *Forever and a Day*; *The Fire Maidens of Catalina*." She nodded at a wall lined with movie posters, all unfamiliar to Leopold but one, glimpsed in passing, which summoned an old, half-forgotten memory of a movie matinee with his mom. It slipped from his grasp as they sidestepped a man pushing a rack of costumes.

There was a shout from up ahead.

"Executive!"

Keeves waited beside a heavy, soundproofed door marked Stage E. As they approached, Leopold could tell that the underling had been running himself ragged since they'd last seen him, his slicked hair mussed and his blotchy face bright red. Arrayed down the hall behind him was a retinue of besuited bureaucrats in gray: three men and two women armed with clipboards and humorless expressions. "Observers from Standards and Legal," Keeves explained under his breath, scowling at the clipboard-wielders. He pushed open the heavy door for the Executive. "They're nearly ready for you."

Leopold couldn't say what he'd hoped to find on Stage E, but as he walked inside the faintly lit room, he realized he'd pictured more than just a cavernous, darkened soundstage. It might've been a thousand square feet or a hundred thousand; beyond a circle of spotlight, the floorboards fell off into featureless black. Crew members wheeled film gear in and out of the shadows. He looked up: Just visible in the rafters was a catwalk, lights and other equipment hanging from it like spider sacs. Against a wall, a row of folding chairs had been arranged for a small group of observers, who were filling the seats one by one.

Leopold hadn't expected an audience.

The mounting pressure was making him break out into a cold sweat, so he focused instead on Emmet, who at that moment was improvising a pep talk—something about how he probably wasn't going to die, and even if he did, maybe they could magic him back to life— while the Executive consulted with one of the suits.

After a minute, she turned to Leopold. "A bit of mandatory unpleasantness." She angled a clipboard toward him. "I'll need your signature on a few lines here. You're sixteen, right? If not, we're going to need the signature of a parent or guardian."

Leopold drew back, he was so offended.

He was almost eighteen. He was over six feet tall. He wasn't made of pure muscle, but years of living under Richter's rule had forced him onto sports teams and into the gym on a regular basis. Documented thoroughly in chapter six of *Think Like a Winner*, his dad's insistence on physical fitness was one of the few Richterisms Leopold could find no fault with. The gym had given him a safe place to exorcise his anger, and in the process, he'd learned how to throw a solid punch at a sandbag, sparing Richter the need for facial reconstruction surgery.

Now, as he prepared to confront a Noxum, he felt almost grateful for his dad's bullshit.

"Yeah," he said tightly. "I'm over sixteen."

"Right," she said, reading the look on his face. "Sorry, I'm required to ask." Her eyes flicked down to the clipboard. "Mostly it's a standard indemnity waiver, hold harmless in case of injury, et cetera. This is not a risk-free endeavor, as I'm sure you understand. But there are two nonnegotiables we have to discuss before proceeding."

Leopold managed a nod.

"First, the test results are binding. If we do determine you're a channeler, you must serve as channeler—for however long it takes to fulfill the obligation. You can't just decide one day that you're tired of the channeler life and go back to your old one."

"I won't," Leopold said decisively, though he realized he had little idea of what the channeler life entailed. Season one had not covered this.

"He won't," Emmet echoed.

"And just so you aren't laboring under any illusions, let me be clear: You'll undergo rigorous training at the Lyceum. It's not glamorous. You'll hardly sleep, and you'll be asked to risk your life, repeatedly."

"I understand," said Leopold, steeling himself. He took the clipboard and signed. Part of him was still convinced he'd be waking up any minute now, back home in the rickety twin bed he'd long since outgrown.

The life he'd outgrown.

"Secondly." The Executive flipped the page. "If you fail—and survive—you won't be given another chance to test. Initial here to confirm you've been informed."

He initialed. The Executive turned to the next page.

"Finally, an image release. For the sake of transparency, and to avoid any suspicion that the channeler might be a fraud or unfair favors have been granted, the test will be filmed and broadcast for public viewing in Sunder."

It was the first stipulation to give him pause. Emmet looked skeptical, but shrugged. In for a penny, in for a pound.

Leopold signed the form.

The Executive took it and handed it to one of the suits. Then she cupped her hands around her mouth and called up to the catwalk. "Are we ready?"

"Ready," a voice answered from the dark.

She turned to face him. "And you, Larry Berry? Are you ready?"

Leopold took a deep breath. "Ma'am," he said, "I was born ready."

THIRTY

Though the lights came on with little more than a whisper, the scene change was so sudden and dramatic he was briefly disoriented—then paralyzed by the feeling that he was standing at the edge of a dream.

To almost anyone else it would've been just a high school cafeteria: the scene of minor traumas, but not enough to make someone dangerously lightheaded. To Leopold this was more than just a startlingly realistic cafeteria set. It was, down to the smallest details, the very place where Max had been surprised with his own channeler test in episode four of *Sunderworld*. It was where he'd faced off against—and killed—a very nasty, very large Noxum.

Given all this, it seemed impossible the Executive had never heard of *Sunderworld*. But Leopold's questions would have to wait. Right now he had to get his head in the game.

He heard a soft, clicking whir from the catwalk above him, the sound like a playing card stuck in the spokes of a spinning bicycle wheel. It was the shutter of a camera, film reels running through a magazine. His every move, every word, was being captured.

He looked up, looked around.

"Holy shit," Emmet muttered beside him. "This is . . ."

"Exactly the same."

"Down to the banners on the wall."

"And the benches. And cafeteria trays. And the little—"

"You know what this means, right?"

Leopold shook his head. The dizzy feeling threatened to overwhelm him.

"It means you know what to do! You've seen this episode a million times! Max had no experience before he walked into this cafeteria, either—and he only had that crappy Vivitar, remember? Probably even worse than the Funcast—"

Keeves bellowed at the room to shut up, then clapped his hands as if calling a meeting to order. Once he had everyone's attention, he crossed his arms. "I'm sure I don't need to remind you people of this," he said, his voice high and shrill, "but no one is allowed to intervene in what's about to transpire, however much your instincts may urge you to do so. Presently, the crew will be casting a safety barrier so the Noxum can't cross into the observation area. As an added precaution, while the test is in progress, please keep your focusers out of sight. As you know, Noxum are infuriated by the lenses."

The few focusers Leopold could see were quickly stashed away. Grips were wheeling two big lights into place on either side of the room. With a sizzling crackle twin beams flared to life, creating what looked like a green force field that stretched from wall to wall, sectioning off the audience from the action. This was called an Arclight barrier, the Executive explained, and Emmet would be protected on the other side of it.

At that, Leopold and Emmet exchanged one last look.

"Nike," Emmet whispered.

Despite the rising terror in his chest, Leopold grinned.

With a parting nod, Emmet accompanied the Executive through a narrow gap in the barrier, which opened and closed at a wave of her focuser. They took seats beside Keeves, surrounded by suits. From the dark wings and the catwalk Leopold heard murmurs and motion, equipment being moved, things being prepared. He wondered, almost casually, what would happen if he died here, then dismissed the thought. He was certain fate had other plans for him. Nothing else made sense. The whole arc of his life had led to this moment.

A large crane rose into the rafters, a bulky cinema camera balanced at the end. He felt the weight of a thousand stares, eyes and lenses tracking his every movement.

Leopold turned away from his gallery of judges and walked into a dream.

THIRTY-ONE

There were chipped brown cafeteria trays on every table, many containing half-finished lunches—soupy mashed potatoes and rubbery approximations of pizza—as if a hundred cliques of shit-talking high schoolers had been magicked away midmeal. In episode four, that's exactly what had happened: A week after Max's first visit to Sunder, his paladin mentor had appeared in the middle of a school day, made everyone disappear, and explained coolly that a Noxum awaited him in the kitchen.

Leopold was moving forward cautiously when he heard a metallic clatter ahead of him. It had sounded like a cymbal crashing to the floor, then rattling until it wobbled flat.

The sound had come, yes, from the kitchen.

He pulled the Funcast from his pocket and gripped it tightly, the cheap plastic flexing in his hands. All he had was the Make It Snow pre-cast, which would almost certainly be useless against a Noxum. He wished he could go back in time and choose something else from 99 Spells. Something aggressive. A bit of death magic, though he was pretty sure death magic wasn't available in the form of a cheap pre-cast. In fact, he wondered if the Executive letting him keep the Funcast might've been a trick, or another test within a test. In episode four, Max had wasted a lot of time trying to defeat the Noxum with his subpar focuser. In the end, he'd tossed away the Vivitar and vanquished the beast using traditional magic summoned with his bare hands. But Leopold's hands had only ever kindled harmless fireworks, and he couldn't convince himself to let the Funcast go. Not yet.

As he neared the serving counter at the back, he struggled to remember the few basics of casting he'd learned from watching the show. He tried to picture the precise movements Max had used: the way he'd planted his feet and thrown out his arms, and how, after a few abortive attempts, he'd produced a bolt of magic so powerful, its kickback had knocked him on his ass. It was strange; *Sunderworld* was no longer Leopold's embarrassing childhood obsession. Now it was the only training he'd ever had for a fight that could cost him his life.

Leopold walked on, his hard-soled interview shoes announcing him with every step. If only he'd known he was getting dressed to battle a Noxum this morning, he might've insisted on sneakers. He rolled up his shirtsleeves like he was in a movie, readying himself for a street fight.

Then, blissfully, he felt a telltale heat building in his hands.

He'd begun to imagine roots hidden there, inside the meat of each palm. Some magical vein that traveled from his heart to his extremities. An anatomy unknown in slacks. *I made it rain in LA in August.* He wondered if a surgeon would notice. If such things showed up on CT scans.

He rounded the counter. Pots of goop bubbled like witches' cauldrons behind a Plexiglas sneeze-guard. Gelatinous rainbows glistened in chafing trays. Wet, smacking sounds echoed through the double doors that led into the kitchen.

Cautiously, Leopold drew closer.

His breaths were coming fast now, his pulse racing to match. He felt energy coursing through him, flowing into his hands. He let the focuser dangle from its wrist strap and pressed his palms together. He'd felt it many times before, the strange heat building along the seams of his scars, these violent tremors in his stomach. But he'd never known what it was.

Now he understood. This was his power.

He approached the doorway and peered into the kitchen: industrial appliances, rows of stoves, their huge vent hoods like gaping mouths. A mess of half-eaten lunch meats littered the scuffed floors. He followed the trail down a hallway, steeling himself as he edged around a corner with the focuser held out before him, his right thumb resting on the Funcast's flimsy plastic trigger.

Down an aisle of refrigerators one steel door hung open, blocking his view of the creature rooting inside it. A carton of melting ice cream flew out and splattered the opposite wall.

Leopold took another careful step forward, the movement nearly imperceptible—

The chewing sounds stopped. There came a low, inhuman snarl. A half-eaten turkey carcass hit the floor and spun across the linoleum, coming to rest at Leopold's feet.

Then, slowly, the creature stepped out.

Sunderworld had studiously avoided depicting Noxum with any real clarity; they were usually rendered in shadow or silhouette. Occasionally there'd be a stomach-churning close-up of some horrible appendage, a gaping maw lined with teeth, or the huge, triple-lidded eye that hid beneath armor in the center of its chest, but never the full form. Which is why, at first glance, Leopold wasn't sure he was facing a Noxum at all.

It was dressed in the gray uniform of a janitor. Though it looked passingly human at a glance, the details were all wrong: the way it hunched and swayed, shoulders and neck at odd, downcast angles; the strange fact of its bare feet, thick yellow nails curling from its toes; the long, scraggly white hair that obscured its face like some aged heavy-metal singer. It let out a strange, satisfied *ahhhhh* and stretched as if waking from a nap, long arms popping as they bent backward at the elbows.

No, this wasn't how the test had started for Max at all.

Leopold was in uncharted territory now.

The thing raised its head, long hair parting like a curtain. Its face appeared to be sliding down its skull: One eye was fully an inch below the other, its nose badly out of place, its mouth crooked and gaping. Then it did something that nearly made Leopold drop his focuser and run: It stuck three fingers into each side of its mouth and pulled. It pulled until its lips became a wide black oval and began to tear. It pulled until Leopold could see something charred and wriggling surging to escape from within, kept pulling until its face split open, tore down the middle, and peeled away like a leathery cowl. Then it kept going, unzipping itself to the crotch before stepping out of its skin and sloughing its human suit altogether, leaving the remains of what had looked like an old janitor crumpled on the floor.

Nothing Leopold had seen on television had prepared him for what he'd just witnessed, and nothing could have prepared him for what stood before him now.

In an ad for Noxum spray he'd seen on Sunder Hill, the creatures were about the size of a puppy and almost as cute. The one Max had fought in his test resembled—inasmuch as they'd shown it at all—an adolescent zombie with retractable talons.

This Noxum looked like all the nightmares he'd ever had as a kid rolled into one horrifying, leathery package: hooves for feet, arms that ended in wolverine claws, ragged wings that protruded from its back like the sails of a ghost ship. It had no face. No head as such. Even without a head it was a full foot taller than him. From the muscled ridge between its shoulders rose a neck-stalk that twisted and bent like a fleshy periscope, as if tasting the air for his scent. Two slits zippered the sides. The headless top was capped by an aperture lined with knifelike teeth, which he supposed was a mouth, and its tough-looking hide was the color of old bone, a mottled white and yellow matted with patches of rough black hair.

It looked like some sightless toothfish pulled from the depths of the ocean.

Most horrific was its singular, cycloptic eye. Three lids of armored muscle split apart in the center of its chest, exposing a dish of clouded, sickly yellow that spanned six inches. That horrible organ was one detail the show had reproduced with unflinching accuracy. It was an eye he'd seen in stress dreams, hovering bodiless over his bed while he lay paralyzed below.

Now. Kill it now.

He tightened his grip on the focuser and centered the creature in its dim, scratched lens. Make It Snow was still locked and loaded. The Noxum took a shuffling step forward and bent its neck-stalk toward him.

Leopold didn't hesitate.

He hit the trigger with his thumb. A surge of power blazed through him and a small blizzard shot from the focuser, numbing his fingertips as it blasted down the aisle and enveloped the Noxum. For a moment the snow was so thick he couldn't see beyond it.

When it cleared, ice clung to everything—the floor, the fridges, the monster. A crystalline skin had formed over its body.

The used pre-cast detached automatically from his lens and dropped, smoking, to the floor.

He waited for the Noxum to move, or topple, or give any indication of life. There was only the sound of crackling ice crystals. Was it possible he'd frozen it solid?

No.

That optimistic notion had only just entered his mind when the Noxum made a high, chittering sound that chilled him to his core, then shook itself free of its icy sarcophagus. Leopold shielded his face as frozen shards pelted the room with stinging hail. When he lowered his hands, the beast was crouched like a runner at the starting line.

It let out a low, guttural snarl, and leapt forward.

THIRTY-TWO

Leopold dodged to one side, then bolted, pulling down the shelves of a pantry unit as he fled. A cascade of cookware rained across the aisle behind him, briefly blocking the Noxum's path. He tore around the corner as he heard a second explosive crash, then glanced back to see a volley of plates shatter against the wall.

Leopold had bought himself only a few seconds.

There was a chance he could still surprise the thing as it exited the kitchen, and surprise was, perhaps, the only advantage left to him. He took up a position near the serving counter, his focuser at the ready. His one pre-cast was gone, but he hoped the device would enhance whatever innate magic he possessed, its lens concentrating the sparks he knew he could make into something much stronger.

The Noxum rounded the corner in full gallop, its ragged wings spread wide. It saw him, bent its neck-stalk in Leopold's direction, and hinged open the mouth atop it to let out a shrill and terrifying scream.

Leopold tensed. He brought his arms tight against his chest and willed some killing power to come forth, imagining a torrent of fire or—as Max had conjured in his own test—a shockwave of death magic that would blow the thing to bloody pieces. When the Noxum was just a short distance away, Leopold cried out and flung his arms forward.

The air rippled around him. A pulse of crimson light flew out of the focuser, the force of which sent him skidding backward into the serving counter. The pulse burst on impact, slamming the Noxum in one of its hunched shoulders and spinning it into a wall.

Leopold looked down at his hands, reddish and limned in sweat. His palms ached like they'd just been sliced open, but there was no visible injury. He could hardly believe it: He had *channeled* something, purposely conjuring power from thin air.

Was someone cheering?

Leopold's elation was short-lived. The Noxum hadn't even been knocked over. It swayed slightly, probing the spot where it'd been hit, more confused than hurt. The armored lids in its chest briefly opened to expose its bulging eye. It studied Leopold with what might've been interest. Leopold knew the eye was its greatest vulnerability, and if he could rocket a blast into its large, black pupil, that might be enough to kill it. He needed to cast again, right away, while the lid was still open, but then the Noxum crouched, muscles rippling along pale haunches, and uncoiled itself in a powerful burst of motion.

It leapt straight upward, spreading its wings as it grappled onto a light fixture. It swung there like a bat, shrieking at him. Its open eye was too far away now, and Leopold couldn't risk wasting a cast at such a distance.

"Come on, Larry!" the Executive encouraged him from behind the barrier. "Be bold!"

Her voice startled him. He'd been so in the grip of the moment, he'd nearly forgotten he was being watched, and the reminder was an added distraction he didn't need. He could still feel his power gathering; he suspected it was too soon to cast again, but when he glanced back at the observers—and registered the tension on Emmet's face—he balled his fists against his chest and, without waiting, let them fly.

Rather than a pulse of energy, the focuser produced a tracer of sparks that fizzled halfway to their target.

"Whoopsie!" he called out, then grimaced. When he heard a laugh from someone in the crew, Leopold seriously considered letting the Noxum kill him.

Whoopsie?

Jesus. And they were filming this.

The Noxum screeched and launched itself from one light fixture to another. One of the pendants detached from its mooring and fell. Leopold dove for cover as the light smashed to the floor, showering a wide area with glass.

Cowering under the table, he took a moment to regroup.

He was angry and mortified. His head and hands ached. He feared his next cast would be even worse than his first. He needed time to think, to recover some measure of strength.

He heard the creature's familiar screech and the leathery flap of its wings, and then an enormous crash shook the room. The tabletop above him shuddered as it split down the middle, a heavy slab knocking Leopold in the head. He was briefly disoriented as glass rained down.

It had dropped another light.

Leopold army-crawled out of the wreckage, his hands and knees sinking into broken shards. He gritted his teeth against the pain, struggling to steady himself as he stood. He might've had a concussion, but he would sooner die than throw up in front of this crowd. He'd already wasted his one moment of weakness on a fucking *whoopsie*. And anyway, if he was going to die, it wasn't going to be under a cafeteria table with his head tucked between his knees.

The creature crept slowly forward, Leopold blinking as he tried to focus. The claws at the end of its arms glinted as they dragged across the floor, leaving deep gashes in the linoleum.

And then its eye, Leopold's only viable target, closed.

Shit.

He wasn't sure what to do. Bolt for cover and wait for the eye to open again? He didn't think he could outrun a Noxum. He wiped sweat from his brow and his palm came away red. He stared at the smear of blood, realizing only then that his hands were trembling.

His dreams hadn't prepared him for failure.

Then a shout rang out: "You got this, Larry!"

Emmet.

His voice had been a shock to the Noxum, too, apparently, because it swiveled in Emmet's direction before taking a step toward the steady green Arclight barrier.

Someone hissed at Emmet to keep quiet, and a spike of alarm went through Leopold. The Noxum hadn't reacted this way to the Executive's voice.

Leopold looked around in a panic, grabbed a baked potato from an untouched lunch tray, and launched it at the Noxum. "Hey! Asshole!"

The potato bounced harmlessly off the creature's back, but it was enough to refocus the thing's attention. The Noxum turned to face Leopold, and now its yellow, pustular eye was open. It clacked its triple rows of teeth, then charged forward, closing the gap between them in a few thundering strides.

Leopold threw his arms out with a cry. He heard what sounded like a thunderclap as a small shockwave rippled around his hands.

The Noxum's eye snapped closed an instant before the pulse hit.

It burst against the creature's chest in a shower of sparks. The

Noxum skidded backward but didn't fall. It didn't even scream. In fact, there was no evidence at all that Leopold had just scored a direct hit with his best attempt at death magic—only a singed patch of hair where the pulse had connected.

Leopold's bones felt suddenly hollowed, the marrow vacuumed out. Maybe he hadn't been desperate enough. Maybe he hadn't been close enough to death to summon death magic.

The Noxum started toward him. Slower this time, shaking off its daze, wary now. Breathless and discouraged though he was, Leopold didn't run. Blood trickled into his eye and he swiped it away. He looked down at the bloodstained focuser in his hands, realizing with dismay that the plastic lens had partially melted. He stumbled backward and tossed it away.

He had nothing left.

Leopold flung out his aching hands anyway, but they channeled only a thin arc of light that curved away uselessly, like a poorly made paper airplane.

He tried again.

And again.

The Noxum was rapidly closing the distance between them. In desperation, Leopold searched the cafeteria for a weapon, grabbing the only solid object within reach: a lunch tray. He held it out like a shield, fully aware of how pathetic he must've looked.

"Don't be a fool!" Keeves shouted from beyond the barrier. "Give up before it kills you!"

"He's right, Larry—it isn't worth your life!" Executive Ramirez called.

The Noxum surged forward suddenly, lashing out. Its clawed arm connected with the tray, shattering it. Leopold scrambled backward, his eyes frantically scanning the crowd. He was searching for Emmet, for a single look of reassurance that he could still be victorious, that he was meant to be here—

He froze.

It was the girl. The one who'd been watching him in the Brite Spot. She stared at him now with an intensity that bordered on terrifying, something like steel in her gaze. The effect was so disconcerting that he hardly noticed when the Noxum swung at him, leaving him no time to react before a second blow struck him in the chest, the force of it launching him through the air.

He landed in a garbage can.

The metal bin swayed, then tipped over with a ringing peal. Leopold couldn't move quickly enough; the blow to his head had cost him his equilibrium. It took a moment to extricate himself from the trash, and another to realize he was covered in food. He felt as if he were wading through mud as he peeled a slice of baloney from his cheek. He brushed a slick of baked beans from his arm. He could smell gravy in his hair. He heard snickers from the crowd as he swiped a glob of macaroni from his shirt.

When he looked up, he saw two Noxum towering before him— until he blinked, and the double image resolved back into one.

The Noxum made a new sound then: deeper, guttural, ravenous. It opened its mouth and vomited a spray of black insects at Leopold, the shock and pain of which startled him from his stupor in an instant. He gave an agonized cry as the insects stung his flesh, scalding him like drops of boiling water, and then the Noxum backhanded him in the face. Leopold heard his jaw crack before he fell, with an echoing wallop, to the ground.

For a moment there was only the pounding in his head, the blinding glare of a spotlight shining from the catwalk, sounds fading in and out. The Noxum approached slowly, blocking the spotlight as it loomed over his fallen body. Leopold knew then that he'd lost. More than that: He was about to die.

"Larry! *Get the fuck up and run!*"

The Noxum spun toward Emmet's voice, its eye slitting open.

"*No,*" Leopold breathed.

This was the second time the creature had taken an interest in Emmet. The first time, Leopold had managed to distract it, but now that Leopold had proven weak and uninteresting, the Noxum seemed unable to resist new prey.

It wasn't towering over him anymore.

Leopold hissed through the pain as he hauled himself into a seated position. He touched a hand to his head, trying to steady the spin as he searched for the Noxum, then spotted it: halfway across the stage, thundering toward Emmet. The Arclight barrier—the wall of green light that was supposed to keep the observers safe—chose that moment to flicker out.

THIRTY-THREE

Chaos erupted among the observers. The suits fled their seats and scattered. A few grips were buzzing around the shield lights in a last-ditch effort to restore the barrier, but after a moment they, too, gave up and ran. Emmet stood frozen, his eyes round with disbelief. Keeves and Executive Ramirez whipped out their focusers.

The Executive moved quickly, casting a streak of angry orange fire that slammed the Noxum in the torso, creating a thunderclap of noise and a spectacular shower of sparks. The beast shrieked, but the cast wasn't enough to stop it. Keeves lifted his focuser next, but the Noxum was faster; with a swipe of its long arms both Keeves and the Executive were flung backward, landing with a crash in the darkened wings.

Now there was nothing between the creature and Emmet. Leopold watched his friend grab a nearby light stand, wielding the pointed end like a spear.

Leopold's body was shaking. Pain radiated from his shattered jaw, his legs, his bloodied hands. He was covered in wet garbage. He was out of magic.

None of that mattered.

Somehow he regained his feet. Somehow he was running, the clarifying terror of the moment narrowing his consciousness to a single point of focus, all else an afterthought.

By the time Leopold reached him, the light stand had been torn from Emmet's hands. His friend had been knocked onto his back, teeth clenched as he cradled his arm, a jut of broken bone visible. The Noxum rounded on Emmet now, and Leopold knew there was no time to think.

So he didn't.

He'd never remember the exact mechanics of the moment, only the adrenaline surging through him as he leapt onto the monster's back. At some point during his dash across the cafeteria he'd grabbed another tray, and now he brought it down over and over again like a flat, flimsy club, battering the Noxum's snapping neck-stalk.

The creature reared back and tried to buck him off. Through sheer force of will Leopold managed to hang on, even as people were shouting, *Move, we can't get a clear shot!* Leopold knew the tray was worse than useless, but he would've tried to murder the beast with a reel of dental floss if that were all he'd had.

Finally, howling with rage, the Noxum catapulted itself backward, slamming Leopold into one of the walls and nearly breaking his back in the process. The tray shattered in his hand. He finally lost his grip on the creature, sliding down into a seated position as pain flared through his body.

The Noxum turned to face him.

Leopold could see down its awful throat as it roared. He became aware of a sharp pressure in his closed hand. With some effort he forced himself to look down, blinking against a burst of stars, and discovered he still gripped one jagged piece of lunch tray. Breathing hard, he clenched his fist tighter, the hard plastic cutting into his flesh. He looked up in time to see the Noxum drawing back its clawed arm, ready to deliver the final blow.

Then, for reasons unknown, it hesitated.

Leopold wasn't sure whether his addled mind had invented it, but he could've sworn he saw something like regret in the creature's uncanny yellow eye—and almost instinctively, Leopold felt his fist relax.

And then the Noxum struck him so hard he heard his ribs break.

Leopold slumped sideways. The creature had him pinned to the ground, and Leopold, who could feel hot blood soaking his shirt, knew this was the end. The Noxum's lurid eye gleamed, a flash of yellow registering in Leopold's peripheral vision.

Marshaling his last ounce of strength, Leopold stabbed the shard upward.

There was a deafening howl. A cry of pain. Then a terrible, smothering weight fell across him, and the world dimmed to a darkened smear.

THIRTY-FOUR

Leopold felt weightless.

He seemed suspended in liquid, insubstantial as he floated, something whispering along his skin. Movement skittered at the edges of his vision, but sleep beckoned, drawing him deeper into the murk.

The dark seemed infinite.

A maelstrom of night terrors, more sensation than image. Locked in a lightless berth on a storm-tossed ship. Trapped in the hot prison of some great beast's mouth. Through it all the feeling of hands moving over him, handling him like baggage; then falling, falling endlessly through black, wind-driven rain.

He felt a sharp burn and winced, then made a noise in his throat: the strangled wail of someone trying to scream while dreaming. The liquid world seemed to converge around him then, compressing until sleep was no longer relief but imprisonment, the sounds in his head no longer soft but searing—then roaring, sharpening to an unbearable crescendo—

He drew a sudden, ragged breath, and his eyes flew open.

"Get me form 5A, partial revision."

"Got his address?"

"It'll be on his ID. Make sure someone has a copy of his license."

The velvet dark was gone, and in its place was nothing but torture.

Agony drowned him in buffeting waves, radiating outward from his chest.

Consciousness, it turned out, was unbearable.

Someone muttered an incantation close to his ear. He heard the metal click of a focuser being adjusted.

"What's happening?" Leopold managed to say, his voice raspy.

White tiles came into focus above him. All around him. He seemed to be on some sort of bed in a windowless, nearly featureless room, the corners wavering in his unsteady vision. Suits crossed back and forth, shuffling papers as they spoke in terse undertones.

A man in a white coat appeared, but didn't look at him.

"Where am I?" Leopold said hoarsely. He tried to sit up and was rewarded with pain so severe it nearly took his breath away. "Who are you?"

The man shook his head. "Best if you don't talk. I'm about to give you a paralytic, and you don't want to get this in your mouth."

"Wait, what are you—"

A bright flash blinded him. Leopold screamed. His heart pounded furiously; there was a metallic tang in his throat, his gut. He was certain his head had caught fire—that every bone in his body had been pulverized—but just when he thought the pain might never stop, it did.

Leopold discovered he could move.

With great difficulty, he managed to push himself up onto his elbows. He squinted against the flare of fluorescent lights, his brain still throbbing in his skull. He was trying to remember more than his name, more than his shoe size and the color of his eyes.

The man in the white coat had turned away.

"Where am I?" he tried again. "What happened—"

"—tell wardrobe to get in here—"

"Not sure what we can do about his shoes—"

"Hey," he said sharply. He sat up straighter, frustration beginning to clear his head. The scrum of bodies around him, too, had begun to clarify, and he scanned the room until he spotted a blurry figure he thought he recognized. "What the hell is going on?"

"Fred's not still on his break, is he? We'll need the car in five, and I'm still waiting on confirmation—"

"I can confirm we were able to locate the vehicle, ma'am—"

"*Hey,*" Leopold barked, his eyes homing in on the familiar face of Executive Ramirez. "Why is no one answering me?"

"—parked on Eighth Street, near Angels Flight—"

"Are you talking about my car?" Leopold realized there were small wires affixed to his temples. He ripped them off, grimacing as the tape took some of his hair, too. "Why are you talking about my car?"

"—tell him not to leave. We'll have the boy sedated again in just a moment—"

"HEY," he finally screamed. "WHAT THE HELL ARE YOU DOING WITH MY CAR?"

The room stilled; the voices went silent.

Leopold scanned the faces around him, some of which he recognized from his test. All wore expressions of surprise, save one.

Executive Ramirez was studying him with pity, and this made him unreasonably angry.

Leopold swung his feet off the bed and managed to stand. For a moment, he thought he might throw up. Instead, he impressed himself by remaining upright and speaking clearly when he said, in a lethal whisper, "What the *fuck* is happening right now?"

The Executive was smiling as she strode toward him, and when she put a reassuring hand on his shoulder, he wasn't sure what to feel. "You're going to be okay," she said, tucking a clipboard under her arm. "You took quite a beating, Larry. We're just trying to make sure all your bones and vital organs are in good working order before we get you out of here."

"Get me out of here?" he echoed. "Wait, where's Emmet?"

Her eyes betrayed a hint of impatience. "His injuries were smaller and easily healed. Don't worry. Neither of you will remember anything that happened tonight."

Leopold realized, with a start, that she was trying to be comforting.

"What are you talking about?" he said, his anger becoming alarm. Her face swam gently before him. "Why won't I remember anything?"

"It's standard procedure. You signed all the waivers—"

"I understand that," he said. He reached out unsteadily, planting his hand on the bed behind him. "I just don't understand why you'd want me to forget I killed a Noxum tonight." At the hesitation on her face, he pressed, "I *did* kill it, didn't I?"

Everyone in the room had gone quiet, just watching.

"Yes," she said carefully. "You did."

"So why would you want me to forget that?"

The door swung open and a suit walked in. "Wardrobe says they've found a nearly identical replacement, ma'am, so we're ready whenever you— *Oh*."

Leopold looked from the man, whose head had turned toward him in sudden surprise, to Executive Ramirez, who was staring at him with the kind of patience reserved for someone missing half a brain.

"We're going to revise your memory, Larry," she said, her tone measured. "It's time for you to go home."

The room began to tilt. Leopold was shaking his head, a tremor moving through his body. "But—I don't understand—I thought you said I killed it—"

"You did," she said again. "But you killed it with a lunch tray, not with magic. Not by channeling. All you proved tonight is that you're commendably valiant in the defense of your friends. Your main talent, however, seems limited to party magic. Useful during Mardi Gras and the Fourth of July, not so much against Noxum. And not, I am genuinely sorry to say, what we need during our present Aether crisis. You failed."

Leopold felt as if his very soul were shriveling.

"As for the mental test," she went on, though he desperately wished she'd stop, "the answer you gave was not nearly as important as the indecisiveness with which you gave it. You lack conviction, generally. But more concerning: You don't even seem to have faith in yourself."

Leopold flinched as if he'd been slapped.

"Your scores did stand out in one respect." She glanced down at her clipboard, and despite everything he felt a tiny shoot of hope poke up from the nightsoil. "Their averageness."

The shoot withered and died.

"I can honestly say you may be the world's most ordinarily magical person. Remarkably unremarkable. Average absolutely to the decimal point. Unspecial by every magical metric."

There was a ringing in his ears, and for a moment he was unsure which interview he was failing, which recruiter or counselor or administrator he was disappointing. Everything she said sounded like an echo of something he'd heard before. Leopold sat down blindly, bracing himself against the mattress. He opened his mouth, then closed it.

"I'm sorry," said the Executive, without malice. "The Aether shortage is too severe. We have no more room in Sunder for sparks of mediocre talent."

And then she nodded to the man in white, and he raised his focuser.

THIRTY-FIVE

He awoke knotted in bedsheets.

Sun fell across his eyes through window blinds and he rolled away from the bright light, feeling vile. His head pounded and his throat was so dry he could hardly swallow.

A strange thought occurred to him.

I'm back.

It was not immediately clear where he was back from. Or what he'd been doing the night before to make him feel as though his brains had been siphoned out, blendered, then poured back in through his ear canal.

He was in his room. That much was evident—though *room*, not *home*, was the word that came to him. *Room* was a leaky, weather-beaten lifeboat inside a house that had never really felt like his. Home was something else.

He attempted to sit up, and his brains sloshed alarmingly inside his skull.

He settled for turning his head, searching for evidence of what might've happened the night before. An empty bottle of cheap whiskey would've explained things, or the baseball bat he'd been beaten with.

No such luck.

Just his bookshelves, neatly arranged. Paperback fantasy novels ordered by series and personal rating. C. S. Lewis on one end, the endless diminishing sequels of *Dragonspear* on the other. Model race cars and Lego contraptions. A smattering of action figures. A telescope he'd built himself out of cardboard and balsa wood. Graveyard of his lonely boyhood passions.

Most other surfaces had been abandoned to chaos, and he liked it that way. His bedroom was the only part of the house that was allowed to be less than spotless.

School notebooks spilled across his desk. Dirty clothes were heaped in a corner. A gallery of monster movie posters papered the wall, mementoes of a cherished ritual. He'd once asked his mom why they only watched old movies and she'd told him that *movies used to be magic*. Leopold hadn't really known what she meant, but he never complained. Movie time meant that, for a few hours, he had his mom all to himself. That was magic enough.

He carefully levered up to a seated position. When his brains had finished sloshing, he disentangled his feet from the sheets and lowered them to the floor. He was wearing shoes. He'd never in his life slept in his shoes. He must've been drunk out of his mind. The poisonous headache, the dimmed-out memories; it was the likeliest explanation, though a little confusing. He'd been drunk only once before and hadn't enjoyed the experience sufficiently to repeat it. He and Emmet often talked a big game about Emmet's dad's bourbon collection, but the thing about bourbon was that it tasted like wood-flavored demon urine. They didn't mention that in commercials.

Of yesterday's disasters Leopold could remember these: disastrous interview, disastrous argument with Richter in the car, disastrous near-accident on Sunset Boulevard. And, he could've sworn, a disastrously ill-tailored suit. He looked down at himself: The shirt, vest, and pants he wore now, though a bit wrinkled from having been slept in, fit perfectly.

He was never drinking again.

Leopold scooted to the edge of his bed, put his hand on the wall to steady himself, and stood. Minimal sloshing this time. His headache had receded such that he could open his eyes all the way.

He shuffled to the window and peered through the blinds. His room was on the second floor, and there in the driveway below was Bessie, his boxy yellow steed, parked at a wonky angle with two wheels off the travertine pavers in the grass. A parenthesis of crushed lawn curved behind her—a serious transgression of the Richter code.

More worrying, though, was how the car had gotten there. He had apparently driven himself home last night, though he knew he wouldn't have gotten behind the wheel if he'd been drinking.

He frowned.

He *never* would've gotten behind the wheel if he'd been drinking.

Feeling uncertain again, he thought, suddenly: *phone.* There would be answers on his phone. He located it among his sheets only to discover it had been turned off. This was strange, because in addition to never driving home under the influence, Leopold never turned off his phone.

Exhausted, he sat on the edge of his bed, then powered up his cell and looked through his texts. There was nothing from the previous day. No texts at all. No calls, either.

Weird.

There hadn't been a day in his adolescent life in which he hadn't sent or received a text.

Leopold closed his eyes. His head hurt too much to play Encyclopedia Brown right now. Tossing the phone down, he hobbled into the bathroom, turned on the taps, and waited for the water to get very hot. He wanted the whole bathroom to fill with steam. He didn't care if it earned him the Don't You Realize We're in a Drought lecture. Leopold wanted to disappear into a cloud of hot vapor and feel his brain melt.

Noting once more the strangeness of his perfectly fitted suit, he undressed and stepped into the billowing steam. He let the near-scalding water pour over him as he soaped his body and allowed his mind to drift. It was Saturday, and he had a shift at the coffee shop that afternoon, which meant he'd—

Leopold's train of thought was interrupted when he noticed a strange discoloration across his ribs. Faintly yellow, like an old bruise.

He touched it and winced. Had he gotten into a fight with someone last night? Or a parking meter? He probed the spot a second time and winced again, the pain oddly fascinating. Each small shock was like pressing a button. Something was stirring to life deep in the folds of his memory. Shaking dust from its limbs.

Unburying itself.

At first it was just the tenor and tone of a woman's voice. Firm but not harsh. He held his hand to his ribs again, but this time something made him hesitate.

He realized, with a start, that he was afraid. Beads of condensation wept down the glass shower enclosure. What was he afraid of? Was there something he was terrified to remember?

Then, with a sharp intake of breath, it all came back to him. He stumbled against the wall, gasping as the memories resurfaced—

Sunder. The test. The Noxum. Each revelation like a sledgehammer to his chest.

The Executive's pained expression as she said, *We have no more room in Sunder for sparks of mediocre talent.*

Leopold slid down the wall and let his forehead bang against his knees, scalding water flowing over him as two words repeated in his skull, echoing louder and louder until they were nearly deafening.

You failed.

He'd finally found Sunder, and Sunder had found him lacking. He'd gained entrance only to be kicked out and banished in a matter of hours, which had to be some kind of record. He'd killed a Noxum and *still* failed. It was a dream come true with a nightmare ending.

He cursed himself, watching water swirl down the drain.

How could he have been so stupid? How had he let himself believe he was some great magical talent—and if that wasn't absurd enough, a *channeler*? Because he'd cast one mediocre spell in an alley? Because rickety old Angels Flight had creaked to life when he'd inserted a novelty coin? Because it had rained unexpectedly and his desperate mind had twisted it into something meaningful?

No: because he was deluded. Because a good friend had told him something he'd desperately wanted to hear and he hadn't questioned it—because he hadn't wanted to.

That wasn't on Emmet. That was all on him.

Remarkably unremarkable.

He let the shame of it sink into his marrow. Richter had been right about him all these years. Larry Berry was nothing special, and his refusal to believe it had nearly cost him his life.

Worse, it had nearly cost Emmet's.

And yet—

Leopold's failure, while devastating, made sense; it aligned with every other experience he'd ever had. What didn't make sense was everything else. Why hadn't his memory revision worked? Why had he been granted a token at all? Why had he found those *Sunderworld* tapes as a kid? And why, for all these years, had he been Seeing into Sunder?

Suddenly, talking to Emmet was the most urgent thing imaginable.

Emmet *knew*. He'd been there too, had gone through everything alongside him. That was something, at least: Leopold wasn't alone in this.

He scrambled out of the shower without bothering to turn it off, wrapped himself quickly in a towel, and rushed into his bedroom. He snatched his phone from the nest of sheets.

The call went straight to voicemail. Emmet's phone must have been turned off, and probably wiped of all recent calls and texts, just as Leopold's had been.

"This is Emmet Worthington's cellular device. If you're hearing this, it's because you've bothered to call me, which is frankly ridiculous, and means you're probably my parents. Just text me, guys. Phone calls give everyone anxiety."

Leopold hung up without leaving a message and tried Emmet's parents, who—partly for emergencies and partly out of nostalgic affectation—still had a landline. Emmet's mom, Laura, picked up after three rings.

"Hello?"

"Dr. Worthington. It's Larry."

He tried not to sound freaked out.

"Hi, Larry. Emmet's sleeping. Still. You guys had a late night, huh?"

"Yeah. Do you think you could wake him up?"

"You're asking me for a favor?" She laughed, surprised. "How about I start: Next time, you two stick to curfew or heads will roll."

"Yes, Dr. Worthington." Leopold winced. "Sorry, Dr. Worthington."

A beat. "Good."

Silently, Leopold banged his head against the wall. "I'm sorry, Dr. Worthington. This is just, uh, really important. Could you wake him up? Please?"

"Speak of the devil, here he is. Like the risen dead."

"Really?" Leopold straightened.

He heard Emmet in the background muttering, "Who is it?"

"Oh, Emmy," Dr. Worthington said pitiably. "You look rough."

"Thanks, Mom. Love to hear that. Can I have the phone, please?"

The phone shuffled from hand to hand.

"Mister Berry." Emmet's voice was thick and gravelly. "What in God's name did we drink last night?"

He sounded like hell, which didn't give Leopold much comfort. There was the sound of footsteps, then a door squeaking shut. The Worthingtons' landline was straight out of an eighties movie, with a long, coiled cord that could stretch all the way into the pantry, and Leopold knew Emmet had shut himself in to talk without being overheard.

"Weird," Emmet said. "I don't smell like booze but I feel like someone took a shit inside my head." His voice dropped to a whisper. "Did we raid my dad's liquor cabinet?"

"No. Listen—"

"Did we smoke? Where'd we even get weed?"

"We live in LA, Emmet, they sell weed at the farmers market. But no, we didn't."

Emmet laughed, then whimpered. "Ow."

"We went to The Stench," Leopold continued. "Remember? Mika's show?"

"Right. Yeah. *Mika.*"

"Your girlfriend."

"I almost forgot I had a girlfriend."

"That bad, huh?"

Emmet sighed. "Someone took a shit in my head, Larry."

For the first time since he'd woken up, Leopold smiled. He fucking loved Emmet.

"Hold up," Emmet said, realization dawning. "Didn't you almost burn down Clifton's?"

He was there, he was almost there. Maybe his memory just needed a jog.

"Yeah."

Now Emmet sounded angry. "What the hell is wrong with you?"

"The list is really, really long." Leopold pushed a hand through his wet hair and started to pace. "Listen, do you remember what happened after Clifton's?"

"Uh, I remember us going back to our cars, I think. Then we must've gotten shit-faced at some point before I fell asleep."

Leopold took a beat, a breath, then just said it: "We didn't go home after Clifton's. We rode Angels Flight."

Emmet was quiet a little too long before he said, "What?"

"I'm saying we rode Angels Flight."

"Bro, did you take something from those D&D guys? They pretend to be straight-edge, but they love to get stoned. One time Jeremiah gave me what he claimed was a clove cigarette, but I saw flying elephants for three hours afterward. *Three hours*, Larry."

Leopold's stomach began to churn. "Emmet. I wasn't stoned. We did ride Angels Flight last night. We used the token I got upstairs at Clifton's—"

"Be there in a minute!" Emmet hollered. Then, back to Leopold: "Sorry. There are waffles happening and people are calling my name."

A slow heat crawled up Leopold's neck. "Just do me a favor and check your pockets, okay? Maybe they forgot to search you before we got revised—"

"Jesus, Larry. What are you talking about?" Emmet said, irritated. "Are you having another episode right now?"

"Would you please just check your pockets?" Leopold said, sounding more panicked than he'd meant to.

"All right. Jeez." A shuffling noise. "They're empty."

"Maybe something fell out in your bed? Can you check your sheets?"

"Larry. *Stop.*" Emmet sounded tired and, more than that, disappointed. "You need to talk to Richter, okay? This isn't cool anymore."

Leopold was beginning to spiral. Everything was crashing, coming apart.

He could feel Emmet slipping away.

"Listen to me," Leopold said tightly. "I'm not having an episode. We really went to Sunder last night. Don't you remember Art? The Brite Spot? 99 Spells? *None* of that rings a bell?"

"Yeah, an alarm bell. Look, I can't do this right now. I really think you need to be in therapy. Unless this is all some elaborate prank, which would just be like, wow, go to hell. But I'm going to give you the benefit of the doubt and assume you're just . . . not okay."

"I'm serious, Emmet—I swear, I didn't remember at first either, but then it all came back to me, out of nowhere, in the shower—"

"I'm hanging up now. I'm tired and I don't feel good and I need to go have breakfast with my family. And so should you, probably."

"Emmet—"

The line went dead.

Leopold stayed still for a long time, shaky hands still gripping his silent phone. Like maybe if he didn't move, the emptiness and shame he was feeling wouldn't obliterate him.

Emmet's revision had worked.

Leopold's had not. And he would never know why because he couldn't go back to Sunder to ask. They'd taken his tokens, made copies of his ID, rolled up the welcome mat. Left him with more questions than ever and no way to answer them.

Worse than all that, he'd lost Emmet. They lived on different planets now, and there'd be no reaching him anymore.

Emmet would never remember.

THIRTY-SIX

He sat in a towel, shivering and paralyzed. For a long time he could do nothing but stare into the middle distance. By the time he became aware of a persistent grinding sound outside his window, his hair had dried and his towel was damp. He stood up automatically, as if his own body were foreign to him, then went to the window and pulled the blinds.

Half the driveway was now occupied by an ugly, hulking tow truck. His old Volvo was hitched up to it, rear wheels hoisted in the air. A man in blue coveralls was climbing into the cab while Richter stood watching with his arms folded.

They were taking Bessie. Hauling her away like trash.

His thoughts turned to static. He threw on a pair of jeans and a white T-shirt and then he was running, shoeless, out of his room and downstairs, past his stepbrother Hal in the kitchen saying *What the actual fuck, Larry*, and then he was outside.

Still running, he shouted *What did you do* at his father's back and his father yelled *Something I should've done a long time ago* as Leopold sprinted past him. He said something else as Leopold ran into the street after the tow truck, but Leopold didn't hear and didn't care.

The tow truck hadn't yet rounded the bend at the end of the block. Leopold screamed for it to stop and waved frantically in hopes the driver would see. Donna Chervil, Realtor to the stars, nearly backed over him with her Range Rover as she pulled out of her driveway. Mr. Khan stared from the sidewalk as his little dog did its business.

The truck picked up speed. Leopold gave chase, still waving like a castaway flagging down an airplane. The one object in the world that still meant anything to him was disappearing, tipping briefly onto one wheel as it skidded around the bend and out of sight.

He made it all the way to the end of the block before finally slowing to a stop, lungs and legs burning, gasping for breath.

Bessie was gone.

THIRTY-SEVEN

Leopold tramped numbly back toward the house. A hedge trimmer buzzed somewhere out of sight, the grating sound like steel wool on his nerves. He was barely holding it together.

In the driveway, Richter paced like a zoo tiger awaiting its lunch. Leopold passed by without a word. Richter pursued him through the front door.

When it slammed behind them, the shouting began.

The hell were you thinking. Look at me when I'm talking to you. Leopold didn't stop. He kept walking through the kitchen, past a stunned Hal holding a sandwich, then a horrified Drake holding a sandwich, his father's voice a battering ram at his back. *Where were you last night. I called you three times. The fucking audacity. And after yesterday's pathetic show. You're going to pay for that grass—*

Through the living room to the stairs. *Humiliated me for the last time.* Up the stairs to the landing. *Maybe you don't care what people think of this family, but I do.* Down the hall toward his room. *I'll make you care.*

None of it landed. Leopold barely heard a word.

He'd just remembered something. There'd been a name printed on the tow truck's door. It was T-something. T-something Towing. In the blur of the chase he'd hardly registered it, but if he could summon the name, then maybe he could find the tow company and his car, and stop the scrapyard from turning Bessie into a cube of crushed metal.

T-something. T-something.

Clouds billowed into the hall, steam from the still-running shower rolling out of his bedroom door like fog. At the threshold a meaty hand caught him and spun him around. His father drew back his arm as if to hit him, then stopped.

Leopold laughed. "Go ahead."

A vein bulged on Richter's forehead. "I should. You deserve it."

"You're right," said Leopold. "Hit me."

His father looked briefly confused, then slowly lowered his arm. Leopold turned away in disgust. He walked into the steam and left his father baffled in the hall.

Leopold pulled a duffel bag from his closet and started throwing things into it. He was done. He had to get the hell out of here.

Richter blocked the doorway.

"Oh, you're leaving, are you? To go where? Homeless—that'll look good on college applications. What, you think the Worthingtons are going to adopt you? Nobody wants a spoiled little shit mooching off them. Put that bag down. I said put it down. If you walk out, don't bother coming back, do you hear me?"

No. He was never coming back.

"See how far your tips from the coffee shop get you. You can go sell yourself on Hollywood Boulevard for all I care. Jesus! Weak. Impulsive. Unmanageable. Just like your mother."

Leopold turned.

"Shut your goddamn mouth."

His father stared as if he didn't recognize the boy in front of him, lips working soundlessly as he fumbled for a reply. Leopold took a step forward and told him to get out.

Richter found his voice. "How fucking dare you."

It should've been you, Leopold thought. *You in that hospital, drowning in your own lungs. It should've been you we buried.*

How many times had Leopold imagined it: his father dead instead of his mother. How badly had he wished for the evil, soul-killing magic that might've achieved that switch.

An old memory clawed at the edges of his mind, then broke over him: Leopold, aged ten, standing bleary-eyed in pajamas at the threshold of his mother's bedroom. He'd seen a light beneath her door and come in to find her wide awake in bed, surrounded by papers and bills, tapping on a calculator. *"Mom? Is everything okay?"*

Mollified by a tired smile and a gentle kiss, Leopold had turned to leave when a familiar sight on his mom's nightstand caught his eye.

He'd stopped cold, then gone rigid.

It was his father's wedding ring: a gold band with a small green gem set into the interior. His mother always kept the ring in a porcelain dish on her bedside table, a memorial to the man who'd walked away from them and started a new family. Leopold had seen it there dozens of times; had asked about it more than once.

A sudden blaze of rage had animated his body. He'd scooped up the ring and thrown it, with all his might, into the hall.

His mom had nearly screamed. *"Leopold, honey, no—"*

"Why do you keep it?" Leopold had cried angrily. *"He doesn't want us, Mom—he abandoned us—"*

But his mom had bolted from her bed and flown down the hall, where she collapsed onto the threadbare carpet, the ring captured once more in her fist.

"Mom—"

"Go back to bed, Leopold," she'd said quietly, her voice trembling.

"But—"

She'd spun around to look at him then, her gaze chilling. *"I said go back to bed."*

Leopold, who'd briefly allowed his eyes to fall closed, opened them again. His father's ruddy face was half obscured by steam, his broad shoulders spanning the doorway.

"Get out," Leopold said again.

He didn't shout. His voice didn't break. But as the words formed in Leopold's mouth, so, too, did a fissure in the ceiling, a crack in the plaster stretching between him and his father like a tectonic fault.

Richter's head tipped up slowly to look at it. When he met Leopold's eyes again, his face had turned the color of chalk.

His voice shook as he spoke. "You were a child. You didn't know her like I did. God knows I tried my best. But she changed, Larry. There was something wrong with her—she was the one who pushed me away, she was the one who forced me out of your life— You have to understand, she wasn't well—"

Shut up, shut up, you fucking liar, Leopold screamed inwardly.

"I wanted to take you with me." Richter was walking slowly toward him, hands up, palms out in surrender. "I wasn't sure you'd even be safe with her. But the court—"

"I SAID GET OUT," he screamed, aloud this time.

Leopold, blind with anger, had lifted his hands only to halt Richter's approach when he felt that telltale heat in his palms, and without warning Richter was flung backward, flying through the doorway and landing in the hall with a crash.

Shaking, Leopold stared at his hands, then at his father. He felt vaguely nauseated as he watched Richter pick himself up, stumbling slightly as he straightened. Leopold hadn't meant to hurt him, and despite having daydreamed about a moment like this for much of his life, he felt no satisfaction now.

"I'm sorry," Leopold whispered.

Richter's chest lifted with the effort to breathe. He said nothing, only shook his head, over and over, before disappearing down the hall.

Leopold stood still for what seemed like a long time. He felt water snaking down his neck and shoulders, and only vaguely registered that the precipitation was coming from the ceiling. Slowly, he looked up.

It was raining inside his room.

THIRTY-EIGHT

Leopold put on boots and packed as the rain subsided, shielding the duffel beneath hunched shoulders as he splashed through puddles forming on his carpet. The walls were sweating and his window had steamed over. Rivulets raced down his bookshelves, the spines of his paperbacks going dark with wet.

He took only what was essential. Socks. Phone charger. Razor and deodorant. Cash tips from the coffee shop he'd squirreled away in the back of a drawer.

He didn't know what he was packing for. All he knew for sure was that he'd spent too many years hoping someone else would save him. Hell, he'd been hoping a magical raccoon might save him. That someone would hand him the key to a world in which he was already chosen for greatness. The crazy thing was, he'd done it. He'd found that other world. He'd cast spells and killed a monster and by any metric of imagination had accomplished something extraordinary. He thought they'd roll out the red carpet and hand him a crown and finally, finally, he'd become someone. Instead, Leopold had been forced to accept that his greatest fear was true: He was average and insignificant, and would amount to nothing no matter the world, magical or otherwise. The Executive had been right.

Leopold didn't believe in himself. Leopold didn't even like himself.

Leopold *hated* Larry Berry.

And now Sunder was dead to him; even the hope of fantasy had been extinguished. Leopold had nothing now, not even delusion. Emmet was lost. His mother was lost. His father—

His father had always been lost to him.

Larry would walk out that door and be forced into a new life, the shape of which he couldn't imagine. He'd walk out, and then—and then what?

And then it came to him. *Tiny's Scrap and Tow.*

He closed his eyes and took a deep breath. At least now he had a plan.

Leopold slung the duffel across his back and gave the room a last look. The steam had wrinkled his school notebooks and caused his monster movie posters to bubble in their frames. He left his old *Sunderworld* tapes where they were, stuffed in the back of his closet.

He hoped they'd drown in the flood.

THIRTY-NINE

His old green bike was wedged between the water heater and a beat-up surfboard in the garage. The frame was bent and the rear tire was nearly out of air. He couldn't find the pump, so he rode it half-flat all the way out of Brentwood, standing up on the pedals to coerce them into motion while the duffel thumped rhythmically against his back. He was winded by the time he reached the gas station on Barrington, where he filled the tire and checked the location of Tiny's Scrap and Tow on his phone.

It had forty-five reviews and one star on Google.

The sky was orange from some distant wildfire. He labored against gusts of Santa Ana wind that sandblasted him with grit and shook the palms overhead into bursts of applause. At a red light he reached down to unspool a fast-food wrapper from his spokes and realized people were staring at him from their cars. Downtown he wouldn't have rated a second glance, but this close to Beverly Hills he cut a strange figure with his duffel bag and his old bike, wearing hiking boots in the summer.

Down Bundy to San Vicente. Down San Vicente past the fancy boutiques and restaurants marked $$$$ on maps until they gave way suddenly to a sprawl of tents and shopping carts. The tow yard was still miles away, in Culver City by the oil fields.

Leopold didn't care. He would've ridden to the next state.

He veered left on Eisenhower and cut through the vast and crumbling VA complex where Richter had taught him to drive stick, then paralleled the veterans cemetery with its stones like a gently undulating sea of white teeth. He knew people who wouldn't drive past it. On misty mornings it looked like a hundred thousand ghosts all rising from their graves.

The city was all ghosts now.

In every neighborhood there lurked some unwelcome reminder of his disappointing life. He began to interrogate his nascent plan. Once he got Bessie back, he'd use the coffee shop cash to fill the tank and— Drive east? North until the needle was on red? And then what?

And then he'd figure something out.

Wilshire to Sawtelle, sand grinding in his gears. Noodle bars and pink motels, birria and phở and dingbat apartments. They stopped building dingbats after the Northridge quake wiped out so many, but there were still plenty left, scattered across the city like little beige time bombs. At the freeway underpass a weathered sign announced that this section of the 10 was called the Christopher Columbus Transcontinental Highway, and he passed into a howling tunnel of gloom. Cigarettes flared in the dark. A shambling cluster of shadows. He splashed through a fetid river flowing from a pair of half-crushed porta-potties, then raced toward the glare of the sunlit world with shouts at his back.

Who needed the Ninth Realm? LA had its own versions of hell.

By the time he reached Culver City, the heat had dried the rain from his clothes and soaked him again with sweat. He turned onto a desolate block of auto body shops squeezed between a concrete riverbed and a range of scrubby hills. At the dead end was Tiny's Scrap and Tow, its imposing fence topped with razor wire.

Leopold dismounted, leaned his bike against the fence, and peered into the vast lot. In an ocean of dismembered cars and oil-sheened puddles, a beastly machine was flattening an old pickup. The crusher growled and whined, sending up flatulent gouts of black smoke as it chewed. Leopold was gripped by a sudden, cold certainty that Bessie had already fallen victim to it, but then he saw rows and rows of undestroyed cars still awaiting execution. She had to be among them. His car hadn't been here more than an hour.

He walked his bike toward the little cinder-block office, then engaged the rusted kickstand. The front door had bars over its bars and a sign that read FORGET THE DOG, BEWARE OF OWNER.

He pushed into a grungy office that was about two hundred degrees despite a ceiling fan that spun like an unbalanced helicopter blade. Two enormous guys were shouting at each other in a language he didn't understand. The one behind the counter stood with his muscular arms crossed, shaking his head in a dire and constant performance of the word *no*. The other, a disgruntled patron, was a biker kitted out in skull-adorned leather. A huge Doberman slept through it all, curled by a side door that led to the tow yard.

As Leopold waited for them to finish their argument, he scanned a wall papered with printouts from a security camera—images of people trying (and failing) to steal cars from Tiny's yard. One was attempting to scale the fence with the Doberman's jaws clamped around his foot. Another was getting Tased while trying to flee, arms flailing cartoonishly.

A small sign above it read TINY'S WALL OF FAME.

Just as it seemed like they were about to come to blows, the biker got a phone call and turned away, whispering with a hand cupped over his mouth.

It was Leopold's turn at the counter.

The hulking figure behind it—the eponymous Tiny, one had to assume—aimed a hardened stare at Leopold. Though some faint self-protective instinct urged him to tread cautiously, as of an hour ago, Leopold had died inside. His fear had died too.

He felt nothing but irritation as he gazed up into the eyes of a man who looked like he might snap someone's neck for fun, and he spoke without hesitation or deference when he said flatly, "You towed my car this morning. A yellow Volvo station—"

"If we towed it, it ain't yours anymore. Somebody sold it for scrap."

"Right. My dad. He did it without my permission, though, and I need it back."

"You want it back, it's eight fifty."

"Eight *hundred* fifty?"

Tiny didn't reply. He was watching a baseball game on a wall-mounted TV. Tiny, it seemed, had a thing for baseball. There was a signed bat on display in the corner.

"It wasn't his to sell," Leopold explained calmly, reining in his frustration. "The title's in my name—"

"So call the cops," Tiny said with a shrug.

The biker shouted *"Not until the arraignment, Ma!"* into his phone, and Leopold leaned in, flattening his palms on the counter as he lowered his voice.

"Look, the car might not seem like much, but it's special to me. I need it."

"Oh, it's *special*. In that case I'll cut you a deal. I'm only gonna charge you eight hundred and fifty dollars, like every other degenerate who walks through my door."

Tiny had produced a toothpick and was dislodging something green from between his molars. His eyes hadn't moved from the screen.

Leopold's jaw tightened. He resisted the urge to grab the decorative bat and smash the television. Instead, he turned away to count his money, hoping it had magically multiplied in the duffel bag while he wasn't looking. It hadn't. His life savings totaled one hundred and forty-six dollars in assorted small bills.

He turned back to face Tiny with the money in his hands. "I can give you this much right now. I'll find a way to get you the rest tomorrow. But I really need my car."

Tiny finally tore his eyes from the TV, a nasty gleam animating them as they settled back on Leopold. "Yeah, no. We don't offer credit. Your car has a meeting with Matilda at"—he glanced at the thousand-year-old computer on the counter—"two o'clock."

"Who's Matilda?"

"The crusher." Tiny pushed up his sleeve. The name *Matilda* was tattooed on his right bicep inside a bleeding heart. "Baby's gotta eat."

Leopold imagined punching Tiny in the face, then figured it would break not only his hand, but his entire arm. Resigned, he said, "Fine. I'll be back before two."

"If you wait till then, it's gonna cost a thousand."

"What? *Why?*"

Tiny shrugged. "Storage fee."

"You just made that up!"

"Maybe I did. And maybe I'm starting to look forward to watching your special car get crushed into an oily pancake. What can I say, I love my job. It sparks joy."

"Love what you do and you'll never work a day in your life," the biker remarked over his shoulder.

"Wisdom." Tiny nodded sagely. "Now get the fuck off my premises."

FORTY

Leopold paced outside the tow yard.

He'd spotted Bessie on the other side of the fence, her yellow nose poking out from a row of beat-to-hell jalopies. A helicopter buzzed over the low hills. How simple all this would've been were he a true spark. Melt the fence with a practiced wave of his focuser. Sleep charms for Tiny and the biker. Cast himself invisible, just for fun. The magically adept bestrode the world wielding real power, but Leopold was just a mediocre nothing whose most notable skill seemed to be ruining upholstery with ill-timed rain showers. His encounter with Richter, of course, had been both alarming and unique; he couldn't explain why it had happened—his best guess was that a lifetime of repressed anger had manifested in a few acts of unintentional magic—but he felt certain it couldn't be replicated. All he knew for sure was that he felt emptied out, his tank so dry he wouldn't have been able to activate even a basic pre-cast. Still, he was desperate to save Bessie, and in this moment of weakness he tried to think of where he might get his hands on a cheap focuser. He knew there were Sundered neighborhoods all over LA—the brochures from Art's booth had promised as much—but Leopold had no clue where their entrances were or how he'd get inside if he found one.

And even if he did—

He imagined dumpster-diving behind 99 Spells for castoffs. Begging random sparks for help. It made him want to die from humiliation.

Why had Sunder left him with this endless, howling shame? Why hadn't they wiped his memories? Was the Aether shortage to blame for the broken tumbleports and failed barriers and faulty revisions? Or was it something else—something about *him*? He punched the chain link fence, scraped his knuckles, and cursed.

And then he turned and stalked back into the office.

Tiny and the biker were berating a third guy, some browbeaten marshmallow of a man with sweat rings around his collar. Only the Doberman noticed Leopold as he crossed the room to the side door, its nose rising from the floor. Leopold shot the dog a *not today* look as he slipped out; it stared back in surprise before lowering its head.

His boots crunched across gravel. Metallic squeals and groans issued from Matilda as she chewed through a minivan. Leopold checked over his shoulder, half expecting to see the Doberman tearing after him, but the office door stayed closed.

He spotted Bessie right away. Halfway down the row of parked cars he saw a pair of booted legs sticking out from under her bumper like the Wicked Witch of the East. One of Tiny's guys was stripping out the catalytic converter.

Much luck to him. Leopold had welded a steel cage over the converter months ago after his last one had been stolen outside The Stench. As Leopold drew close, the guy gave a startled "Who's that?" and began to scramble out from beneath the car.

Leopold never slowed his stride.

He pulled open the driver's door, tossed in his duffel, and slid in after it. He hit the locks just as the guy stood up, his eyes dark-ringed and furious. The man tried to yank open the passenger door, and when that didn't work, he started pounding on the window.

Only then did Leopold realize he didn't have his keys.

He checked his pockets: empty. He checked the sun visor and the cup holder and the ashtray. He would've seen them if they'd been on his nightstand where they belonged, but in his tunnel-vision focus on getting his car back it hadn't occurred to him to locate, prior to leaving the house, the object that would've made the car *start*. He couldn't think of where else they might be, due primarily to the fact that he still didn't know how he'd gotten home last night. Had the Executive portaled him back into bed somehow? Had a Sunderian underling driven him and Emmet back to their respective homes and arranged everything just so (car parked shittily in driveway, etc.), and if so, *what the hell had they done with his goddamn—*

Ah. They were dangling from the ignition.

The man—who'd briefly disappeared—now reappeared in the distance wielding the decorative baseball bat from the office. This was a worrying development.

Leopold jammed the clutch, turned the key. The engine wouldn't start.

He swore.

He heard the guy shouting as he approached. Leopold turned the key again and again, looking up in time to see the baseball bat smash the passenger-side window. Safety glass exploded into the car just as the engine sputtered and came alive.

Leopold released the clutch and hit the gas. The tires sprayed gravel. The car fishtailed and shot away, one of Bessie's hubcaps flying off as he took a corner.

The exit soon came into view: a section of fence on rollers. Leopold hit the brakes and skidded to a stop in front of it, a plume of dust engulfing the car as the automatic gate began to trundle open. In the rearview mirror, he saw Tiny sprinting toward him; the Doberman and bat-man weren't far behind.

Leopold revved the engine. The gate's torturous pace was killing him. Tiny waved a long-handled socket wrench, and now the dog was outpacing the guys, barking like a rabid beast. Leopold pictured himself on Tiny's Wall of Fame, bloodied and bitten—

The fence opened. The gap was just wide enough for the Volvo to lurch through, mirrors scraping as the wheels juddered over the roller track. Leopold shot off down the street, knuckles going white as he gripped the steering wheel.

At the end of the desolate block he turned onto Jefferson Boulevard, which despite its six wide lanes was nearly as deserted. He kept checking the rearview, certain that one of Tiny's tow trucks was about to appear behind him, and to be safe he veered onto a side street and then up into winding, treacherous hills. The scene changed around him, and before long he was in a landscape of unmarked streets, oil derricks, and dry scrub. He drove until the road turned to washboard dirt and dead-ended at a stand of volunteer pepper trees. Only then did he hit the brakes, slamming the pedal down with all the finesse of a heart attack.

Leopold sat there a moment, the hot engine crackling, his blood pumping like mad.

In the space of a few hours he'd told Richter to go to hell, physically assaulted his dad by accident, gone head-to-head with a possible biker-gang boss, and stolen a car. His own, granted, but still.

A day ago Leopold wouldn't have thought it possible.

This alone was reason to feel victorious, except that he seemed incapable of emotion just then. He sat there, numb, his hands trembling slightly, listening to the furious thrum of his heart and the shudder of his breath. Victories like these—against his dad, against potential gang bosses—meant nothing if he couldn't pick up the phone and tell Emmet.

He swallowed hard.

What a waste of his life it had been, pining for magic. Sunder was supposed to save him. Instead, it had cost him everything that mattered.

A sudden buzz cut the silence.

Leopold pulled his phone from his pocket, scanning the first few words of Richter's text—*get your ungrateful ass back here*—before a swell of anger nearly prompted him to throw his phone out the window. Instead, he tore open his duffel bag and stuffed it deep inside.

He let out a shaky sigh, then sat back in his seat. Out the window was a classic LA vista: ugly oil derricks set against a smoggy grid of gray streets. The chirrup of cicadas rose from the grass, harsh and alien. This city didn't seem magical anymore, even if pockets of it actually were.

A bone-deep exhaustion settled over him, and his eyes, casting downward, fell upon something in the footwell of the passenger seat. Amidst a tide of broken glass lay a rectangular, spiralbound book.

Thomas Bros. Los Angeles Street Guide, new edition for 1987.

It must have flown out from under the seat during his great escape.

Something compelled him, for the first time in years, to do more than just jam it back into its hiding place. He stretched to pick it up, let the glass fall away, and flipped it open. On the title page, as always, was his mother's inscription:

To Leopold. Just in case.

His eyes held those five scant words, written in a road atlas years before he'd even had a learner's permit, and a chill swept through him. Not once, in all these years, had he actually looked through the book. Larry Berry was an expert at running from his feelings, and he'd always lacked the courage to turn the goddamn page.

He turned it now.

At once, he saw the doodle: In blue ballpoint above the table of contents was a man with a big nose peering over the top of a wall.

Kilroy.

Leopold dropped the book, heart pounding as he looked up, out the windshield. He pushed both hands through his hair as a terrifying feeling welled up inside him—something perilously like hope.

"Leopold," he could almost hear his mother say. *"Pay attention."*

Bracing himself, he returned his eyes to the page. A thorough scan revealed a small, easy-to-miss asterisk penned in blue beside one of the section headers.

His hands shook as he turned to page thirty-four.

It was a grid map of Hollywood, the scope of its territory highlighted in pale pink and divided into squares of equal size. These were marked A–F from left to right and 1–6 from top to bottom. In the upper margin his mother had written:

Seats where we saw Frank.

Leopold stared at her looped handwriting, his mind drawing a blank. *Frank.* Who the hell was Frank? And then he felt an old, dusty memory surfacing.

A darkened room. A summer afternoon. He and his mother sitting together—*where?*

Suddenly he had it.

Frankenstein. Bride of, to be exact: the first monster movie she'd ever taken him to see. The one that had started their weekly tradition.

It was a clue only he could've understood. They'd seen *Bride of Frankenstein* at their favorite theater: the New Beverly. He looked down at the map still open in his lap. It was at the intersection of Beverly and Formosa. Grid D-6.

His mom was leading him somewhere.

The prize at the end of Monica Berry's scavenger hunts was always something inexpensive but fun: a new pack of markers, a handmade certificate entitling him to one movie with Mom and extra butter on their popcorn. Whatever was waiting at the end of this chain of clues was likely to be something equally sweet but insignificant, ruined from years of weather exposure if it was still there at all. He didn't care.

One last game.

His future could wait a few more hours.

FORTY-ONE

After a few dead ends and wrong turns he found his way out of the hills. He avoided Jefferson and the area around Tiny's, checking his mirrors perpetually for tow trucks. It seemed unlikely that Tiny and Friends would hound him across the city over what was, to them, a few hundred dollars' worth of scrap metal, but his definition of what was unlikely had been very much in flux lately, so he took no chances.

By the time he got to Hollywood he'd begun to relax a little, and as he parked outside the New Beverly, he was cautiously optimistic that Tiny had better things to do than chase down one belligerent teenager—and if he didn't, that he'd be merciful enough not to break Leopold's driving leg.

Leopold looked up at the theater and fought the impulse to feel something. He hadn't been back here since she died. He'd never gone to another old monster movie or revisited any of the grungy theaters they'd frequented, and it felt strange to return without her.

He tucked the Thomas Guide under his arm and stepped out of the car. In this small way, at least, she'd be with him in spirit.

The New Beverly hadn't changed; it was the same shithole it had always been. Someone was sleeping off a bender outside the ticket booth. A driver leaned on their horn across the street, setting the appropriate mood, an ambience complemented by the funk wafting from overflowing trash bins near the entry doors. The red paint was peeling off the building and the marquee was missing letters. Leopold almost smiled.

Taste th Blo d of Dracula

Leopold approached the ticket booth, where, in lieu of hello, a sallow-cheeked man in a Hawaiian shirt told him there was no discount for movies that had already started. Leopold begrudgingly forked over eleven bucks and walked inside.

There were only a few people in the theater, their heads silhouetted against the screen, where an actor in cheesy vampire makeup was tiptoeing through a graveyard. Leopold stood at the rear, letting his eyes adjust to the dark.

Seats where we saw Frank.

They'd always chosen the same seats: three rows from the back, next to the aisle. Optimal viewing angle and distance. At the moment they were empty, so he went and sat down, the chair creaking as he lowered into it. He wasn't sure what to look for. He checked around the seats, then underneath them. Nothing but sticky floor and stale popcorn.

He felt like a fool.

Of course there was nothing. She'd written the note years ago. Whatever she'd left for him to find was long gone. It was a dead end.

He'd let himself believe another fairy tale.

With a sigh, he ran his hand along the underside of the chair, his heart no longer in it. Someone in the movie screamed. He felt the familiar bumps of hardened gum, nearly retracting his hand in disgust when, suddenly, he experienced a stab of pain. He'd nearly cut his palm on a slim piece of metal.

Leopold slid out of the seat and let it flip up. The object in question became clear once he got out his phone and turned on the flashlight: a thick rectangular magnet. Its heft was notable, but the object was the same color as the seat and practically invisible unless you were looking straight at it.

With some difficulty, he pried it off. A playing card slipped out from behind it and fell to the floor.

GO FISH, it read, beside a smiling cartoon goldfish.

For a moment, Leopold just looked at it. It had been there five years—five years at least, since that was the very latest his mother could have placed it. Five years, waiting for him to find it.

An actor on-screen said, "My God, it's *you*!"

The soundtrack played a jangly dramatic chord as Leopold picked up the card and turned it over. Another fish, but that wasn't the important part. Something was written in the blank space, in blue ballpoint.

49 C-5.

With the card and magnet clasped in his hand he walked as calmly as possible through the lobby and then dashed outside to his car—where he promptly opened the guide to page 49.

It was a map of Venice. His finger traced along the top to C, then down to 5.

Page 49, grid C-5. The neighborhood surrounding the old canals near the beach. He and his mom had lived nearby. Not in C-5, but close.

He knew what he was supposed to do. He could feel it as clearly as if she were standing beside him.

Go fish.

FORTY-TWO

The sun was sinking toward the sea as he drove west on the
freeway, blinding him through the dirty windshield. He exited at Lincoln, fought traffic all the way from Santa Monica, and parked on a street bordering the canals. They were all that remained of what Venice had been a hundred years ago, when it was a fanciful real estate developer's dream come to life and gondolas were the main mode of transport. Now the canals were a missable grid of stagnant waterways that led nowhere, spanned by humpbacked pedestrian bridges and befouled by hordes of ducks. Many Angelenos didn't even know they were there. But this small, strange place had been special to Leopold and his mom; they'd walked along the canals all the time, young Leopold chasing the ducks and playing in the neighborhood's one tiny park.

He zipped the Thomas Guide into his duffel bag, then slung it across his back. (Venice's smirking motto was "Where Art Meets Crime!" and there was no need to tempt fate any further by leaving the bag inside a car that was already sporting a broken window.) As he walked, Leopold flipped the playing card absently between his fingers.

Go fish.

His first stop was the Canal Market, a little bodega that sold snacks and tackle equipment, where Leopold bought a spool of fishing line before embarking on riddle number two.

He navigated the narrow sidewalk alongside Linnie Canal, low and fetid after a spell of hot and mostly rainless days. There was no one around. He mounted a pedestrian bridge—their old favorite because it was closest to the little park—and in the middle he stopped and looked down over the railing. His mother often hid metal trinkets in the shallow water, after which they'd spend whole afternoons "fishing" for them. As with the New Beverly, he hadn't been back here in years, and he found his sudden, unplanned return strangely unsettling.

This time, though, he knew exactly what to do.

Leopold uncoiled some fishing line, tied it around the heavy magnet he'd brought from the movie theater, and cast it into the canal. Through the brackish water he could make out a shape, dark and square, and after a few attempts, he felt the magnet latch onto it. With some effort he hauled up his treasure, twisting and dripping at the end of his line.

He'd caught an old lunchbox. A vintage model, metal and dented.

Leopold set it on the railing, wiped away some of the mud, and got another surprise: It wasn't just any old lunchbox. It was *his*, the one he thought he'd lost in the fourth grade. The rusting face of a zombie from *Dawn of the Dead* had nearly flaked away, but it still made him smile.

He wrenched the thing open.

Where once it had been home to Cheetos and turkey sandwiches—lettuce bagged separately so it wouldn't wilt before lunchtime—now the lunchbox contained only stars. Dozens of plastic, mud-stained, glow-in-the-dark stars—the kind kids stick to bedroom ceilings. They fell all around his feet, over his boots, into the dark water.

As a boy, he'd had hundreds.

His mom had helped affix them to the walls of the potting shed in the scrubby backyard of their old house, a place he'd once used as a fort. Leopold's breath caught at the realization. These puzzles never had more than three steps, which meant he must be close to the finish line now.

His mom was leading him home.

FORTY-THREE

The last traces of dusk were draining from the heavens, and for
a fleeting minute the grungy streets of Venice turned a rosy, dying
pink. Pushing away memories of Sunder, Leopold flipped on the
headlights, veering around double-parked cars and sun-drunk beach-
goers weaving home in the twilight.

He was hardly present behind the wheel. Their old house had
been sold long ago; strangers lived there now. Fortunately, the shed
was accessible from the alley.

It was fully dark as he turned onto Amoroso. He scanned for their
old house but couldn't find it.

At the end of the block he made a U-turn.

Had he missed it? Was it possible he'd been gone so long, he'd
forgotten what it looked like? Leopold had avoided the neighborhood completely since the last terrible afternoon he'd spent sitting on
the sidewalk, waiting for a key to Sunder that never arrived. Still, it
seemed strange that he'd forget.

On his next pass he drove more slowly, taking inventory. The
homes of old neighbors glowed invitingly, windows lit from within.
There was what everyone had called the Pink House, occupied by a
coterie of friendly Hare Krishnas. Then the house covered in glued-
on shells and colorful broken tiles. Next door to that, a green one with
porthole windows that used to be a church. It had belonged to their

next-door neighbor, a watchful widow named Helen Morse, who'd lived on Amoroso since the beginning of time. And then—

Then nothing.

Then an empty lot.

Leopold screeched to a halt and stared out his shattered window in disbelief. He hadn't missed it; their house was gone. All that was left was a broken foundation and weedy hummocks of dirt. An architectural firm's sign was planted near the sidewalk. R+H PARTNERS, COMING SOON.

In a daze he got out of his car and wandered into the rubble, the spectral image of their old bungalow rising up before him. He followed the gravel walk to what had been the front steps, then picked his way through chunks of broken concrete into the footprint of the house. His bedroom had been here. The living room there. Without walls it all seemed impossibly small. He hadn't realized until that moment how much he'd depended on the house's continued existence. He'd reconciled himself to the idea of it being bought and sold, but he'd never imagined anyone profaning the place with a wrecking ball. Now it was just a tract of scarred ground.

He walked into the ghost of the backyard, scabbed with unwatered grass, to the place where the shed had once stood. All that remained was a lone sycamore tree, one whose branches hadn't been able to hold his weight, gifting him his first broken bone.

Leopold's throat tightened.

He stood there, grieving as he stared at the dirt, when suddenly a light flashed over him. He turned sharply, raising his arm against the dazzling beam. It shone from the yard next door, over the top of a thorny bougainvillea hedge.

"What are you doing there?" came an old woman's shout. "No trespassing!"

"I didn't mean to trespass," he called back, squinting. "I just—I used to live here."

There was a jangle of bracelets as the light played up and down. A lengthy pause. Then—

"Leopold?"

"Mrs. Morse?"

She lowered the flashlight. He could see her now, gray hair in a messy bun, peering cautiously at him through huge, round glasses. She'd seemed old when he was a kid. Now she was practically a relic, her eyes rheumy and searching, a wobble trilling her thinned voice.

"Come over here and let me get a look at you!"

Leopold moved toward her, careful not to trip in the uneven dirt. Upon closer inspection, he saw that she wore an oversized T-shirt that read *NO NUKES*.

A warm feeling came over him.

Mrs. Morse was an old sixties radical who grew her own vegetables and marched in every protest. Her lime-green cottage had once been charming. Now it had the sagging, tired look of a place that would show up on Zillow in a few years billed as *An Investor's Dream!* Her living room smelled like lentils and incense, which he remembered because she'd babysat him occasionally when his mom had to work late. His mom would return the favor by inviting her over for tea, and Mrs. Morse would regale them with stories about running into Jim Morrison or Ken Kesey back in the days when the hippies ruled Venice.

"How are you, Mrs. Morse?" he said over the bougainvillea. "Your hips still bothering you?"

"They tore it down," she replied, never one for formalities. "Crying shame. It was a fine little house. 1920s. No one gives a rat's warty ass for history anymore. They're going to put up some modern monstrosity. It makes me want to puke." Her gaze circled him before landing on his face again. "My hips are made of titanium now. Knees, too."

Leopold smiled. "Nice."

"Heard your mom passed on."

"A long time ago."

"I was real sorry to hear it. She was a good lady, and no surprise there. Both your parents were great people."

Leopold stifled a laugh. "Uh, yeah. I mean, yeah, my mom was. Thank you." He cleared his throat. "Anyway, I hope I didn't scare you. I was in the neighborhood and thought I'd say goodbye to the old house."

Her chin rose. "Oh?"

"I might be leaving town for a while."

She didn't ask where. Instead she said, "Have you checked under the sycamore?"

Leopold froze. "What?"

"You show up here under the cover of dark without a word, and for no good reason. Odds are you're here to find something. And I'm pretty sure what you're looking for is under the sycamore."

"How do you"—he blinked—"how did you—"

"I saw your mom out there one day, burying a box."

"My mom?"

Mrs. Morse nodded. "This was just before she got sick." She raised the flashlight, aiming its beam at the only thing in the yard that hadn't been flattened—the massive, weak-limbed tree.

"You can borrow my shovel."

FORTY-FOUR

Leopold sat in his car, the streets dark, the glaring lights of an In-N-Out his only real source of illumination. He hadn't opened the envelope yet.

"*A lead-lined envelope,*" Mrs. Morse had called it.

It'd been tucked away inside a rusted tackle box. He'd unearthed it after a little digging under the sycamore tree, then looked over his shoulder to find Mrs. Morse standing there, staring. She'd clicked on her flashlight and nearly blinded him.

"*Jesus,*" he'd gasped, rearing back.

"My late husband was a photographer," she'd said, nodding at the heavy black envelope in his hands. "He used those fancy sleeves to protect his film when he went through airports. They're rainproof, fireproof, X-ray proof—probably nuke-proof." She'd canted her head, eyes narrowing slightly. "Your mom must've wanted to make sure you had until the end of time to find it."

She'd waited then, expectant, for him to open the package.

Instead, Leopold had mumbled a half-assed apology and nearly twisted an ankle bolting out of the yard. He'd jumped in his car and driven himself here, to this half-empty parking lot redolent of cheeseburgers. His reasons were two:

First, he hadn't eaten anything all day.

Second, he'd needed to get away from the prying eyes of Mrs. Morse.

His stomach chose that moment to grumble cantankerously, and Leopold promised himself he'd hit the drive-through just as soon as he dealt with the massive, super-important, potentially life-changing thing in his hands.

He took a deep breath. No pressure.

Finally, he unclasped the envelope. Inside were two pieces of paper, nothing more. The first was a note written on lined stationery. He lifted it with halting reverence, his fingers tracing the words as his eyes moved across the page.

Dearest Leopold,

You're nearly there now. Sorry for all the steps, but I had to make sure no one but you would get this far. You'll know what to do next. I wish I could say more, sweetheart, but we have to be careful.

There's something I need you to find.

> *Love, love, love,*
> *Mom*

Leopold read it again. Then twice more. His pulse seemed to slow.

The message was written in the same blue ballpoint as the other scribbles he'd found, and judging by his mother's shaky scrawl it had been composed in a state of either infirmity or extreme anxiety.

He didn't understand. What was it they had to be careful of? Why such paranoia? Had her mind really started to go in the end, as his father had implied?

Just before she got sick.

He took a breath, setting all that aside for the moment, and picked up the second piece of paper, which turned out to be a page torn from the Thomas Guide.

At the top it read *Key to Map Sections.*

In the corner was a legend, various symbols denoting highways, streets, railroads, and city boundaries. The page contained no further clues; nothing was circled, no arrows had been drawn. Just a few stray marks in the left margin: two curls of blue pen and a line, interrupted by the torn edge.

What was he missing?

He grabbed the Guide from the seat beside him and opened it, scanning its pages for secrets.

For the first time, he noticed a faint blue mark on the inside cover. He glanced at the legend page again, then at the marks along its tattered edge. He held one page beside the other and the marks lined up, merging to form a face. A little man with a big nose peering over a wall.

Two halves of a Kilroy.

The book felt suddenly warm to the touch. He was wondering if he'd imagined it when a faint pulse of energy crackled inside the car, and he could've sworn the In-N-Out sign flickered for an instant. Then, as his breath caught in his throat, the legend page bound itself back into the book.

The Kilroy, unsevered now, almost seemed to wink at him. The box at the top right, *Key to Map Sections*, was larger than it had been a minute ago.

New symbols had appeared inside it.

The first was a field of faint blue dots, beside which was written

Boundary of Incorporated Sunderhoods. The symbol below that was an *e* inside a red circle: *Entrance.* Beneath the circled *e* was a directional arrow interrupted by exclamation points:

The final symbol in the legend box was a blue star: *You are here.*

Goosebumps rose across his arms, his neck, the entirety of his scalp.

"What the hell is this?" he said out loud.

As if in reply, the Guide's pages began to turn by themselves, fanning the air until they settled on a map of Venice. And there he was on page forty-nine, his position marked by a blue star pulsing faintly near the end of Washington Boulevard.

A sibilant string of profanity escaped his lips.

He stared at the map for a long time, struggling to process what he was seeing. The Guide was obviously enchanted; it was a magical artifact gifted to him by his mother. That meant she'd known about Sunder—had been involved, somehow, with magic—

Suddenly, a path glowed to life beside his little star, the —!—!—!—> extending across the map. The symbol pointed east on Washington, stretching from his current position all the way to the edge of the page. It shone and faded, shone and faded, insisting.

Guiding him.

He turned the page. The glowing blue arrow tracked east until it reached the end of that map, too—and the one after that. He followed the symbol, turning pages until the marked path came to an end downtown, terminating at a large field of pink dots with a red, circled *e* at the edge of it. *Entrance.*

An entrance to Sunder Hill.

Leopold slumped in his seat, his eyes unfocusing as he gazed out the windshield. A streak of neon blazed in his peripheral vision, the glare of a motel sign in the distance. There was so much he hadn't known about his mother, so much she hadn't told him. He felt strange: terrified but excited, betrayed but hopeful. He had a thousand questions. His confidence was shattered. He felt infinitely alone. He didn't want to go back to Sunder. He wished Sunder had never existed.

There's something I need you to find.

"Okay, Mom," he whispered.

FORTY-FIVE

He crossed the night-shadowed city with the Guide open on his lap, alternately stuffing his mouth with french fries and taking bites of a double-double cheeseburger. He was driving with his knee, looking down now and then to check his progress. Like a GPS, the star moved with him across the map, the —!—!—!—> symbol always leading the way.

Washington to La Cienega; La Cienega to Olympic; Olympic through the glitzy neon carnival of Koreatown to the ragged edge of Pico-Union. A smog-yellow moon rose through a wispy veil of clouds. He shoved more fries into his mouth. In classic LA fashion, traffic thickened for no apparent reason, and to avoid the worst of it he cut down a side street. Immediately the map shook and fluttered in his lap, and the arrow symbol, marking the path from which he'd strayed, began to glow an angry red.

"All right, calm down," he muttered, finishing his double-double as he hooked a quick U-turn back onto Olympic.

The instant he returned to the path, the Guide settled down. The arrow symbol returned to its previous calm shade of blue.

Leopold drove the rest of the way without deviating from the recommended route, taking every turn demanded of him. The farther he drove, the more the streets narrowed, downtown's high-rises looming ever closer. He wound a snaking path up to Union, then crossed under the 110 freeway and entered the Second Street tunnel, the long, concrete sarcophagus that cut beneath Bunker Hill. Greenish lights blurred overhead like Morse code. A pair of motorcycles roared past, filling the tunnel with fumes and thunder. Leopold looked down at the Guide to confirm he was nearing the *e* symbol, then got a shock.

Earlier, he'd been so intent on the journey that he'd only glanced at the destination. He'd assumed the entrance to Sunder Hill would be near Angels Flight—on the other side of the tunnel. But the *e* was smack in the middle.

Peering more closely at the map, he saw that the entrance was actually down a short spur of tunnel that veered off to the left, not far ahead of him. There was only one problem with this: He'd driven through the Second Street tunnel a hundred times, and he knew for a fact there *was* no left turn. No turn in either direction. It was straight as an arrow, walls all the way.

His head snapped up at the resonant blare of a horn. Leopold jerked the wheel straight, moving so quickly he nearly knocked over his soda. Putting himself to rights, he pretended not to notice the middle finger offered in his honor, averting his eyes as the offended car sailed past, still leaning on its horn.

More cautious now, he scanned the tunnel ahead.

He was rapidly approaching the theoretical entrance, but the walls were solid as far as he could see. No STOPPING ANYTIME was painted in huge letters along the left side. His eyes darted again to the Guide. Now a few words had appeared above his glowing arrow.

Exit boldly, 500 feet.

There, ahead of him on the left, the wall now shimmered, slightly translucent. Through what looked like a sheen of heat waves, he could just make out another spur of tunnel. And then he was upon it, and there was no time to second-guess anything.

He floored the gas, yanked the wheel left, and exited boldly.

To an operatic chorus of horns he cut across oncoming traffic, steeled himself for sudden impact, then sailed through the half-transparent concrete. A snap of static electricity crackled as a flash of blue light danced across his windshield, and then he was through, stomach lurching as the tunnel ramped upward precipitously. He rounded a sharp curve before leveling off.

Only then, as brake lights came into view, did he think to let his foot off the gas.

Leopold came to a skidding stop at the end of a short line of cars, his heart thudding, french fries littering the dashboard. It was the second time that day he'd channeled The Fast and the Furious, and he hadn't even seen those movies. If there was much more of this in store for him, he was starting to think maybe he should. He remembered to breathe, straightened his spine, and scanned the scene out his windshield. In front of him was a weathered pickup truck with a bumper sticker that read STUDENT DRIVER—one of many vintage cars, he noticed, idling in the queue. At the front of the line was a booth, a guard, and a gate. Beyond that seethed a wall of gray mist.

Leopold had arrived at some kind of checkpoint.

The gate arm rose and an old Volkswagen van puttered through. The mist split open to receive it, then churned shut again after the van had passed. As the line of cars inched forward, Leopold felt a twinge of doubt. How, exactly, was he supposed to get in? What would he tell the guard? What if the guard knew he'd been banished from Sunder?

He looked down at the Guide. It offered no advice.

Channeling Richter, Leopold pulled up to the booth wearing his most accommodating smile—which faltered as soon as the guard swiveled in her chair to face him.

It was Rochelle. The winged old lady from the underground parking garage.

He still owed her a nickel.

"*You.*" She glared. "I know you from someplace."

Leopold briefly squeezed his eyes shut. Of all the people she must've seen in that parking garage on a daily basis, he couldn't believe she remembered him. "Yeah, listen, I'm sorry about that. I can pay you now, if you've got change—"

"You an actor?" A pair of glasses hung from a beaded chain around her neck. She put them on and peered at him skeptically. "Where've I seen your face?"

"I'm not an actor." Leopold frowned. "We met yesterday. In the parking garage."

A car honked impatiently.

"Nah," said Rochelle. She was tapping her chin when, suddenly, her face lit up. She reared back on her stool, cackling loudly. "Holy hell, you're the *whoopsie* kid!"

Leopold felt the blood drain from his face. "What?"

"I saw you on TV! You're that shit-for-brains who thought he was a channeler!"

"I, uh, don't know what you're talking about," Leopold said, suddenly feeling sick, "but if you could just let me through—"

"No chance, you were banished," she said, wagging a finger at him as she picked up a heavy black phone. "They'll want to talk to you. Pull over to the side, you're blocking traffic. Sunder PD will be here in two shakes."

She raised the gate and waved him over, still laughing.

"*Shit*," Leopold hissed as he shifted into first gear, casting a last glance down at the Guide.

Yet again, it offered no help.

"Ahoy, Clarence!" Rochelle was shouting into the phone. "You'll never believe who just pulled up to my gate! No. *No*, dummy. I'll give you two guesses, and the first one don't count—"

"You know what," Leopold muttered, hitting the gas. "Fuck this."

He swung a hard left to circle the booth, but the turn was too tight, and he had to brake before hitting the wall. Rochelle leapt out of her chair, wings ruffled and thrashing as she shouted into the phone. Leopold managed to extricate himself with a beautifully executed three-point turn, set to the soundtrack of a dozen wailing car horns. But just as he was about to speed away, wheels spinning, his car refused to budge.

The mist had attached itself to his bumper and was dragging the car backward. Leopold kept his foot planted on the gas. After a tire-squealing moment the mist's hold broke and he shot away, past the booth and back down the curving tunnel, Rochelle waving a fist in his rearview. A thick gray tendril pursued him, snapping at his window like a cobra until it could stretch no farther.

Finally, the mist evaporated.

He skidded back into the main tunnel, merged with normal traffic, and sped out into open streets as fast as LA would allow. Only when he was several blocks away did he pull over. He sat there breathing like he'd run a race, cold sweat beading his brow as he checked his mirrors for rogue appendages of mist.

Leopold's head fell back against the headrest, his adrenaline slowly fading, leaving in its place a cold, terrifying humiliation.

"You're that shit-for-brains who thought he was a channeler!"

Apparently, he was famous.

He remembered signing those waivers—remembered the Executive explaining that the test would be filmed and broadcast to the public—and yet he'd never truly considered what failure might look like. He'd never considered failure at all. He'd been so damn sure he was special.

Leopold dragged his hands down his face.

It would've been easier, of course, to have left Sunder behind forever. Ideally, they'd have revised his memories like they were supposed to. Then he might've gone on being a mediocre nothing in privacy—a privilege it hadn't occurred to him to be grateful for. But for reasons he didn't understand, his mom needed him to return to a world that seemed to know his face, his choices, and the precise dimensions of his stupidity.

And yet.

Larry Berry had failed many things in his life, but he couldn't bear to fail his mother.

He bent to retrieve the Guide. In all the chaos it had fallen to the floor again. He opened it to downtown Los Angeles, then located his glowing blue star.

"Well?" he said to the map. "What am I supposed to do now?"

In response, it shuddered. Beside the blue route that had led him down the tunnel, the words **Easy Way** appeared. Then a second route glowed to life, this one marked by a new symbol:

$$-X-X-X->$$

This path led from his current location to the other side of Sunder Hill, where it narrowed to a thin and twisting thread—no more than a hiking trail—that ended at a red, circled *e*, almost too faint to make out. Beside this more ominous-looking entrance appeared the words **Hard Way**.

With a reluctant shake of his head, Leopold shifted the car into first gear. He supposed nothing good in his life had ever been easy.

FORTY-SIX

Hard Way led him to the other side of the hill, where he was forced to leave his car in a sketchy parking lot by the freeway overpass. He Clubbed the wheel, grabbed his duffel bag, and got out. The hiking trail commenced in the scrub behind a power substation, its transformers humming and snapping in the night air. Unencumbered now by clouds, the moon cast a ghostly glow across the barren scenery. He followed a thin dirt track up the hill, so steep in places he had to stash the Guide and haul himself along by the spiky underbrush.

Halfway up the incline he paused to recover his breath. The freeway spread below him, a gleaming vein of endless, stuttering brake lights. A chilly breeze rustled the sage and sliced through his thin cotton T-shirt. For the second time in as many days, he wished he had a jacket.

Finally, he crested the hill. The trail dead-ended at a chain link fence from which hung a menacing octagonal sign. Trespassers Will Be Prosecuted to the Fullest Extent of the Law.

He blinked, felt a slight pressure build in his ears, and the sign changed.

Hungry Mist. Enter at Your Own Peril.

Now he could see a wall of gray swirling beyond the fence. He stared at it for a moment, recalling a scene in episode five where Max actually *befriends* a patch of semi-sentient mist, but he knew nothing about angry mist of the border-control variety.

He pulled out the Thomas Guide and double-checked the path ahead. **Hard Way** led to the very spot where he stood, then continued on past the fence and the mist. Leopold stuffed away the Guide, steeled himself, and jumped it—in the process activating what sounded like a gentle alarm. Once he'd landed on the opposite side he spun around, searching the dark for the source of the noise.

A small, red bell.

Someone had tied it to the fence.

Unsure what to make of this, he turned to face the mist—a boiling, opaque barrier that stretched away endlessly in both directions. He heard a low, menacing rumble from within, and as he deliberated whether to be afraid or very afraid, he was startled by a shout.

"Somebody rang?"

It was a man's voice, hoarse but loud. It had come from beyond the mist.

Leopold hesitated. "I did?"

"Who's that?"

"Larry."

"*Who?*"

"Larry!"

"You coming through or what, Larry? I don't have all night!"

Leopold looked around. "Coming through how?"

A pause. "You got legs?"

"Uh—"

"If not, no problem, we'll do this a different way—"

"I've got legs."

"Then why are you asking stupid questions, Larry? *Run.* And try to hold your breath!"

Leopold sighed, stifled his irritation, and then—holding his breath—gave it a running start. The next thing he knew he was enveloped in it, mist dimming his view in all directions and clinging to his limbs like molasses, arresting his momentum to such a degree that after a few strides he struggled to move forward even an inch. The mist's roar was nearly deafening now, and he could only just hear the man shouting, *"Grab my hand!"*

An outstretched arm appeared before him, and Leopold grasped it. With a sudden heave, he was pulled through to the other side.

Leopold stumbled out into tall grass. He took in a deep lungful of night air, then tried to assess his surroundings. He was in a small clearing. A cracked asphalt path led away through a copse of trees.

"Okay there, Larry?" The man who'd helped him was standing a few feet away in a patched coat and a furry, flap-eared cap. He untied a bandana that had been wrapped around his nose and mouth and stuffed it away in a pocket. The man was walleyed and had a thin beard that grew in disconnected patches, as if he'd suffered repeated shaving accidents. Despite all this, he looked pleased with himself as he untied a rope from his midsection and let it drop. The other end was staked into the ground behind him.

"I think I'm okay, yeah. Thanks."

"Good thing you didn't try that without me." He flashed a gap-toothed smile. "Check yourself for clingers."

Leopold looked down at himself. "Clingers?"

The man nodded at Leopold's boots. "You don't wanna take any of that with you."

Leopold bent to see a wisp of mist lingering on his boots, wriggling up his laces like an inchworm. He shuddered and shook it off, then stomped the squirming tendril under his heel for good measure, as if trying to kill a spider.

There was a snort of laughter. "I think you got it."

Leopold composed himself.

"I'm Harney. Over there's French," he said, gesturing to a wooden bench beside the path, where a man piled with blankets lay curled and snoring beside a guttering lantern. "French, we got a customer. Rouse yourself."

"Customer?" Leopold echoed.

Harney grinned. "Do I stand here in the cold night for my health?" He let out a hacking, asthmatic cough. "I do not."

French stirred, the blankets falling away as he sat up and let out a hacking cough of his own. He wore a disheveled uniform with DEPT OF BORDER SECURITY AND MIST MAINTENENCE printed on it.

"Right." Leopold frowned, feeling naïve. "Of course not."

Harney shoved his hands into his pockets and rocked back on his heels. "That'll be fifty dollars, please."

"*Fifty?*"

"Fee for services rendered." French hooked a thumb toward the mist. "Of course, we can always toss you back into the churn."

Leopold glanced behind him as the mist let out a particularly hungry-sounding rumble, then then returned his eyes to the men. "I can give you thirty."

Harney exchanged a look with French, who was screwing a small flat cap onto his bald head, then turned back to Leopold. "Then that'll be thirty dollars, if you please."

Leopold pulled a few bills from his duffel. Thirty bucks represented a sizable chunk of his total fortune, so it hurt a little as he pressed the money into Harney's hand.

"Appreciate your business," Harney said as he pocketed the cash. "Exit through the trees. And don't forget to tell your friends."

Leopold turned to leave, only to discover French staring at him.

"Now wait just a minute," the man said, rising from the bench as his eyes narrowed on Leopold. "I'll be a street conjurer's monkey. You're him."

"I'm not anyone," Leopold said, a small dread building as he backed away.

"You're right, French." Harney shuffled closer to Leopold, inspecting his face in the moonlight. "It *is* him."

"I don't know what you guys are talking about."

"Don't worry," Harney said with a calculating grin. "We won't tell a soul. Do we snitch on clients with whom we do business? We do not."

"So, which way you headed?" French asked.

Leopold couldn't have told the man even if he'd wanted to. He'd put all his faith in the enchanted and slightly cantankerous Thomas Guide, which at the moment lay still and silent in his duffel.

He only shook his head before walking away.

Harney called after him. "Piece of advice, friend! If you go back to a sunderhood you've been banished from, it won't rest. It'll keep trying to spit you out, like a bit of undigestible meat."

Leopold slowed a moment, looking back.

Harney gave him a pitying look. "You're an error in the system now."

FORTY-SEVEN

Before long, he was bathed in pink light.

The trees had cleared like curtains parting, and in the distance he glimpsed a familiar neon blur. Leopold cracked open the Guide, double-checking his position along the easterly, abandoned-seeming end of what was called Vigdor Street. The glowing path that stretched ahead of him was still marked **Hard Way**.

He tucked away the map, then readied himself.

The evening breeze shook a stand of skeletal bushes. Leopold crossed from wild, scrubby grass through cigarette graveyards and unkempt medians. He jaywalked through a district of lonely warehouses and factories, then straight into the main strip of Sunder Hill, its familiar sights and smells jeering at him from all directions. The street was alive with shoppers and pedestrians. He kept his head down, passing landmarks he recognized. Norm's MagiPawn and the portable hole in its window, still available for financing. Art's information-post-slash-tumbleport-station, Art himself inside, patronless, dusting the counter. The Brite Spot, bustling with patrons. Its bell jangled as a customer exited, the enticing smells of greasy food that escaped reminding Leopold, with a sharp pang, of a more hopeful time.

Larry Berry of yesterday seemed like a distant memory.

Keeping his eyes averted, Leopold ignored the aggressive offers of a street vendor selling cheap souvenirs from a pushcart. The Guide wanted him to walk three blocks down this, the busiest stretch of Sunder Hill, before turning onto Bradley Street. Clearly, the Guide had no idea Leopold was both a laughingstock and a wanted man.

He'd just have to be careful.

So committed was Leopold to keeping his head down that he was nearly run over by three teenagers on skateboards, who seemed to be propelling themselves by means of a cheap focuser. He ducked into an alley and flattened himself against a brick wall. Taking a breath, he finally allowed himself to look up. A billboard shone brightly across the street. Beside a picture of a three-eyed man peeking over a pair of sunglasses, it read STAY VIGILANT. IF YOU SEE SOMETHING, SAY SOMETHING.

At that exact moment two beefy guys in tan uniforms strode toward him down the alley, one carrying a burlap sack tied shut with a knotted chain. Leopold could do nothing then but turn his attention to a heap of trash near his feet and hope to go unnoticed.

Something inside the sack rustled, jangling the chain.

"Don't worry," one of the men said as they trundled past. "Thing's out like a light. Probably dreaming about eating someone's cat."

Realizing they were talking to him, Leopold risked a look in their direction. Stitched on the backs of their uniforms was *Balthazar's Pest Control.*

He knew then: There was a Noxum in that bag.

It had to have been a small one—maybe one of the minor, "residential-grade" subspecies that could be repelled, if the ubiquitous advertisements were to be believed, with a few spritzes of Noxum spray. Leopold had his doubts—as he now knew from experience, some of the deadliest looked perfectly unthreatening at first glance, and he shuddered, remembering the nightmarish janitor stepping out of his skin suit.

The creature let out a sudden hiss and clawed at him from inside the bag. Leopold spun away to face the wall.

"Sorry 'bout that," one of the guys called over to him, laughing. "Little bastards won't even let you take a leak in peace, huh?"

Leopold made a strangled sound.

"They're in rare form lately," the other guy added. "Something's got 'em all riled up."

"On a busy week we get two, three callouts, but lately we've been getting two or three a *day*. This little sweetheart came up through a lady's shower drain while she was shampooing her hair. Nearly chewed one of her toes off."

"Wow," Leopold said noncommittally. His eyes were still fixed on the wall. He was, theoretically, supposed to be taking a leak, but this did nothing to deter the conversation.

"Last job of the day, at least. Not sure what's gotten into them. Must be an error in the system . . ."

They wandered off, out of sight and earshot, those last words ringing in Leopold's ears. It was the same thing Harney had said to him.

You're an error in the system now.

"—error in the system, apologies for the Aether glitch. You're on with Jakey—"

"—and Jamila!"

"So don't touch that remote!"

"That's right, folks. You demanded and we're here to deliver a two-hour, commercial-free marathon—"

Leopold looked around, trying to locate the source of the perky voices. He peered through split fingers as he moved toward the sound. An eerie feeling blazed through him as he left the alley and approached a familiar storefront.

He came to a halt in front of the display.

Just last night he'd stood here. Just last night he'd been hypno-tized—no, *inspired*—by the glaring pyramid of boxy television screens. Now he watched, horrified, as new footage unspooled before his eyes. His hands fell, dead weight, to his sides.

"Mother*fucker*," he breathed.

"—you say, Jamila? We've been polling callers all night, but I know everyone wants to hear from you: When do *you* think it all started going downhill for Lunchtray Larry?"

Jamila flashed a knowing smile at the camera. "Glad you asked, Jakey."

They cut to a clip of Leopold looking overconfident in the rem-nants of his filthy, ill-fitting suit, the grotesque Noxum swinging from a light in the rafters. Leopold watched, dread mounting, as on-screen Larry balled his fists against his chest like a moron—as if he were a superhero from a comic book—then let them fly. This theatrical gesture was undercut by the pathetic results of his focuser, which pro-duced a limp spray of reddish sparks that fizzled out midair.

"Whoopsie!" cried yesterday's Larry.

Jamila and Jakey, their talking heads gleaming on a dozen screens, burst into peals of laughter, pearly teeth flashing as they guffawed.

"I think we need to watch that again—"

Leopold watched himself say *Whoopsie!* over and over, his legs crossing in the aftermath like a little boy who needed the bath-room. The chyron on the bottom of the screen read *Lunchtray Larry: Channeler Test Gone Wrong. Phone lines open. We want to hear from you!*

Leopold stepped back, disoriented, as the din of the streets around him rose in his ears. He heard the bustle of shoppers (*Whoopsie!*) and the blast of a car horn. A raucous burst of laughter. (*Whoopsie!*) Leo-pold stumbled, startling as hands pushed at him. He spun around, breathing fast, realizing too late that he'd (*Whoopsie!*) bumped into a couple on a late-evening stroll. Leopold heard one of them shout, their voices indistinct, and he practically ran back to the darkened alley, deaf to all but his thundering heart as he sank against its filthy wall and slid to the ground.

A tide of humiliation swept over him like nothing he'd ever experienced. No lecture of Richter's had ever made him feel so unworthy; no clichéd high school indignity had ever made him feel so small. He'd never seen himself reflected this way—had never seen himself in such a pathetic light. All these years, he'd believed his efforts at faked confidence had been fooling people. He'd thought he'd been putting on a pretty good show.

He hadn't realized the world could see straight through him.

Mortification coiling in the pit of his stomach, Leopold heaved himself upright. He'd been many things in his life—passive, pathetic, indecisive—but he resolved, then and there, that he'd never again be a coward. He turned and stalked back down Vigdor Street the way he'd come, head firmly down until he reached the souvenir cart he'd passed earlier. Working quickly, he searched its racks of trinkets until he found an LA Dodgers cap and a cheap pair of knockoff Ray-Bans. He ripped off the tags, donned the hat and glasses, and tossed the tags onto the little counter.

"How much for these?" he asked, avoiding the vendor's gaze.

Leopold didn't hear the man's reply. He was frozen in renewed horror, his eyes having landed on a rack of novelty T-shirts, all of which bore the same image—*of him*.

Below a grainy black-and-white photo of Lunchtray Larry, legs crossed like a drunken ballerina, was a single, boldfaced word.

WHOOPSIE

He wasn't just famous in Sunder. He'd become a fucking meme.

"—but if you get a keychain, too, I'll knock off five bucks," the vendor was saying.

"No thanks," Leopold muttered, placing the bills on the counter.

There was a loud *cha-ching* as the register opened. "If you're interested in the shirts," the vendor went on, counting the cash, "I'd grab one before they're gone. It's a limited print run—"

"You know what," said Leopold, forcing a smile. "Keep the change."

Leopold continued on toward Bradley Street, taking his time now as he kept an eye out for paladins or Sunder police officers. He didn't care if he looked ridiculous wearing a hat and sunglasses at night. In fact, Leopold was surprised to find that he no longer cared about much of anything.

He'd already hit rock bottom.

The map forced him to retrace his steps, which meant soon he was passing the electronics store and its pyramid of TVs again, still rehashing his myriad humiliations. Leopold forced himself to stop and stare at his own image—at the version of himself he was determined to leave behind.

Leopold of Yesterday was holding up two broken halves of a lunch tray, and then, one quick cut later, peeling baloney from his face as he climbed out of a trash can.

"What an idiot," muttered a woman who'd paused to watch.

"You can't blame the poor guy," said the man beside her. "I guess everyone thinks they're the hero."

Leopold, swallowing against a knot of emotion, turned and kept walking. It was a surprising relief to discover that, having been stripped wholly of his dignity, he was left only with fire.

FORTY-EIGHT

Leopold looked down at the Guide in his hands, then up at the building in front of him. Again at the Guide. Once more at the building.

He'd arrived at his destination. He could practically hear the GPS voice in his head.

It was nothing like what he'd expected. Then again, he wasn't sure what he'd expected. The building was straight out of a horror movie, exactly the kind of thing an LA developer would salivate over: a once-grand three-story Victorian with its paint peeling scabrously, balcony clinging to the façade by a few bent nails. It wasn't abandoned, though maybe it deserved to be. Lights shone in the first- and second-floor windows, and a sign above the porch read:

GOLDIE'S ROOMING HOUSE
UNHAUNTED ROOMS TO LET
REASONABLE RAT s

Casting a paranoid glance behind him, he climbed five crooked steps to the porch. An old man in an old suit smoking three cigarettes regarded him suspiciously from a folding chair, as if weighing whether Leopold was a door-to-door salesman or an off-duty murderer. Leopold checked to ensure his hat was covering his hair, then adjusted his sunglasses and pushed open the front door.

He entered a cramped and funereal reception area: creepy porcelain statuary in the corners, threadbare floral carpeting, roses dried black in dust-skinned vases. Skittering sounds echoed behind the peeling wallpaper, and Leopold surrendered to an impulse to place his hand against it, the panel so soft with mold he could feel the patter of tiny feet from the other side.

He approached the check-in desk, imprisoned inside a wire cage. Within it sat a giant, rawboned clerk who looked like he hadn't risen from his chair in years. He reclined with his shoes propped on the desk, slurping take-out noodles while chuckling at a small, squawking television before him.

A sign on the cage advertised rates for monthly, daily, and forever.

The clerk didn't bother glancing up. "All we got left is haunted rooms, top floor, no elevator, hot water from five to seven a.m., bathroom down the hall," he said, his eyes on the TV. "It ain't the Ritz."

Leopold was about to reply when he heard a familiar voice.

"Whoopsie!"

The man wheezed with laughter between slurps, a fine mist of soy sauce spritzing the air. "Jackass."

Leopold's jaw tensed. "Mind if I look around before I decide?"

"Knock yourself out."

Beyond the desk was an arrow-shaped sign that read GUEST ROOMS and pointed up a staircase. To the left, an arched doorway opened onto a common room, where a chandelier cast pallid light on a collection of sad characters. Leopold drew farther into the room. It smelled of stale, trapped air. A few elderly people dozed in armchairs around a barely going fireplace. A woman who might've been in her second century of life shuffled back and forth past a grandfather clock, obsessively adjusting the aperture on a cracked focuser, conjuring only faint traces of light in the process. An age-darkened oil painting of a shipwreck hung above a piano with half its keys missing. He wondered if the place was a rest home for aged sparks. At the very least, it appeared to be a refuge of last resort, a catchment for the unwanted and the desperate.

When Leopold was satisfied no one was watching, he pulled out the Guide. His blue star pulsed gently at the rooming house on Bradley Street, where the **Hard Way** path appeared to end. Now a small addendum had appeared at the top of the page.

Kindly turn to Appendix A.

Flipping to the back, he found the appendix and a diagram of the rooming house, a new blue star glowing inside a roughly rectangular floor plan of the space he currently occupied.

Then, before his eyes, a fresh route brightened to legibility.

It led from the common room to the staircase, then traced a path to one of the upper-floor guest rooms. Several warnings interrupted the path as it ascended:

Take-great-care—!—!—!—to-proceed-unobserved—!—!—!—>

With a jolt, he realized he was within a few hundred feet of whatever his mom had meant for him to find. He felt at once an ache and a longing. For all that was. For all that might've been.

For whoever he might be on the other side.

Leopold adjusted his clothes, squared the duffel on his back, and tucked the Guide under his arm. With a last look at the distracted desk clerk, he mounted the stairs as quietly as its groaning steps would allow. His heart was racing now, his mind reeling with the possibilities of what lay ahead.

The Guide wanted him to go to the third floor.

Reaching the landing of the second, he detected motion down the hall and shrank into a dark corner. He waited until an old woman shuffled into one of the rooms, then closed the door behind her.

He continued up the next flight of stairs.

Each step produced a little shriek, as if the building itself were objecting to his ascent. He grew only more anxious as he climbed, sensitive to the slightest sounds and movements. A prickle at the nape of his neck alerted him to something—a presence somewhere below—and he sped up, taking the stairs two at a time until he reached the top, where he backed into a wall, chest heaving. He hesitated, listening for the approach of footsteps or the chatter of some stray guest, and only when he was convinced he was utterly alone did he turn his gaze once more to the Guide.

The marked path continued past a series of doors and around a corner, where it terminated at a circled *e* symbol. He checked one final time to make sure no one was near, moved down the hall as quickly and quietly as he could, took a sharp left, and arrived at the endpoint. Steadying himself, he looked around—this section of hallway seemed decidedly unimportant—and then down at the Guide. The entire page had blanked; there was no floor plan anymore, no map. All that remained were a few lines of bold text, red ink bright against a page that was now warm to the touch.

> **Five paces east. Knock three times on the knotted panel. Not too loud. Follow the passage to its end. Then four paces forward, three left, kneel, and knock again.**

That was all.

The ink, vivid when he'd first begun to read, was already fading. He chased all else from his mind and scanned the words twice more, reading slowly and whispering each step aloud.

By the time he'd committed it to memory, the page was blank.

FORTY-NINE

Leopold had done precisely as the Guide had instructed, and still he was baffled. He stood now before the knotted panel, on which he'd knocked three times. Nothing had happened. He wasn't sure whether he should try knocking a fourth time.

Leopold was starting to freak out.

"Open, goddamn it," he whispered, tossing a look over his shoulder. The hallway was still mercifully vacant, but his panic was reaching a crescendo. His pressed his hand flat against what was, theoretically, an entrance, hoping he might be able to push it open through sheer force. When this, too, failed, he could no longer rein in his alarm.

"Shit, shit, *shit—*"

Each word accompanied by a strike of his fingers.

Only then, miraculously, did the panel slide away, but Leopold was more relieved than triumphant.

He pushed through the gap and crouched into near darkness, proceeding on hands and knees through thick dust in what appeared to be an old ventilation shaft, or something like a crawl space. The dust, combined with a muggy, clinging heat, made it difficult to breathe. Worse, the passage narrowed as he went, and soon he was flat on his stomach, forced to shimmy past unsnapped mousetraps and nets of cobwebs while dragging the duffel behind him with one foot. Weak light gasped through cracks in the boards that brushed his head, sufficient to identify the occasional rodent corpse but little else. He was squirming around an abandoned wasp's nest when he heard the panel slide closed some distance behind him.

If he suffocated here, he thought, they'd never find him.

After what felt like an interminable stretch of darkness, he thumped against what he hoped was the end, and then another panel swung open directly overhead. He stood up and burst through it, gasping for air. At first he thought only of breathing, head swimming as he filled his lungs. Only then did he allow himself to freak out in full: the claustrophobia, the spiderwebs he'd snagged in his teeth, the stench of mildew and that sharp, clinging *eau de* decomposed rat still lingering in his nose.

Blinking steadily, horrors gradually abating, he looked around. He'd emerged from the floor in the middle of what appeared to be someone's hotel room. Leopold hoisted himself the rest of the way out of the hole in the floor, then reached down for his duffel, which he hung across his chest before standing.

Squares of pale moonlight on floral wallpaper. The narrow bed was made, sheets tucked tightly, an oversized Hello Kitty T-shirt draped carefully over the edge. A stack of books teetered on a nightstand. There was no en suite bathroom, just a leaky sink in the corner, its drip like an irregular heartbeat. An old wardrobe had been left cracked open, allowing a view of a few neatly hung clothes. Most conspicuous of all was the suitcase by the door, as if the owner was preparing for a quick exit. Whoever was staying here didn't intend to stay long. They had that in common.

Four paces forward, three left, kneel, and knock again.

It occurred to him, with some trepidation, that the Guide's instructions had not indicated how long his paces should be, or what "forward" meant relative to previous directions. Apprehension was clouding his head, making it difficult to focus. He pressed his eyes shut, and in the brief stillness an old song popped into his mind unbidden.

> *Come on, sparks, it's time for adventure*
> *A secret passage in a wizard's tomb*
> *Magic spells and treasures to find*
> *Monsters lurking in your room*
> *Get your key, heed the call*
> *Sunderworld, Sunderworld awaits us all!*

He let out a low, bitter laugh. It had once been the theme song to his life, hummed in moments of quiet, sung aloud in the shower. It sounded ridiculous to him now.

He forced his thoughts back to the task at hand.

Four paces forward, three left, kneel, and knock again.

He regarded the passage from which he'd emerged. He'd found the knotted panel easily enough, so he figured an average stride-length should suffice. Forward probably referred to the direction he faced when he'd stood up from the hole, which was the same direction he'd been facing during his belly-crawl through the passage.

He took four careful, even steps forward, turned ninety degrees left, then took three more steps until he stood atop a section of gently warped floor that looked like all the other parts of the gently warped floor. He knelt down, ready to tap three times, when he heard an unprompted click, then the mechanical *thunk* of a tumbler turning in a lock. He was confused for a moment, wondering how the panel had anticipated his knock.

Then he realized: It wasn't the floor.

Someone was opening the door to the room.

He looked around frantically, considered diving under the bed or into the wardrobe, then realized that if he did, he'd lose the spot he'd worked so hard to find. He leapt to his feet just as the door swung open, then stiffened as the stranger entered, his head ringing like a struck bell.

It wasn't a stranger, exactly. It was *her*.

The girl from yesterday. She'd watched him from a corner booth at the Brite Spot, arresting him with both her beauty and her suspicion. Later, she'd appeared like a phantom in the middle of his test. He'd never forget seeing her face right before he got backhanded into a trash can by a Noxum. And now this, his third sighting: Of all the neighborhoods, all the flophouses, and all the rooms in Sunder, she just happened to occupy the one that contained his mother's secret. This could not be coincidence. He'd suspected it, of course, the second time he'd seen her, but now he was certain.

She'd been following him.

The absurdity of the situation was clear even as his eyes narrowed. He stood now in her room, by all accounts the asshole who'd inadvertently broken into her private space, yet he felt an unnerving flash of anger as he realized that, all along, he'd been marked.

"What the hell are you doing here?" they both shouted at the same time.

She went still for an instant, lips parting in shock, then quickly found her voice. "This is my room," she said, her green eyes wide with outrage.

"Why have you been following me?" he shot back.

He couldn't explain it—couldn't explain why his many frustrations sharpened to a point aimed in her direction. But it had just occurred to him that, other than Art, hers was the only face he'd seen repeated in Sunder.

"Are you out of your mind?" she was saying. "You broke into my room, and instead of apologizing, you're yelling at me?"

"I'm not yelling," he said. "And I'm sorry for breaking into your room. I didn't know it was your room."

"Then get the hell out!" she shouted, flinging her arm at the open door behind her.

"No."

The girl went slack with disbelief. "You must be insane."

"I'm going to ask you one more time." His jaw tightened. "Why have you been following me?"

"Why don't you tell me what you're doing in my room?"

"No chance." Leopold was probably angrier than he should've been. He felt a strange heat gathering in his chest as he watched her, the way she slapped her dark bangs out of her eyes, the way she stood there insolently, all five feet of her vibrating with rage. She was wearing a heavy, forest-green cloak pulled straight from the bins of a discount Halloween store. All she was missing was a pointy witch's hat, a jack-o'-lantern trick-or-treat bag, and a parent to chaperone. If he hadn't been so angry, he might've thought it was cute.

She turned and slammed the door shut.

Which was startling.

She took a careful step toward him and reached into her cloak. Leopold felt the hair rise along his arms. Was she about to murder him? Did it matter? If she forced him, somehow, to leave this spot, he'd lose everything anyway. He was so close, inches from an opportunity that might never come again if he let it slip away.

No, he wouldn't leave without the thing he'd come for.

"Now, I'm going to ask *you* one more time," she said, drawing out her hand. It held a focuser, small and tarnished with age, its lens glimmering with some spell that was already locked and loaded. "What the hell are you doing here?"

"Wow." Leopold was almost impressed. "You're really willing to kill me over this," he said quietly. "You must be a really excellent person."

"You have no idea," she said evenly. "I don't know who put you up to this or how you got in here, but if you turn around right now and crawl back where you came from, Larry"—she nodded to the open trap in the ground—"I'll think about letting you keep your face."

"My name isn't Larry."

"I know," she said flatly. "It's Lunchtray Larry."

His eyes flashed. "My name," he said, "is *Leopold*."

Quickly, before he could change his mind, he tapped his boot on the floor three times.

She let out a horrified gasp as a small panel flipped open at Leopold's feet. He dropped to his knees, reached into the hole, and fished out a velvet box the size of a thick paperback. It was substantial, and as he weighed it in his hands he experienced a sudden lightheadedness, like a long-distance runner nearing the finish line.

He recognized the box. He knew it quite well, in fact.

It had belonged to his mother.

"Put that down," the girl hissed, fear lighting her eyes.

He met her gaze slowly, glaring with a righteous indignation he'd felt only one other time in his life—that morning, when he'd faced down Richter.

"Why do you have this?" he demanded.

"Because it's mine, you idiot."

"Liar," Leopold said furiously. "This belongs to *me."*

Now she panicked, her focuser all but forgotten. "Okay, wait," she said, backing away. "Don't open it— You don't understand—"

Leopold was done listening.

He shot the girl a defiant look before flipping open the box, and for a vanishing instant, he saw the object whole in a gleam of moonlight. It was a focuser—unlike any he'd seen, the width of his hand but nearly flat, the gold circumference of its housing etched with delicate aperture markings, its thin lens glinting—

The girl screamed.

Leopold looked up, startled, to see her diving for cover. A high, metallic sound snapped his attention back to the box, where the focuser had risen from its bed of velvet to hover in the air. Six sharpened spikes popped out around its housing like little teeth, and then it flung itself at him, hitting Leopold square in the chest.

He reeled from the impact, dropping the box and gasping as he was seized by a sudden shock of pain. Razor-sharp barbs cut straight through his clothes to embed themselves in his flesh. From the fallen box came a flash of blinding light and searing heat, and with that a crash so obliteratingly loud he thought his head was cracking open. He clung to consciousness long enough to feel himself being lifted off his feet and blown across the room, and then the world and everything in it was blotted out, lost in black, gone.

FIFTY

One by one, like lights dimming up on a darkened stage, Leopold's senses returned to him. First, the smell of frying sausage. Then coffee, its enticing aroma coaxing him from a deep hole. As the roaring in his head dulled to a loud hum, he could identify the puttering of a coffeemaker, the pop and spatter of oil in a pan.

Someone was making breakfast.

His eyes slit open. Once he'd blinked away a stubborn blur, he was greeted by the sight of an unfamiliar wood-beamed ceiling. Overstuffed bookshelves climbed a pale green wall. Mismatched chairs clustered around a weather-beaten coffee table. Morning sun filtered through a curtained window, the mop-top fringes of palm trees visible outside.

Daytime.

He'd been out the whole night.

The girl's face swam into view, her green eyes shimmering among dark spots in his vision. "Leopold?" she was saying, peering down at him. "You awake?"

He tried to summon a reply, but his chest felt like a tin can being crushed. His head throbbed painfully as a burst of fireworks went off behind his eyes. As it faded, scattered floaters appeared in their place. He dipped his chin to look down the length of himself. He was stretched out on a lumpy brown couch, his tall frame occupying all of it.

"Leopold? Can you talk?"

He must've mumbled some word of affirmation, because she looked profoundly relieved.

"You're okay," she said, exhaling. Then, over her shoulder: "He's okay!"

"I thought you wanted me dead," Leopold managed to say.

"Not yet." A fleeting grin. "My reaction might've been premature."

He tried to frown but laughed instead, the sound hoarse and weak. "Where the hell am I?"

"My uncle Norm's place," she said. "You hungry? He makes a killer breakfast."

A spasm of pain branched across Leopold's sternum, taking his breath away. His hand went to his chest, where it encountered something alien and metallic. It was the same object that had sprung out at him like some nightmarish jack-in-the-box: what appeared to be a focuser, a disc of gold and glass four or five inches in diameter, vacuumed tight against the mangled fabric of his blood-speckled T-shirt. He pried at its edges with rising urgency, remembering the shock he'd felt as its spikes had dug into him, but his fingers could find no purchase.

Gritting his teeth, he forced himself partially upright just as a new character came into view: Over the girl's shoulder he saw a scraggly, slightly absurd-looking man with wild, graying hair and a short goatee. He wore, of all things, a pair of puffy red oven mitts and a striped brown bathrobe.

"Go easy, brother, go easy." The man hurried forward, concern on his face as he said, "You had a hell of a night. Can you sit up all the way? Let's sit you up."

Then he and the girl were sliding their arms beneath Leopold, lifting him until he was seated with his back against the couch. The girl smiled as she knelt in front of him, her energy strangely intense, eyes darting between Leopold and the uncle.

Her attitude made no sense.

Just last night she'd been threatening him with death, after which he'd nearly gotten them both killed. He could see the singes and burns from the explosion on her cloak, even on the high-necked shirt she wore underneath it.

Which reminded him: *manners.*

"Hey—thank you," he said, feeling awkward as he looked her over. "I basically blew up your hotel room and you—I mean— Wait." His brow furrowed. "Why did you save me?"

Color heightened in her cheeks. "I didn't save you."

"You could've left me to die," Leopold pointed out. "Or get picked up by the cops. Sunder has cops, right?"

"Yeah, and you would've deserved it, too." Something shone in her eyes, a secret depth of humor. "Some creep breaks into my room, then tries to steal from me?"

"Hey, I didn't steal from you—"

"A thief *and* a liar? Impressive. I can't believe I wasted a port-cast rescuing you—"

"Isabel!" Her uncle's bushy eyebrows shot up. "You cast your way back here? How many times have we talked about this?"

Leopold clung to this scrap of information: Her name was Isabel.

Her cheeks flushed brighter. "It was an emergency."

"What about the gateway watch I made for you?"

"You said it was only designed to transport one person at a time. Plus I had to take his bag, my books—anything the police might've used to identify us—"

"Right," Norm said, relenting with a nod. "That's why you've been so exhausted." He sighed roughly. "Well, please don't ever do that again."

"I won't." She leaned over and gave her uncle a kiss on his craggy cheek. "Probably."

Looking beleaguered, Norm tugged off his oven mitts. His fingers were festooned with rings of all types, as eclectic in style as the weather-beaten furniture scattered around the room. He turned to Leopold and said, with no preamble, "Close your eyes."

"Why?"

Norm pinched some powder from a small jar and blew it into Leopold's face.

Leopold responded with something between a choking sound and a violent cough—but before he could unleash a word of profanity, the pains in his body began to subside.

"Feel a little better?" Norm asked.

Leopold blinked, then nodded gratefully, testing his joints.

"Brain salt. Packs a punch, huh? It's my own patented recipe—can practically bring the dead back to life. Which, lucky for you, wasn't necessary." He laughed, the mound of graying, curly hair atop his head quivering, then squirreled the jar into his bathrobe. He looked like a benevolent madman crossed with a past-his-prime surfer, his skin tanned and leathered from a lifetime of sun exposure. Isabel, grinning practically ear to ear, looked like an adorable elf.

Leopold couldn't help smiling back. He felt a little dopey and couldn't decide which weird thing—the brain salts, the focuser suctioned to his chest, or Isabel's disarmingly sunny disposition—was responsible for the endorphins now flooding through him. He realized he had no good reason to trust either of them; the fact that Isabel had saved his life was obviously a point in their favor, but he'd yet to make sense of their motivations. He squinted as he looked around at the cozy, cluttered living room, then tilted his head at Norm. "This is your place?"

"Surpassingly excellent deduction." Norm spread his arms expansively, and Leopold saw that under his bathrobe he wore pajama pants and a well-worn Metallica *Ride the Lightning* shirt. "You find yourself in my humble casa. The Chateau El Royale apartments, finest magical accommodations this side of Cahuenga."

"Are we in a sunderhood?"

"Yes, indeed. Hollywood. Had to get you out of Sunder Hill before our cops snapped you up. My name's Norman—call me Norm—and I believe you've met my niece, Isabel."

Leopold didn't bother telling Norm he'd already figured out their names.

"So." Norm nodded at him. "You're Larry, right?"

The warm feeling vanished.

Leopold gestured to the kitchen. "I think your eggs are burning."

Norm jumped up and bolted out of the room, shouting, "Damn, I left the burner on!" while Isabel stifled a laugh.

Then it was just the two of them. It was a little awkward for Leopold, sitting across from someone who'd so recently threatened to kill him, but Isabel seemed to be struggling even more. For some reason, she couldn't seem to look directly at him, and when she finally risked a glance, her eyes betrayed her mood. This was a fascinating discovery for Leopold, who'd never been fluent in the language of girls; but even now, as she studied the floor between them, he felt almost as if he could read her thoughts: She was dying to ask him something.

He was determined to beat her to it.

"Why didn't you kill me?" he said, the words coming out more sharply than intended.

She'd been about to speak, her lips parted. She sounded surprised when she said, "You seem disappointed."

"I'm just trying to understand," he said. "I'm not ungrateful."

"If I tell you the truth, will you promise not to be an asshole about it?"

"No."

This earned him a grin, which made him smile in turn. And now he was getting distracted again.

"Okay. The truth is, I only saved your life because"—she looked down at his shirt, and the object embedded there—"well, it turns out you're kind of important."

Leopold's hand rose to touch the focuser, fingers brushing glass and cold, inhuman metal. He'd never been described as *important* by anyone, ever. It was nearly as disconcerting as the thing on his chest.

"Important?" he said, finding his voice. "Important how?"

She canted her head at him, then shrugged. "You were able to activate the object."

Stunned, Leopold opened his mouth to reply, but before he could think of what to say, a shout came from the kitchen.

"All right, kids! Breakfast's ready!"

FIFTY-ONE

Briefly, blissfully, Leopold was lost in a domestic daydream. He'd been watching Norm wheel around the cluttered, sunny kitchen in a *Kiss the Cook* apron, the sound of popping grease and smells of cooking food filling the room with warmth. On the pink-tiled counter, a standard-issue coffeemaker percolated beside odd-looking appliances of unknown and possibly magical function. Swooping chrome letters spelled *MagiFreez* across the fridge door, which was covered with magnets, recipes, handwritten lists, and kid art, presumably vintage Isabel. Contemporary Isabel ferried steaming dishes and platters to the table. Before long, Leopold's plate was piled with scrambled eggs, generously buttered toast, and hash browns, all dusted with what Norm had called "Aether flakes," which glinted like spun sugar in a slant of windowlight. The whole scene felt like a delicate fantasy that would crumble at the slightest disturbance, so Leopold sat completely still and tried to ignore the drumbeat of *the object, the focuser, the thing on your chest.*

It turns out you're kind of important.

He risked it all for a bite of fried potato, forking one from his plate and popping it into his mouth. A quiet *wow* escaped his lips.

Despite everything that might've put a damper on his appetite—the million questions pinballing through his brain, the object, the questioning that awaited him—Leopold ate like eating was going out of style.

Rather than a kaleidoscope of changing flavors, Norm's eggs and toast and potatoes actually tasted like eggs and toast and potatoes—but perfect ones. He wondered if it was Norm's cooking or there was something about the Aether he'd dusted over everything, which, in addition to effervescing delightfully on his tongue, made Leopold feel like his bones were growing more solid with each bite. He even felt a little bit of that old familiar heat returning to the pit of his belly, like his reservoir of magical energy, shallow though it might have been, was slowly refilling.

"Glad you're digging the food, man," said Norm, chuckling into his coffee mug.

Leopold pulled his elbows off the table, attempting table manners at the eleventh hour, then pushed back his empty plate. "That was dellicious. Even better than the food at the Brite Spot."

Isabel frowned. "Uncle Norm's cooking is way better than that slop."

Speaking of which: The Brite Spot was the first place he'd seen her, and he still didn't know what she'd been doing there, watching him.

"Compliment accepted, Iz." Norm practically gleamed. "In another life I would've had one of those cooking shows. *Forkin' Around with Norm.* I actually worked up a whole pitch for it, but every studio in town passed." After a moment he muttered, "Their loss."

"You said there's Aether in it," Leopold said, noting the warmth still radiating through him.

"Just a touch. All natural, though, not the synthetic crap most restaurants serve nowadays. Gives your Aether levels a healthy, long-lasting boost, especially when they've been drained from overuse." He shot a disapproving glance at Isabel, then looked back to Leopold. "Does wonders for your hair and nails, too."

Leopold suddenly tensed, then yelped, startled by a spasm of pain across his chest. The focuser, which had been dormant for some time, had flared to life with a sudden, searing heat.

"You okay?" Isabel said, rising from her chair in alarm.

"Yeah," said Leopold, still wincing. The metal cooled as quickly as it had warmed, and gradually he relaxed. "I'm fine."

"You sure?" Isabel asked, and at his repeated assurance she sat down again.

Norm waved his fork at the two of them. "Not to worry. I checked the thing out while you were sleeping. Plus, I inspected it thoroughly long before you activated it. I'm sure it's uncomfortable, but it shouldn't be harmful to the wearer." He laughed breezily. "If it was, you'd be dead already, amiright?"

"Right," Leopold said uneasily. "I don't suppose you could tell me what it is? Or does?" He shifted in his chair. "Or how to get it off me?"

"Well." Norm took a contemplative sip of coffee. "The thing is, we don't exactly know." He took another sip. "In fact, we were hoping you could help us test out some theories."

Leopold rubbed absently at the metal ring on his chest. "What kinds of theories?"

Norm leaned back in his chair and crossed one leg over the other, a fuzzy slipper bobbling off the end of his big toe. "Well, let's start with some backstory: We discovered the object three weeks ago. It showed up at my shop late one night, left on the doorstep with no explanation. Boxed in a metal crate."

"No note, nothing," Isabel added. "Though it's not entirely weird for things to get dropped off like that, given my uncle's line of work."

"I'm in the asset revival game," Norm explained.

"You've heard of Norm's MagiPawn," Isabel said. It wasn't a question.

"Wait, you're *that* Norm?" Leopold sat up a little straighter, gaping at the apron-clad man before him. Emmet would lose his shit if he knew.

"Hear that, Iz? You're living with a celebrity!"

Isabel rolled her eyes.

"So, yeah," Norm went on, still preening. "Sometimes people give me things to sell on consignment, but even the ones who want to remain anonymous leave a note, a hoped-for price, some cryptic way to contact them . . . but here's this crate, and no nothing." He stood up suddenly and crossed to the kitchen window, then peeked outside before sliding the pane shut. "Can't be too careful," he murmured. "The walls have ears around here. Sometimes literally."

Instead of returning to his seat, he began to pace.

"As soon as I opened it, I knew it was something special. The materials, the craftsmanship." He shook his head, in awe just picturing it. "I've seen, handled, bought, sold, dismantled, and repaired just about every kind of enchanted, cursed, or charmed object you can imagine, but never anything like this. This is a diamond of the first water. From the looks of it I figured it was a focuser, but I haven't gathered enough evidence to prove or disprove the theory. All I know for sure is that it was forged from ancient, extremely rare materials. Custom-made, no doubt, by a very heavy individual. And you can bet your ass there are similarly heavy individuals who'd do just about anything to get their hands on it." His tone lowered, darkened. "That's why we moved it. Strangers were showing up, sparks I've never seen in Sunder before, sniffing around my shop with no intention of buying anything. I got the idea they were looking for the object, so we stashed it at Goldie's, where no one goes if they can help it, and booby-trapped the thing."

Leopold gaped at him. "*You* blew me up?"

"You blew yourself up," Norm corrected him.

"And most of the room," Isabel added.

"But not the object itself," said Norm, pointing at Leopold's chest. "Totally unscathed."

"Wait, what about the rest of him?" Isabel was staring curiously at Leopold.

"What *about* the rest of me?"

"Your head's still attached to your body."

"And you're upset about that?"

"Don't get me wrong. I'm glad you weren't decapitated." She turned her attention to Norm. "But shouldn't he have been more . . . dead?"

"The blast wasn't supposed to be lethal," Norm said. "You can't interrogate a dead thief."

"But it blew up in his hands, and he still has all his fingers." She glanced at Leopold's hands, as if to verify. "Is it possible the object's some kind of shield?"

"Seems unlikely, but I can't rule it out." Norm scratched his chin. "I'm still betting it's exactly what it appears to be—a focuser. One we couldn't get to work." He looked at Leopold. "But you did."

Leopold peered down at his chest, at the torn cotton and dried blood of his shirt. "I don't think this is the definition of *working*."

"Yeah, but you got it to do something," Norm insisted. "I analyzed it with every magical device known to sparks—and a few that aren't. Couldn't find a seam, sigil, rivet, button, or fingerprint. Or get so much as a shiver out of it, no matter what I did."

"But when *he* touched the thing," Isabel said, "it just flew out at him, like magic."

"Probably was magic," Leopold pointed out.

Norm whistled. "Wish I could've seen it."

"And I wish you'd told me there was a secret passageway under the floor," Isabel countered, wandering over to the kitchen counter.

Norm, who'd been clearing the plates, looked slowly from Isabel to Leopold, eyebrows raised. "There was a secret passageway under the floor?"

"Uh." Leopold cleared his throat. "Yeah."

Norm returned from the sink, shrugging off his *Kiss the Cook* apron as he dropped into the chair across from him. "So," he said. "Larry."

"He prefers *Leopold*," Isabel said over her shoulder.

Leopold considered proposing to her right then.

"Leopold. Cool. I dig it." Norm was nodding at him. Despite his constant motion, Norm had hardly taken his eyes off Leopold since he'd regained consciousness. Now Norm leaned in, staring, intent as an X-ray. "You're new here. You barely know your way around Sunder Hill, right?"

Leopold narrowed his eyes. "Right."

"But you knew there was a secret passageway under the floor of Goldie's."

Isabel, who'd been clanking around inside the open fridge, stopped to listen.

Leopold only nodded.

"So." Norm leaned in further, voice dropping. "Who told you where to find it?"

There it was. The beginning of an interrogation.

Leopold regarded Norm and Isabel carefully. Had these people saved him, healed him—made him an enormous breakfast—only to pry information from him? And what would they do once they had it?

"No one told me," he said after a beat.

Norm sat back in his chair, folding his hands atop the rolling hill of his stomach. Gone was the jovial, carefree surfer; now his eyes gleamed sharply. "I find that kind of hard to believe, little dude."

Isabel kicked the fridge shut with a bang. "The object had only been in that room a few days. There were obfuscation spells all over it—"

"If we're launching an investigation," Leopold said, cutting her off, "maybe first we should talk about why you've been following me."

Norm's brow wrinkled. He turned to look at Isabel. "You were following him?"

"I wasn't!"

"You *were*," Leopold insisted. "First, at the Brite Spot—"

"Is it a crime to eat dinner?"

"Then, at my test—"

"That was purely for entertainment."

"And then you show up in the exact room I need to search—"

She huffed, exasperated. "You barged into *my* room and blew up *my* things in order to steal *my* object—"

"I can't steal something that already belongs to me!" Leopold exploded, the sudden boom of his voice bringing the conversation to a halt.

Isabel stared at him, slightly stunned, but Norm looked delighted.

"Belongs to you, huh?" said Norm. He glanced at Isabel. "That explains a lot."

"He could be lying," she muttered, now glaring determinedly at the wall.

Norm considered that. "My wild guess is he isn't. Also—" He frowned suddenly, confused. "Wait, you were banished, which means you must've gotten your memory revised. So why do you remember being tested, and meeting Isabel, and—"

"It didn't work, obviously," Leopold said. "They screwed up."

"Figures." Norm sighed. "Trust our elected officials to do something simple—"

"Whatever." Leopold shoved away from the table and rose to his feet. "Thanks for breakfast. I think it's time for me to go."

No one tried to stop him as he walked away, picking through the disarray of Norm's apartment in search of his duffel bag. "Hey, where the hell is my—"

"Map?"

Leopold froze, then spun around. His stomach sank. Norm was holding up his mother's Thomas Guide, the expression on his face just triumphant enough to piss Leopold off.

He stalked back into the kitchen. "You went through my things."

Norm looked almost offended. "Of course I went through your things."

"What gives you the right—"

"You nearly blew up my niece!"

"You stole my shit!"

"You stole *my* shit—"

"Choose a new word, guys, this is gross—"

Leopold tried to swipe the Guide from Norm, who jerked it out of reach. Leopold briefly considered decking the guy.

Norm made a show of flipping through the Guide, then made an appreciative sound. "This is some high-grade shit, little dude—"

"What did I say about—"

"Stuff," Norm corrected. "This is next-level enchantment for a kid who massively, catastrophically failed his channeler test." He looked up at Leopold. "I have, like, a billion questions for you, Lunchtray Larry."

"Fuck," Leopold whispered, dropping his head into his hands.

"1987 edition, right?"

"Congratulations, you can read. It's right there on the cover."

Norm smiled. "You know what's not on the cover? The brand of the enchanter."

Now Leopold looked up, frowning. "What? Who cares?"

"I care, little dude. I care a lot. Rare, enchanted objects are my stock in trade. Don't dis the biz."

Norm had risen to cross the room and was rifling through one of the cabinets. When he turned back to face them, his right eye had grown to three times its size, and Leopold recoiled.

"What the hell is that?"

"What? This?" Norm gestured to his eye as he strode back to the table. When he sat down, it became obvious that he'd strapped some sort of device to his head. It looked like a cross between a monocle and a fishbowl—which, upon closer inspection, was filled with water and swam with tiny orange guppies.

The guppies turned to stare at Leopold in concert.

"I call this an optical expositator," Norm explained. "It allows me to see beneath the surface layers of magical objects. Shows me something about how they were made, and sometimes, by whom. It didn't reveal anything about the object on your chest, but it showed me a hell of a lot about this Guide."

Despite his better judgment, Leopold sank back into his seat at the table.

If Norm had information about the Guide—and perhaps, by extension, his mom—Leopold was willing to listen. And *then* he'd deck the guy and get the hell out of there.

Norm turned the Guide over in his hands. "This particular work of magical cartography was enchanted with a 1930s-era Barnack Leica Aether focuser. There are maybe three such focusers in existence, most in the hands of collectors. Someone with access to serious gear made this. Someone connected. Someone talented."

"I've never heard of an enchantable street atlas," said Isabel, crowding behind Norm to look over his shoulder.

"Because they're almost as rare as 1930s-era Barnack Leicas," said Norm. "There's only one edition that's enchantable, and that's the '87. A map like this can lead you to a targeted object no matter where it is. Even if it moves from place to place, the directions will adjust accordingly."

"And find hidden passages in the floor?" said Isabel.

"Yep. And if we'd kept the object in the shop"—he looked up at Leopold—"your Guide might've found a way to break in there, too."

Norm opened the Guide and held it up to his eyepiece, hemming and hawing with little sounds of interest. The fish pointed this way and that, synchronizing with the movements of Norm's eye as he scanned page after page.

"Aha, here you are!" he said after a minute, and then he turned the Guide to show Leopold what he was looking at.

It was a diagram of Norm's apartment.

A blue star pulsed at the center of the kitchen. There was no path anymore, and as of now, no further instructions. Norm whistled through his teeth. "This really is primo spell-work, my friend. I'd say it's about five, six years old, judging from the rate of Aether decay."

Five or six years.

Right around when his mom had died.

"Now." Norm turned his enormous eye and its staring fish toward Leopold, then tucked the Guide under his arm. "I'm gonna need you to tell me where you came across this little beauty."

Leopold worked his jaw as he studied the curly haired eccentric.

Norm's brown bathrobe had little pink flamingoes all over it. His goatee was flecked with bits of egg. Only now did Leopold notice that Norm's pajama bottoms were decorated with marijuana leaves. His eyes, however, were clear and determined.

"Norm," Leopold said calmly. "Are you threatening me?"

"Yeah, little dude." Norm was smiling now. "I am."

"Why?"

"Because I don't trust you."

"Neither do I," Isabel piped in.

Leopold leaned forward. "I don't trust either one of you."

"Good. We're all in agreement," said Isabel, biting into a triangle of toast. "I love it when we're all in agreement. Makes it easier."

"Makes what easier—"

Leopold gasped as the object on his chest heated once more without warning. He tensed, gritting his teeth through the pain.

Despite their show of toughness, both Norm and Isabel leapt out of their chairs.

"You okay?" Isabel said, her fingers alighting on Leopold's arm. He was grateful for the point of contact, grateful for an excuse to focus all his attention there, where she touched him.

"I'm fine," he said, the heat fading, pain subsiding. His hand fell away from his chest. "Just got lightheaded for a second."

"You're sure this thing isn't going to hurt him?" Isabel asked.

"I'm sure." Norm focused his fishbowl eyepiece on Leopold again. "It's got zero death magic."

"It wouldn't have death magic," said Leopold, closing his eyes on an exhale. "She wouldn't have done that to me."

"Who?"

Leopold looked up, surprised by his own foolishness. "No one," he said.

Isabel crossed her arms, frowning at Norm. "Okay, maybe we should switch to good cop. Bad cop is getting us nowhere."

"Bad cop got us a *she*," countered Norm, looking affronted. "Bad cop got him to admit the Guide belonged to him! I'm about to crack this kid—"

"No, you aren't," said Isabel and Leopold at the same time.

"Fine." Norm sighed. "You're up, Iz."

But before she could ask him anything, the interrogation was interrupted by a familiar, insistent buzzing noise.

Leopold straightened, then turned to face the living room. In the silence it became clear that the sound was emanating from his duffel bag, which he could see now atop the cluttered coffee table.

It was his phone.

"Hold that thought," said Leopold, rising from his chair.

"Bad cop wouldn't have let him leave the table to take a phone call," Norm grumbled.

FIFTY-TWO

Leopold plucked the phone from his bag, meaning only to turn it off, but the screen was lit with dozens of all-caps texts and alerts for missed calls, an enormous backlog that had for some reason only just started coming through.

Most were from Richter. That his dad had tried to reach him was not surprising; Leopold had run away from home and stayed out all night. What shocked him was the sheer volume of texts and voice-mails, along with missed calls from both Emmet and, strangely, Emmet's mom.

"You're not planning on skipping out on us, are you?" Norm called from the kitchen. "You try to leave, bad cop will have to chase you down."

Leopold almost smiled, then returned his attention to the phone. An argument of car horns drifted through the apartment's thin glass windows. He ignored Richter's voicemails—he didn't feel like being screamed at just then—and scrolled to the beginning of his dad's texts instead. They started out angry, predictably enough, their time stamps beginning a few minutes after Leopold had flung Richter out of his room and ridden away on his bike.

10:57AM: I had every right to do what I did. Come
downstairs and face me.

11:10AM: You left???? Get your ass back here NOW

11:11AM: You're grounded for the rest of the summer

11:21AM: Make that the rest of your life if you don't
answer me

11:29AM: Running away from your problems won't
solve them.

11:31AM: I knew you were an entitled little shit. I didn't
realize I'd raised a coward.

Leopold rolled his eyes. He almost swiped away from Richter's text thread, but the tone of the next message—and the few after that, sent hours later—kept him reading.

2:46PM: Answer me, Larry. Pick up your phone.

3:10PM: WHERE THE HELL ARE YOU

3:45PM: Son, this isn't funny.

Son.

The messages cycled between rage and fear, threats—then, finally, surprisingly, something like vulnerability.

At 5:45, a flurry of missed calls and increasingly desperate texts.

5:45PM: ARE YOU CRAZY?? You could have been
KILLED

Someone had called him. Tiny? The police?

5:48PM: I'm at the tow yard! Where are you????

Leopold was amazed: His father, normally the world's most emotionally lazy man, had actually left the house to go looking for him.

> 5:55PM: I talked to the tow company, you're in deep
> shit with ME but they've agreed not to report this
> to the police
> 6:00PM: This is your dad. Larry, please answer, need to
> know your status

Your status. Rigid, toxically proud Richter-speak for *are you okay?*

He'd been operating under the assumption that his dad wouldn't really care that he was gone. That some part of Richter was glad to be rid of him.

Shockingly, he'd been wrong.

Then again, maybe his father's concern stemmed partly from the fact that Leopold was under eighteen and legally still his responsibility. Either way, he'd gone to the trouble of tracking him to the tow yard, asking after him, even paying off Tiny, who had surely demanded some exorbitant bribe to let the matter drop. He tried to picture self-important Richter throwing his weight around in that scruffy office with socket-wrench-wielding Tiny and Friends, but he couldn't summon the image; it was un-picturable.

> 7:44PM: You can't just disappear like this. You're
> scaring me.

Then, at 8:30 p.m.: The police found your car in some parking lot in the hills. I don't know if you even have your phone with you anymore but call me. Wherever you are, I'll come get you. Please.

That simple, plaintive word made Leopold's stomach knot. *Please.*

There was one final text, at 10:55 p.m.

It's been twelve hours

Free-floating, desperate, emotionally inscrutable. Was he angry or terrified? Or both?

And that was it. End of thread.

Leopold's first reaction was resentment. He tried to remember the last time his dad had said a caring word to him, anything that carried even the subtlest whiff of *I give a shit*. But now that Leopold was maybe hurt, maybe in danger . . . now he could bring himself to thumb-type the word *please*?

Way too little. And way too late.

He let the phone, and the hand holding it, fall to his side. Somehow he'd arrived at the window, and through the sheer curtain he could see a Spanish-style courtyard jungly with potted palms, a small, kidney-shaped pool at the center. A dark shape swam lazy circles beneath the surface, in no apparent hurry to come up for air.

He decided to believe Richter cared, or evinced caring, only because Leopold's disappearance could make trouble for him in the form of police inquiries and hospital stays and, if worse came to worst, funeral plans—and he was an important man with a reputation to manage.

Leopold could untangle the rest later.

A siren wailed outside. Leopold tensed as it sped by, then had a realization that sent his heart racing. He was a wanted man in both Sunder *and* slack LA.

To be safe, he knew he should turn his phone off altogether, but he wanted to look through the notifications from Emmet and Emmet's mom first. They'd come through earlier that morning, not the previous night, which meant Richter had probably recruited them in his quest to find Leopold. He considered calling Emmet's mom just so she wouldn't worry, but he'd seen enough police procedural shows to know he couldn't reach out without running the risk of giving away his location. If the police were looking for him, they might be able to trace his call. And what would he do if cops suddenly descended on the El Royale apartments? Where would he go then?

"Hey, is everything okay?"

Isabel had ventured out of the kitchen. She stood beside a boxy TV propped on a cocktail cart, frowning at him.

Leopold shifted to look at her, struck again by her beauty. She was outlined in sun, dust motes suspended in a slash of golden light that cut across her green eyes, which were wide with something like concern—but he didn't trust it.

"Everything's fine," he said, turning away.

He felt her approach, the weight of her presence tangible as she drew near. Norm was puttering in the kitchen, pretending not to listen. The two of them stood side by side, staring silently out the window. A murder of crows circled a nearby telephone pole.

"You're in trouble, aren't you?" she said quietly.

He shook his head, feeling suddenly restless. He glanced at the phone still clutched in his hand. "I thought slack tech didn't work in Sunder."

"Phones never work in Sunder Hill," she explained. "They occasionally work in other sunderhoods because their veils and boundaries are more porous."

"Right." He took a breath. "Well. I need to go."

"Where?"

Leopold closed his eyes. He wanted to laugh.

Nowhere.

He didn't even have Bessie anymore. He tried to imagine calling his dad, then crawling back home, back into the revolting skin of Larry Berry and the suffocating limits of that world. The iron fist of Richter that had reined him in. The fantasies that had always ruled him. He couldn't return to that. He wouldn't.

An escape from Norm's apartment would achieve nothing. Running from this wouldn't save or spare him, wouldn't remove this thing from his chest. Wouldn't reveal a path forward.

Clearly, his mom wasn't finished with him yet.

For a moment there was a lull in the clamor outside, horns and the screech of a garbage truck fading to a hush, as if some cosmic sound mixer had dipped the city's master volume to zero; as if Los Angeles itself was holding its breath.

"Leopold," Isabel tried again. "Do you think—"

Leopold, who'd been fidgeting with his phone in his hands, suddenly dropped it. Isabel moved quickly to catch it, and in the process one of her sleeves slid partway up her forearm, revealing a tracery of knotted pink lines. The scars twisted around her slender wrist until they disappeared beneath the fabric of her cloak.

She straightened slowly, the alarm in her eyes belying her outward calm. She handed him his phone without a word, then tugged down her sleeve.

"What happened?" he asked, nodding at her arm as he pocketed the phone.

"What's going on with you?" she deflected.

Leopold exhaled, returning his eyes to the window. He had no one to count on. No one to trust. Nothing, really, to lose. "My dad thinks I might be lying in a ditch somewhere," he said softly. "And now he's got the police looking for me."

She was quiet a moment. "I'm guessing that means he doesn't know about Sunder."

Leopold shook his head.

"What about your mom?" Isabel asked. "Does she know?"

"My mom is dead."

He said it like he always did, bluntly, as if the words meant nothing, cost him nothing to say aloud, required nothing of the hearer. He waited for Isabel to look away, the way most people did. Most people were intimidated by death, freaked out by the intensity of mom-loss and semi-orphanhood. But Isabel didn't flinch.

"When?" she asked.

He turned and met her eyes. She didn't look afraid or devastated. In fact, she was smiling a little.

"When I was twelve."

"Hey, mine too," she said, her smile growing.

Against his every instinct, Leopold found himself unclenching. "What do you mean?"

"Both my parents died when I was twelve."

"Both of them. Damn." Leopold shook his head. "At the same time?"

Now she looked away, nodding at the window. "In a fire. Lab accident."

"That's why you live with Norm."

Again, she nodded. Leopold was still, studying her as she watched the distant hills.

"I'm sorry," he said finally. The death of one parent had nearly broken him forever, and despite having a father who was essentially a stranger, he couldn't imagine losing both. "That's a shitty way to lose your parents."

She laughed a little when she said, "It really is. Efficient, though."

Their eyes met fleetingly then, long enough for some fragile, unsayable thing to pass between them. A bright spark of shared understanding, of agonies so large they refused expression, of pain untranslatable to language.

Then a truck blasted its horn outside, and Los Angeles resumed.

The phone in Leopold's pocket buzzed, and Isabel's smile returned. "So popular this morning."

The incoming call was from Emmet's mom, and it was her third of the day. Leopold's finger hovered over the button. He wasn't sure whether to answer. He *wanted* to answer. If Dr. Laura Worthington was calling him this much, something was definitely wrong—but he worried, again, that the police might trace his location.

The ringing stopped; now came the double buzz of a voicemail.

Leopold felt Isabel's eyes on him as he stepped away to listen. Hearing Emmet's mom speak always made Leopold feel like he was a kid having a sleepover in Emmet's basement. Dr. W would pop down around midnight, instruct them sternly to go to sleep, and leave a tray of snacks behind. Her voice had that same firm go-to-bed timbre now, but she sounded frayed and anxious, too.

"Hi, Larry, it's Dr. Worthington again. I need you to call me back right away. Something's wrong with Emmet. He hasn't been himself since yesterday—the morning after you two were out so late. He's been really spacey, and he's saying things that don't make sense. I just need to know what you did, where you went. Is it possible Emmet hit his head somehow? Did you . . . take something? I'm beyond anger at this point, Larry. I just need to know how to help him. Call me. We're worried. Thanks."

Leopold was reeling.

Something's wrong with Emmet.

It wasn't like Emmet's parents to call him like this. They trusted their son and almost never freaked out, so whatever was going on had to be serious. But Leopold had talked to Emmet on the phone only yesterday, and he'd sounded like himself—a little out of it, maybe, but that was to be expected from someone who'd just had his memory revised.

He played Emmet's last voicemail, time-stamped sixty-seven minutes ago.

"Mister Berry, it's Mister Worthington. Again. Are we shooting today, or what? You're not answering, so I'm gonna assume you're on your way to the location." *Shooting today.* A sick feeling gripped Leopold. "You'd better be, because I spent half the night packing fake blood into these new squibs I got. They're real ones from an actual movie set and completely illegal to use without a permit, which means they're gonna be frigging awesome. It was supposed to be a surprise, but whatever. I can't find the extra paladin costumes anywhere, though, so I hope, uh . . ." He mumbled something unintelligible, and there was a dull crash in the background like he'd knocked something over. "What the hell, who rearranged my room? Where are my nunchucks? Anyway, I hope you called Tom and Erica, because I don't have their numbers on my phone for some reason, and I don't want to recruit any more randos to be extras. And remember, we're shooting at Hollywood Forever this time, not Pan Pacific Park. I'm leaving in five. See you soon—"

After another dull crash and a muttered curse, the voicemail ended.

Leopold listened to the message one more time to make sure he'd heard it correctly, then played Emmet's other two messages. The first was about collaborating on homework for a class they'd had together—freshman year of high school. The second was somehow even more worrying, and consisted mostly of Emmet laughing strangely, trying and failing to remember why he'd called, then finally whispering, *"Larry, what's happening,"* before hanging up.

Leopold stood gripping the silent phone, horrified.

Emmet thought they were still in Mr. Bostich's Intro to Chemistry class. He thought they were still making *Sunderworld* videos.

Holy shit. Emmet thought they were *fourteen*.

Leopold jammed his phone into his pocket and turned to find his boots.

FIFTY-THREE

"What's wrong?" Isabel's fear was palpable, her rigid frame an exclamation point as she followed Leopold toward the couch. "Something's wrong. Uncle Norm," she called out. "Something's wrong with Leopold!"

Norm came shuffling over in his bathrobe, half a chocolate-chip cookie melting in one hand. "What's going on? Hey, now," he growled, "what did I say about skipping out on us—"

Leopold was hopping around, his foot stuffed into one boot while he scoured the floor for its mate. "I have to go. Emmet needs me. They messed up his brain."

"Who's Emmet?" Norm asked.

"Is that the guy who was with you at the Brite Spot?"

Leopold nodded. "Where the hell is my other boot?"

"Here, it's wedged under—"

He and Isabel both bent to retrieve it and clonked their shoulders together. Leopold attempted to put the boot on while standing, lost his balance, and did a controlled fall onto the couch.

"Wait a second. Slow down." She dropped onto the cushion beside him. "What do you mean they messed up his brain?"

Leopold laced as he spoke. "Emmet's memory is all screwed up. His parents are flipping out." He spared her a brief, worried glance.

"He thinks we're fourteen and still making *Sunderworld* videos. He's headed to the Hollywood Forever Cemetery right now to meet me for a shoot."

"*Sunderworld* videos?" Norm brightened. "You know about *Sunderworld*? I haven't heard anyone mention *Sunderworld* in years—"

"Uncle Norm," said Isabel, frowning.

"Right," he said, popping the rest of the cookie into his mouth. He spoke while he chewed: "Bad time."

Leopold finished lacing his boots, stood up, and looked Norm in the eye. He'd ask *Sunderworld* follow-up questions later. "If I bring Emmet back here, can you fix him?"

"Whoa, I don't know about that, little dude." Norm took a step back. "Depends on the memory enchantment they used, the revisionist . . . Rewiring the brain is serious magic. Plus, you need a license for that kind of work. If I go digging around in his head, I might mess things up even more—" .

"What about Jamal?" Isabel suggested.

"The hypnotist?" Norm wiped a chocolatey hand on his robe, considering. "It's a good thought, Iz. A real good thought. I'd say it's a definite maybe."

Leopold crossed to the window in a few long strides. "I'll take a maybe," he said, his mind reeling. Emmet was out there somewhere, thinking he was fourteen.

And it was all Leopold's fault.

He twitched the curtain, checking for cops. The courtyard was empty. He glanced back at Norm and Isabel. "I'll try to be back in a couple of hours."

"No way." Norm was shaking his head, his salt-and-pepper curls bouncing. "We can't just let you go running around, Lunchtray. If it weren't for the seven protective enchantments I put on this place,

Sunder PD would've come to arrest you an hour ago. You'd be getting *Clockwork Orange*d at Department HQ right now, your head in a vise while some flunky puts veritas drops in your eyes. You think they messed up your friend? Just wait till they get ahold of you"—he nodded at Leopold's chest—"now that you've got something that interests them."

Leopold stilled. "Something that interests them? You mean this object might have something to do with the Sunder government?"

"Were you not listening when I said *heavy individuals*?" said Norm, flinging out an arm that almost knocked an old camera off a shelf. "Who did you think I meant? There are only three kinds of people who could source enough Aether to create something that powerful." He counted on his ringed fingers. "Shady, shady, and *a channeler*."

A flicker of emotion went through Leopold at the word *channeler*. He snuffed it out.

Isabel stood up from the couch, her studied cool eroding, and positioned herself between Leopold and the door. "We're in this together now," she said, watching him. "Don't do anything stupid. Please."

"Together?" Leopold echoed. "I don't even know you two."

Norm crossed his arms. "The object may have attached itself to you, my dude, but it appeared on our doorstep. Mine and Isabel's. We're just as much a part of this as you are."

"Oh yeah? What happened to good cop, bad cop?"

"We'll finish the interrogation later," Isabel said. "I promise I'll be really annoying."

"And I'll order pizza," said Norm, who was, somehow, biting into another cookie. "I've got a coupon for deep dish."

"You know I hate deep dish," said Isabel, making a face. "I want to try that new place, the one on Ivar—"

"Guys?"

Norm and Isabel turned to look at him.

"I'm leaving."

Again, Isabel blocked the door. "If you leave, you might not make it back. There are two different police departments out there looking for you now, and thanks to the explosion you set off at Goldie's, you're a higher priority for the Sunder PD than when you were just, you know, a guy whose worst day ever was caught on camera." She inched closer. The power of her full attention was hypnotic. She tapped the metal ring on his chest, and he could've sworn he felt that small touch reverberate through his rib cage. "Mysterious, powerful devices of unknown origin don't just show up on doorsteps and bind themselves to barely magical people—"

"The Executive called me 'remarkably unremarkable,'" Leopold said dryly. "'Average absolutely to the decimal point. Unspecial by every magical metric.' If we're going to insult my abilities, let's quote an expert."

Isabel laughed. Leopold cracked a smile.

"I'm serious," she said finally, softly. "This could mean something."

"Listen, I want to figure out what's going on as much as you do," he replied, eyes returning to the door. "But first I have to help my friend. Emmet's a danger to himself, and I can't trust that he'll make it all the way here on his own, even if I give him turn-by-turn directions."

"Fine," said Isabel with a sigh. "If you're dead set on this, I won't stop you. But I'm coming, too."

"Isabel!" Norm cried. "No way you're going anywhere after what happened to you last night— You still need to rest—"

"And I don't need a babysitter," Leopold added.

"No," said Norm, turning on him. "She's right, you can't go alone.

You need someone who knows their ass from a portable hole in the ground. *I'm* coming with you."

"You can't," said Isabel. "You've got that *thing*, today, remember?"

Norm wavered, then raked a hand through his curls. "Shit."

"What thing?" asked Leopold.

"I've got to meet with my old parole officer," Norm muttered. "In fucking Redondo Beach. I *hate* Redondo Beach."

Leopold's eyes widened, but Norm waved it off. "I did a stint in Salton State a few years back for possession of 'unauthorized magical devices.'" He added air quotes and a scowl. "Bureaucratic overreach at its finest. Long story short, I owe my parole officer a huge favor, and he happened to pick today to call it in."

"Don't worry," Isabel said, "my uncle's not a criminal."

"Not unless absolutely necessary," Norm added with a wink.

"Right."

"So." Isabel fixed her eyes on Leopold. "We've got a deal?"

"No."

Isabel frowned. "You won't last ten minutes without me."

"Listen," Leopold said, his impatience rising. "I might be Lunchtray Larry, but I killed a Noxum with that tray, okay? I'm going to be fine."

Norm's rich laughter filled the room. He clapped Leopold on the shoulder and gave him a little shake. "I think I like this guy."

"Yeah," said Isabel, still smiling. "I think I do, too."

FIFTY-FOUR

In the end, Isabel got her way.

She and Norm had conferenced in the kitchen, exchanging heated whispers before she'd emerged looking pleased with herself, after which a sullen Norm had barked at Leopold to follow him into his bedroom.

"You gotta change your clothes, Lunchtray. Both sets of cops will have a description of . . ." He'd taken in Leopold's burned and bloodied outfit. "That."

Alone now, Leopold studied himself in the mirror of Norm's surprisingly neat bedroom, frowning at his bare chest. He often frowned at himself in mirrors, but this time the focus of his displeasure wasn't his unruly hair or moderately developed pectorals but the thing centered between them, encircled by shreds of the bloodied shirt he'd been forced to scissor away.

Interestingly, he no longer felt a barely containable urge to tear the thing off his body.

"How're things fitting?" Norm called from behind the door.

"Uh, fine," Leopold called back. "Be right out!"

He turned to the clothes Norm had left on his paisley-sheeted waterbed. A pair of baggy, beige drawstring pants. A washed-out shirt that read *Lollapalooza '94*. A burnt-orange, fraying-at-the-elbows track jacket. Though Leopold appreciated the gesture from a veritable stranger, he pushed aside Norm's pile of weed-scented garments in favor of a few wrinkled basics from his duffel bag. Already he'd spent several minutes cleaning himself up in the bathroom—grateful he'd remembered to pack a razor and some deodorant—but he would've killed for a hot shower, had there been time.

He pulled on a gray Henley and a pair of black jeans, then finger-combed his reddish-brown hair. The one thing he'd lost in the madness of yesterday was his crappy Dodgers cap, and with a sigh of resignation he searched through Norm's offerings for a suitable replacement.

The only real option was a beanie.

It was pink, with a smiling cartoon cat embroidered on it. The cat, naturally, was giving everyone the middle finger.

Norm and Isabel were in consultation in the living room when Leopold emerged. They were sorting through a range of what looked like home-brewed magical devices on a console table. Norm muttered as he pointed to a pair of tea-brown dice, and Isabel said something affirmative in reply as she skimmed them off the table and dropped them into a pocket of her cloak.

"I'm ready," Leopold said.

Looking up, they broke into wide smiles.

"You wore the beanie!" Norm laughed, flashing a double-barreled thumbs-up. "I've got the matching slippers, too, man, if you want to borrow them."

"I'm good, thanks."

"I never pictured you as a stoner," said Isabel. "You look like you might try to sell us a dimebag outside a bowling alley."

"I was going for 'someone who wasn't blown up recently,'" Leopold said, high-stepping an overflowing laundry basket on his way across the room.

Isabel, on the other hand, hadn't changed much.

"Do you wear that every day?" Leopold said, meaning the cloak.

"Only when there's a chance I might need to defend myself," she said, shrugging. "Which is most days."

She selected a slim, serrated knife from the tabletop and slid it into a sheath on her belt. Holstered beside it were what appeared to be a looped rope, an old TV remote, and a small can of spray paint, among other, less-identifiable objects.

"A ready-for-almost-anything kit. My own design." Norm waved a hand at the items like a game show host. "Noxum repellant, a chant scrambler for low-level curse deflection, and a befogger for quick escapes—plus a few other goodies." He winked at Isabel. "Just in case."

Just in case.

Leopold couldn't help but think of his mother. Absently, he lifted a hand to the focuser, the outline of which he could feel through his shirt.

He wouldn't let her down.

Leopold had started to follow Isabel to the door when Norm caught his elbow, pulling him aside.

"Need to bend your ear about something," he said, his expression suddenly grave. "It's about Izzie."

"Oh," said Leopold, looking ruefully at the door. "But Emmet—"

"My niece is strong, confident, and smart as hell—it's easy to get fooled into thinking she's as bulletproof as she pretends to be. But she isn't," said Norm, low and serious. "In fact, she's not well."

Leopold hesitated, remembering the web of scars he'd seen trailing up her forearm. "She's sick?"

"Not exactly." Norm glanced at the entryway, where Isabel knelt partly out of view, lacing up her boots. "She has this sort of . . .

situation. She wouldn't want me getting into all this with you, but it's important that you know: Casting can be very dangerous for her."

"But she carries around that focuser. She cast us halfway across the city with a port spell last night."

"She got lucky. She could've been seriously hurt." Norm shook his head. "Look, I forced her to give up her focuser today, but even a cheap pre-cast could cause an injury. That's why I make devices for her and load them with high-potency Aether. It's of a purity you can't find anymore, powerful enough to allow Isabel to use a bit of magic to protect herself—but without really casting."

Unsure how to respond, Leopold just nodded.

Norm leaned in, his voice dropping to a whisper. "The true bastard of it is, she's really goddamn good. Naturally she gets frustrated, tries to outsmart her condition. It never works. She's put herself in the hospital more times than I care to remember."

"The hospital?" Leopold echoed.

Norm's eyes narrowed on him. *"Do not let her cast."*

"Okay, yeah, sure," Leopold said, frowning. "I won't. I promise."

Norm's face relaxed just as Isabel stood up and turned to face them. "Everyone remember to use the bathroom?" he said cheerily.

FIFTY-FIVE

"Holy *hell*, this place is gorgeous," Leopold said under his breath, craning his neck as he and Isabel walked through the grand lobby. The El Royale was an old Hollywood beauty—past its prime, perhaps, but a beauty nonetheless, with a dozen heavy iron chandeliers suspended from its soaring, wood-beamed ceiling, hand-painted Spanish tile in abundance, and an ornate, splashing fountain in the center of the floor. Sparks of all types buzzed around, picking up packages at the doorman's desk and chatting by a wall of mailboxes that stretched high out of reach. Puzzles of prismatic light fell across the floor through stained-glass windows, each depicting some scene from Sunder history. Had Emmet been there, he would've forced them to stop so he could analyze every detail, cross-referencing them against his voluminous knowledge of LA's history. Of course, if Emmet had been there, they wouldn't have been in such a hurry.

Leopold quickened his pace, the dread in his gut growing heavier with each step.

"The beauty's a trick," Isabel whispered as they rounded the fountain. "The El Royale was built on top of an old Noxum containment pit, way down in one of the sub-basements. The building was meant to be a sort of cap. If it wasn't so fancy, nobody would've wanted to live here." She hesitated, glancing at him; Leopold's mind was elsewhere. "You've still got those sunglasses from yesterday, right?"

Leopold put them on and pulled his beanie low.

They exited through wrought-iron doors. Leopold felt a light pressure tug at his limbs, as if he'd walked into a giant spiderweb. He pushed forward, was released with a barely audible *pop*, then stumbled outside feeling lightheaded, like he'd experienced a sudden and dramatic change in altitude.

"That's the veil," Isabel explained. "It's an enchantment we use to protect the building from overly curious slacks. Their eyes slide right past it."

"*Cool*," he enthused, looking back at the invisible barrier.

The exit led not onto busy Cahuenga Boulevard but into a narrow alley, all the better to hide the comings and goings of the building's Sunderese tenants. Buntings of colorful laundry swayed overhead, drying on lines stretched between the El Royale's beautiful façade and that of its unremarkable—and almost certainly unmagical— neighbor. In this part of town, spark and slack seemed to be shuffled together, cheek by jowl.

Leopold's phone buzzed. It was a text from Emmet.

Where u at? Pretty chill here just dead ppl around
haha 🪦🧟😄

Emmet, unnaturally punctual for a teenager, was already at Hollywood Forever, a touristy cemetery packed with dead celebrities. Leopold's chest tightened at the thought of his addled friend spending the next twenty or thirty minutes there by himself. Emmet was so chatty, he'd probably end up making friends with the grave-tender and whatever funeral mourners happened by; who knew what trouble he might get into.

"Emmet's already at the cemetery," Leopold said. "We need to hurry."

He composed a quick reply as they sped to the end of the alley.

Be there soon! Meet by Johnny Ramone. Don't talk to anybody.

Emmet replied right away with **ok why** and Leopold typed **just don't** and Emmet sent an animated GIF of a dancing bear that made no contextual sense and only deepened Leopold's worry.

The sky sprawled open at Cahuenga, smog like a bathtub ring smearing the horizon. Tar-stained palms lined both sides of the wide avenue, a parade of shabby cheerleaders shaking their pom-poms for five lanes of indifferent traffic.

Isabel pointed south. "We'll take Cahuenga to Santa Monica to Hollywood Forever. Sunder public transport doesn't reach the cemetery, so walking will be fastest. We just need to make a pit stop first. It'll only take a minute."

"What? *No*—"

"Yes."

"Why?"

"Because I need to get something. Something that's saved me more times than I can count." She looked at him with a gleam in her eye. "*Snacks.*"

"I'm not hungry," he said flatly.

Isabel grabbed his hand and pulled him off the sidewalk. "These aren't regular snacks," she said. "Just trust me."

He supposed he did trust her to some extent, because he allowed her to drag him across the street at a dead sprint, Isabel's cloak flying out behind her as they dodged knots of cars and a speeding city bus. Even after they'd made it to the other side she hardly slowed, guiding him around a tangle of tipped shopping carts and into the parking lot of a grungy strip mall.

It looked like every other grungy strip mall in town, save one detail: the sagging inflatable wizard on its roof.

A memory sparked, sudden and vivid, of a man pulling a tooth from his own mouth, then using it to feed a parking meter that opened a glowing cavity in the pavement. Leopold had seen it happen not three weeks ago, right here, through the window of his idling Volvo.

An eerie feeling crept over him, like he was treading in his own ghostly footsteps.

He and Isabel went into a convenience store called Jae's Cash & Dash, squashed between a strip mall psychic and a tire shop. As an automatic door hissed open to admit them, Leopold felt a minor tug, like a half-strength version of what he'd felt leaving the El Royale.

This place, too, was veiled.

The Cash & Dash was deserted except for a hipsterish Asian guy manning the register. The items on offer appeared to be standard— beer, wiper fluid, air fresheners—until Leopold spotted the sign above aisle seven, which read OCCULT, MISCELLANEOUS. Beneath those words in faint palimpsest, Leopold could make out the sign as it must have appeared to slacks: PET FOOD, EXPIRED.

Compared to the rest of the store, aisle seven was in a sad state, its shelves picked over like a miniature 99 Spells that was about to go out of business: a disorganized rack of pre-casts in plastic packages, dusty tabloids shuffled with what looked like spell books, a few focuser accessories but no actual focusers. Wasting no time, Isabel headed straight for the snacks, grabbing a bright-orange bag of Flamin' Hot MagiCrisps and something that looked almost exactly like Raisinets but instead were called Abracadabs!

"What do these do?" Leopold asked, trailing her to a lighted drink fridge.

Isabel chose a neon-green energy drink and pushed the frosty can into his hand. "They give your Aether levels a quick boost. It's all junk food, so the effect doesn't last long, but it's better than nothing. Even using my uncle's devices can dig a hole in your levels that could leave you weak if you've barely done magic before. Best to be prepared."

Remembering the awful, hollowed-out feeling that had come over him during his channeler test, Leopold nodded and looked down at the can of Aetherblast Xtreem he was holding.

"Chug it and meet me up front," she said, already heading for the register.

Leopold popped the top. It made a sound like a .22 rifle shot and sprayed purple sparks up his nose. He fought back a sneeze, then took a cautious sip. After an involuntary full-body shudder, a strange and pleasant sensation of simultaneous heat and cold coursed through him. He decided it wasn't half-bad.

Leopold's phone buzzed. Another text from Emmet.

Update: bored, hungry. Think I'll hit Astroburger. Text me ur order.

DON'T LEAVE ALMOST THERE, Leopold texted back, a lie. I'm bringing food.

The food part wasn't a lie, though he wasn't sure what would happen if a nonmagical person consumed Aether-laced snacks, and this wasn't the day to find out.

In response, three dancing dots appeared on his phone screen, then disappeared.

Leopold's anxiety spiked.

FIFTY-SIX

As he approached the register, Leopold interrupted a surreptitious exchange between Isabel and the clerk. The clerk, who wore oversized glasses and had his hair slicked back in a pompadour, had just passed Isabel a small package wrapped in white butcher paper. Leopold would've assumed it was a sandwich, except the Cash & Dash didn't have a deli counter.

He decided to let Isabel have her secret, whatever it was.

"Leopold, this is Jae," Isabel said quickly, stuffing the package into her cloak. "He and Uncle Norm went to college together."

"Nice hat," Jae said with a smirk. He turned to Isabel. "Doesn't Norm have the same one?"

"Yeah. He's got the slippers, too."

"Uh, nice to meet you, Jae," Leopold said, holding up the half-finished Aetherblast. "Hope it's okay that I already opened this."

"No problem," Jae said, then started bagging the other stuff. "Oh man, Abracadabs! These are addictive. Have you tried the green tea flavor yet?"

"I want to, but you're always out of stock."

"They don't always make it onto the shelves," Jae said with a wink. "Next time I get a shipment I'll hang on to some for you."

Leopold tugged Isabel aside. "Hey, Emmet's getting restless. I'm worried he's going to wander off unless we get there soon, so unless you've got a flying car parked somewhere around here, we need to call an Uber."

She frowned. "Flying cars are illegal. What's an Uber?"

"You've seriously never heard of Uber? It's a ride-hailing app—"

She cut him off. "No apps. We don't do apps."

"We?"

The register dinged. "Sparks don't," Jae said, pushing their bag across the counter. "Slack tech doesn't play well with Aether-based magic. Brings out the ghost in the machine. I put this stuff on your tab, by the way."

Isabel nodded gratefully. "Thanks, Jae. And hey, if anyone asks, you never saw us, okay?"

"You got it," Jae said.

They were about to go when they heard the loud, distinctive squelch of a radio from the walkway outside.

They all turned toward the sound.

The squelch came again, followed by a voice saying, "Ten-four, base. They were seen entering a convenience store on Cahuenga . . . approaching now . . ."

Leopold tensed. Isabel's expression darkened. She asked Jae if there was another way out of his store.

"Afraid not," he said, "but if you hurry, I've got a stockroom." He jutted his thumb at an open doorway behind him, a curtain partially screening a cramped space stacked with boxes.

The automatic door whooshed open. Leopold ducked behind the counter just as the cop entered, but Isabel didn't make it in time.

"Isabel Alvarez?"

It was a weary, *I should be on my lunch break* voice.

"Um, yes?" Isabel answered.

The cop asked Isabel if she'd seen a tall kid in a gray shirt, black jeans, and hiking boots. She said she hadn't. Leopold scrunched a little lower, feeling like a jackass for hiding while Isabel had to endure an interrogation.

"Then maybe you can explain why someone called our tip line a few minutes ago," the cop said, "about a person matching your description running across Cahuenga with a person matching his description."

Leopold took stock of Jae, whose casual slouch beside the register betrayed no fear.

"Oh, *him*," Isabel said innocently enough. "He came up to me on the street asking for directions. Said he was looking for a bus stop. I knew where it was and didn't see any harm in walking him there. You know the one on Selma?"

A scratching sound. The cop was writing something down. "Uh-huh."

"He didn't seem suspicious or anything. He walked with me for like a block, but then something scared him and he ran off. I think he saw a police car."

"You should know there's a warrant out for his arrest. He's not only here illegally but wanted in connection with an incident that occurred last night in Sunder Hill."

Isabel, cool up to now, sounded nervous. "Well, that's everything I know."

Leopold glanced at the stockroom, its half-curtained entrance only a short crawl away. Then he risked a quick peek around the counter. Instead of a uniform, the cop wore a wrinkled leather jacket and a tie. A serious-looking, pistol-gripped focuser hung from his belt. Isabel stood with her cloak partly open, its array of magical devices just within Leopold's reach.

He began to form something like a plan.

Leopold raised the unfinished can of Aetherblast to his lips—he'd never set it down—and silently chugged the rest of it.

The cop was questioning Jae now. "You see anyone matching that description?"

"I didn't, Rick."

"Detective Samuels. You can't call me Rick while I'm on duty."

"No such kid came in here, far as I know. Detective Samuels."

The detective's radio squawked. "Base to Samuels. We've got a second positive ID on the girl and the kid. They were seen entering the Cash & Dash."

Leopold's pulse began to race, but he didn't know whether the increasingly dire situation or the Aetherblast was responsible for the effect.

"Base, I'm on location at the Cash & Dash. About to do a sweep. Requesting backup."

"Ten-four, Samuels. Dispatching now."

"Both of you stay where you are." Samuels's tone had gone from bored to pissed. "I'm going to execute a search of the premises."

Samuels muttered an incantation and something hummed to life. A reddish beam swept across the ceiling. Whatever he was using, Leopold assumed it was capable of discovering a barely magical boy crouching behind a counter.

"I'll help you search," Jae offered. "There's a bathroom and a broom closet past aisle seven, and you'll need my keys to get in to them."

"All right. But the girl stays here. Hands on the counter where I can see them. No funny business, no casting."

Leopold scanned Isabel's holstered devices. He then reached out, wrapped his fingers around the hilt of her slim, serrated knife, and drew it carefully from its sheath. This, he knew from *Sunderworld*, was a limiknife, a tool capable of cutting through solid walls. Isabel tried to bump his hand away with her elbow, but she couldn't take her hands off the counter.

"Can I at least call my uncle?" she said.

"*No,*" Samuels barked.

His red beam swept the ceiling. Leopold started crawling toward the stockroom, the knife gripped in his right hand. Isabel attempted to hook him with her foot, but he pulled free. Passing the stockroom's curtained doorway, he glanced back: Isabel stood marooned at the register while the two men walked off down the main aisle. If Samuels turned around at the wrong time, he'd have a direct line of sight, so Leopold would have to work fast. And while he was sure cutting a hole through the wall was the best way to save them, he was less certain that the technique he'd seen on an episode of *Sunderworld* years ago was technically correct—or that, even if it was, he could pull it off.

There was only one way to find out.

Leopold crawled to a gap between shelves, knelt before the exposed cinder blocks, and pressed the tip of Isabel's knife to the wall.

Nothing happened.

He applied more pressure.

Just as Leopold was imagining what the inside of a Sunder jail cell might look like, the handle of the knife began to heat in his hands. The Aether he'd consumed seemed to come alive inside him—a powerful, slightly intoxicating sensation that sizzled in his veins. Then, as if the wall were made of softening butter rather than concrete, the blade sank in to the hilt.

Now: *down.* That's what he'd seen Max do. In the show, it'd been as easy as cutting cake. But as Leopold gripped the knife and tried to drag it toward the floor, he realized the show had not been entirely accurate on this point.

A few seconds later, he'd managed to bring the knife down only a few inches. It took nearly a minute of sustained effort to reach the floor, his hands shaking as a slim gap finally opened in the blade's wake. Daylight glowed through gauzy, dew-dappled webbing, and from the other side he could hear city noise.

He stopped, unsure what to do next—at this point in episode five ("The Unsubtle Knife") Max had made a gap large enough to escape through. Leopold's was hardly wide enough to accommodate one leg.

Getting desperate, he turned to look at Isabel. She stood at the register with her back to him. The detective's balding head bobbed down the Occult Sundries aisle behind Jae, his searchlight scanning windows and walls. Soon, they'd be returning.

Leopold pulled the knife from the wall, and its blade faded from red hot to cool silver. He didn't know what to do.

"Give me my damn knife back."

Leopold spun around so fast he nearly toppled a tower of boxes. Isabel was right behind him—but she was also, he confirmed with a baffled glance, still at the register.

Which was impossible.

His eyes darted between the two Isabels. "How—"

"Doppel-Buddy," she whispered.

The Isabel at the register turned to honor its maker with a grin, and Leopold recoiled. One of its eyes drooped alarmingly below the other, its nose took a sharp left where Isabel's was small and slightly upturned, and its lips were pulled into a snaggle-toothed grimace. It looked just like Isabel—if her face had been put through a laundry press. "I know, it's not great," Actual-Isabel said, "but I had, like, twenty seconds to make it because you were over here about to rip a hole into the Ninth Realm. In which case we would've had much worse things to deal with than one surly cop."

"What do you mean, the Ninth Realm—"

"Never mind." She snatched the knife from his hand. "Just keep watch while I fix this."

Wielding the blade's tip like a pen, she set about making adjustments to Leopold's work with the quick, confident strokes of a calligrapher. Back at the register, Doppel-Isabel swayed on its feet, a video game character whose player had abandoned their controller.

With a silent shudder, the gap in the wall began to expand. After a few seconds, Isabel tapped the blade against the concrete and the expansion halted. It was just wide enough for them to squeeze through, one at a time.

"Damn," Leopold said, awestruck. "You're good."

"My sigil-work is okay," she admitted, clearing diaphanous, cottony webbing from the gap with the flat of the knife. The webbing fell to the floor, where it immediately disintegrated to ash. "My spellwork is better."

The red beam was tracking toward them across the ceiling. Isabel urged Leopold toward the opening. "You first," he said in flat refusal.

She almost laughed as she wedged into the gap. "And I thought chivalry was dead."

As she wriggled through to the other side, Leopold saw Doppel-Isabel wander away from the counter and into the aisles. They were officially out of time.

Hastily, he followed Isabel through the wall.

FIFTY-SEVEN

Leopold emerged into a shaded breezeway that separated the Cash & Dash from the psychic next door. He'd hoped they'd be able to reach the rear of the strip mall and escape unseen down an alley, but from here the only way out was straight through the parking lot to Cahuenga. Back inside the store, they could hear Samuels yelling at the Doppel-Buddy. In a minute he'd see its face up close and realize he'd been tricked.

"I've got to close the wall," Isabel said, flipping a small switch embedded in the knife's hilt. "If they realize I used a limiknife, Uncle Norm will be in deep shit." She began to draw the gap closed, making rapid, stitch-like gestures across the opening. "These things aren't technically legal."

She'd only been working a few seconds when they heard the pitched wail of an approaching siren. The backup Samuels had requested was about to arrive.

Isabel finished her work and returned the limiknife to its sheath. Leopold leaned around the corner of the breezeway to make sure the coast was clear, and together they ran into the parking lot, ducking behind a pickup truck as a police cruiser skidded to a halt in front of the Cash & Dash. Two officers in blue got out. Leopold recognized them as Sunder PD not by their blue uniforms, which were nearly identical to those worn by the LAPD, but by their complex holsters and circular badges. One hurried into the convenience store while the other stood guard, watching the lot.

Now there was no way out.

"Any chance we can make a run for it?" Leopold asked.

A flapping sound snapped their attention to the sky. A pair of enormous crows were circling high above. Isabel shook her head. "Those aren't normal birds," she said darkly. "They're Watchers— spies enchanted by the Department. They're covering the exit in case we make it to the street."

Leopold swore under his breath, then cast a hopeful glance at her cloak. "In that case, I don't suppose you brought a portable hole."

"Nope," she said. "You?"

"Fresh out," he joked. Then something occurred to him, and he said, "When someone puts a tooth in a parking meter and a hole opens in the ground, what's down there?"

"Utility tunnels, stuff like that." Her eyes narrowed. "Why?"

"A few weeks ago I saw someone put a tooth in one of those." He nodded to a row of meters on the far side of the lot. "You wouldn't happen to have any loose teeth, would you?"

Isabel stared at him with ill-concealed astonishment. "Yeah," she said. "Uncle Norm always makes me carry some, just in case." She dipped a hand into one of her pockets and drew out a molar, ambered with age. "But—look—those kinds of entrances aren't usually veiled—we'll have no cover at all—"

"We've got no other choice." Leopold plucked the tooth from her hand. "Stay low and come with me."

Her mouth set in a grim line, Isabel hesitated only a moment before she said quietly, "Lead the way, Lunchtray."

They darted from parked car to parked car until they reached the row of meters, then crouched behind an old newspaper box—the only thing sheltering them from direct view of the cop. The newspaper dispenser read *Los Angeles Times* but also, in a veiled underlayer, *The Sunder Prism.*

Leopold took the opportunity to look around.

There were at least twenty parking meters, and he wasn't immediately certain which was the right one. Closing his eyes, Leopold cast his memory back to his view out Bessie's window—to the man with the tooth and the shop he'd been closest to.

"The birds are circling," Isabel whispered. "The cops will be able to pinpoint our location any minute now—"

Suddenly, he had it.

His eyes flew open. *That meter. In front of the vacuum repair shop.* It looked like all the other meters but for one detail, which resolved into perfect clarity only as Leopold focused on it: Below a slot that accepted coins was a second opening, square-shaped and blue.

"There," he said, pointing. "It's that one."

Isabel nodded, her jaw tight.

Leopold's blood pumped in his ears as they ran the short distance. Wasting no time, he pushed the molar into the square slot. Immediately the meter emitted a low hum and the asphalt in front of it began to shimmer, then ripple.

There came a cry of alarm from behind them. They spun around to see a stupefied woman shouting incoherently, dropped shopping bags at her feet, waving her arm at the rift now splitting the pavement. Pedestrians stopped and stared, disturbed by the commotion. Sirens blared nearby, and the crows overhead clamored for attention as two, then three Sunder cops came running.

Leopold urged Isabel forward.

The hole had widened enough to expose a ladder, its lower rungs vanishing into darkness. Isabel paused to stuff something that resembled chewing gum into the tooth slot, which quickly expanded to cocoon the entire meter.

She'd only just placed a foot on the first rung when the crack of a focuser rang out. They ducked for cover as a bolt of blue shot overhead, leaving a scorch trail in the air and shattering the shop window behind them.

The street erupted in chaos, passersby now screaming in terror.

Leopold scrambled down the ladder after Isabel, nearly losing his grip on the steel rungs as his head disappeared below the level of the asphalt. The hole was already beginning to ripple shut overhead when someone shouted "LARRY BERRY!"

Against his better judgment, Leopold looked up.

Samuels stood above them, his legs straddling the fast-closing fissure, his face warped grotesquely through the lens of his focuser— which was aimed straight at them.

The lens brightened suddenly, blindingly, a spell firing off just as the hole snapped shut, muting Samuels' angry shout, blocking his cast, and suffocating the last rays of daylight.

And then all went dark, and they were lost in an inky, bottomless gloom.

FIFTY-EIGHT

The ladder's cold metal numbed their hands as they descended, rung after slippery rung, into a black infinity. They still had no idea if what waited below was a dead end—or something far worse. After what seemed an eternity, a whisper of light appeared beneath them.

They stepped off the ladder onto a rough concrete floor, then took a moment to catch their breaths. Leopold's heart was beating fast, and Isabel leaned back against the ladder, her cheeks flushed. They were at the end of a long, narrow corridor, weak lights embedded in rough stone walls that trailed away around a blind curve. The words *Transportation Dept.* were stenciled at their feet in orange spray paint. On the floor a bit farther down the corridor was a bold *No Trespassing*.

Leopold glanced back up the ladder. "That thing you did to the parking meter—"

"A Stick-all. It should render the meter inoperable for a few minutes," Isabel said, though she sounded less than certain. "I think."

They looked at each other, then at the path ahead.

They broke into a run.

Before long the corridor ended, opening onto a small, unadorned subway platform. They slowed to a stop, pausing for a moment to gaze around them apprehensively. The ceiling was oppressively low, the floor filthy and skimmed with trash. There were no wall tiles spelling out the name of the station, no turnstile, no benches. The only indication that this was, in fact, a subway station, was the lone trolley car that sat waiting on a short section of track between two black and yawning tunnel arches.

Looking at the car sent a dislocating shudder of déjà vu through Leopold. It was practically identical to the trolley he'd almost smashed into on Sunset Boulevard, only this one was painted industrial gray rather than a dull, weathered red. Emblazoned below its roofline were the words MAINTENANCE CAR.

"Sunder has a subway?" Leopold said, finding his voice.

Isabel was shaking her head as they approached the car. "Hardly. A short section of our trolley system goes underground, but there's no entrance around here. This must be a maintenance tunnel for emergencies. I've heard rumors about them, but I never knew for certain where any of them were."

She shot him another wondering glance, which only deepened his unsettling déjà vu. Leopold felt certain then that witnessing the man insert his tooth into that parking meter, weeks ago, could not have been random; that someone—or something—had wanted him to see it. He shelved this strange idea for later consideration, and together they stepped into the subway car.

The interior looked like Angels Flight without the stairs: wooden benches spanned the car from end to end and hand straps hung from the ceiling. Occupying the front was an unmanned operator station surrounded by buttons and a big brass lever.

"I don't suppose you have any idea where this thing goes," Leopold said, heading straight for the operator station.

"It makes a bunch of stops," Isabel said, peering at a route map she'd located on the wall, pasted below a peeling advertisement for an insomnia curse reversal service. "Franklin and Beechwood . . . De-Longpre and Seward . . . Santa Monica and Vine . . ."

"That's just a few blocks from the cemetery," Leopold called over his shoulder. He was searching for a token slot among the buttons, starting to feel hopeful again.

"Right." She joined him at the panel. "Now if we can just figure out how to start this thing—"

Leopold gave up on finding a slot and simply shoved the big brass lever forward with both hands. Immediately the engine thrummed to life below their feet, and then—without any warning or PA announcement—the car let out an alarming series of creaks and lurched forward.

They let gravity pull them down onto the nearest bench, going slack with a mixture of relief and exhaustion as the platform blurred out of view. The car juddered and swayed, pushing their shoulders together. Leopold felt a familiar lightheadedness as they passed through a veil and the windows went dark.

When he'd recovered enough to collect his thoughts, something disturbing occurred to him. He had, in the space of half an hour, totally screwed up Isabel's life.

The impact of this depressing realization must've been printed all over his face. "What's the matter?" she asked almost immediately, angling toward him on the bench. "We're okay now, we made it. And Emmet's going to be fine—"

"It's not that." Leopold hung his head. "It's just— Shit, Isabel, I'm sorry. They're not going to leave you alone after this. You lied to the cops. Ran from them. They know who you are now, and that you've been helping me—and I'm some dangerous fugitive, apparently—"

"Leopold," she said, holding up a hand. "It's okay. I knew the risk I was taking—"

"What if they come to your house?" he insisted. "Try to arrest you? Norm's already on probation or something—"

"*It's okay*," she said again, emphatically. Her look of concern was gone; her expression was now one of soft surprise. "Uncle Norm and I have dealt with a lot worse over the years. He and I always take care of each other. You don't have to worry."

Leopold gave a small nod. "I'm sure that's true," he said quietly, fixing her with a steady look. "But I will anyway."

Her eyes rounded before she looked away, staring at her boots as she smiled. "Uncle Norm and I appreciate your concern."

A small, sharp feeling flared to life inside him, the sensation both painful and joyful. Through the window behind her a flurry of yellow sparks lit the dark, then vanished.

When Isabel looked up, her face had changed. Her smile had become a grimace, her brows knit together. Her hands had balled into fists.

Leopold tensed.

"I'll be fine," she said, waving away his concern as she grimaced in pain. Her cheeks had gone a deathly pale. She pressed one hand hard against her side.

"What do you need?" he said urgently. "What can I do?"

"You can stop . . . freaking out," she said, her breath coming in uneven gasps. "And you can get me . . . that vial . . ." She nodded down at her belt. "With the black liquid."

Hurrying, he flipped open her cloak. Secured with a snap between the looped rope and the old TV remote was a small glass vial in a leather pouch.

"This one?"

She nodded. He unsnapped the piece that held it in place and drew it out. A splinter of wood floated in murky liquid. The vial was etched with the word *Enceladus* and stoppered with a cork.

"Need to drink," she said, her voice barely a whisper.

He opened it, careful not to let any spill as the car leaned around a curve. She was fading by the second, and it was scaring the hell out of him. He slid a hand behind her neck and raised her head until her lips met the bottle. She took a sip, paused, then took another. Isabel squeezed her eyes shut and clenched her jaw like she'd swallowed poison, but after a few seconds her face began to relax.

Her eyes opened.

She took the bottle from his hand with a faint *thank you*, then took another sip of her own accord. She grimaced again as color began returning to her cheeks.

"Maybe we should get you to a hospital," said Leopold.

"They couldn't help me anyway. And I'm fine now."

"You're not fine. Nothing about that was fine. What just happened?"

She took another sip. And then he realized.

"The Doppel-Buddy," he said.

She nodded, then squinted at him. "So Norm told you."

"Yeah. But I don't get it . . . That was a pretty minor spell, right? Not like portaling us across the city."

Then again, in the aftermath of that escape he'd been unconscious. He had no idea what torments she might have endured before he awoke.

"I didn't think it would be this bad," she said. "But the effects of multiple casts are cumulative, like radiation exposure. I guess I needed more time to recover from last night." Shaking her head in frustration, she pushed up the sleeve that covered her right arm. Beneath was the maze of pink scars he'd noticed earlier, but now there was a new one: red, angry, and tracing a crooked line from wrist to forearm.

"God. Isabel." His chest constricted at the sight. "Why do you—if you know it's going to hurt you—"

"Most are from when I was younger. And angrier, and stupider." She tapped a drop of the murky liquid from the vial onto her fresh wound. It hissed like a branding iron. She winced as a curl of smoke rose from her arm. "And sometimes you don't have a choice."

He looked at her, letting a moment pass before he said, "What do you mean?"

Isabel hesitated, returning his gaze for only a moment before her eyes darted away. She capped the bottle, stowed it back in its holster, then yanked her sleeve down again.

"Isabel." His mouth pulled into a grim line. "Please. I need you to promise me you won't cast anymore."

The windows flashed from dark to light as the trolley emerged briefly from underground, and for a moment Leopold couldn't see her against a blinding blast of sun. He shaded his eyes, and when she came into focus again, she had a curious, slightly bemused look on her face.

"What?" said Leopold.

"Nothing." Isabel turned away as the window dimmed.

"Look," he said with a sigh, "whatever happens, whatever the situation is, we'll deal with it some other way. You don't need to cast. You can count on me—I've got your back."

Her eyes were heavy and uncertain, as if she wanted to say something but wasn't quite sure how to begin. Then she turned suddenly to look out the window, where a new subway platform came flashing into view. She reached up to pull a cord that ran along the ceiling and a sign came alight above the operator's station: STOP REQUESTED.

With a squeal of brakes, the trolley began to slow.

FIFTY-NINE

With the empty subway car idling behind them, they hurried across another small, bunker-like maintenance platform. A low corridor led to a steep concrete staircase. Halfway to the top Leopold felt pressure build in his ears, then release as they passed through a veil. At the landing there was a posted reminder about hiding focusers and extinguishing any visible spells. They pushed through a metal door and stumbled out into blinding sun and traffic noise.

Leopold pulled his beanie low and donned his sunglasses. They were on Santa Monica Boulevard, across the street from a bustling carwash and a payday loan place, only a few blocks from the gates of Hollywood Forever. With a bang the heavy door slammed shut behind them. It had no exterior handle and was built into the side of an aggressively anonymous two-story building, its windowless edifice betraying nothing of the secrets that lay within. Leopold scanned the blank door and surrounding wall for a slot, a keyhole, or some other method of reentry, but there were none.

There'd be no going back this way.

They headed for the cemetery, inexplicably beheaded palms striping the sidewalk with their pencil-thin shadows. As they dodged pits and potholes, Leopold's spiraling thoughts returned to Emmet. Once they got his friend to safety—and found a way to help him—Leopold would figure out what the device suctioned to his chest was for. There'd be time to discover what his mother had wanted from him— and what other purpose the Thomas Guide was meant to serve in his life, if any.

There would be time for all of it, he promised himself.

Leopold and Isabel walked alone into the cemetery, through a flank of iron gates, past a wooden sign carved with an infinity symbol and words veiled from slack eyes: ALL-REALM RESTING PLACE.

They crossed an expanse of manicured lawn where peacocks roamed, fanning their tailfeathers for tourists, and hurried into the cemetery proper. Beyond a few rows of modest graves by the entrance, the cemetery was dominated by ostentatious crypts and tombs, their size appropriate to the egos of the old-Hollywood moguls and movie stars whose bones they contained. They avoided a tour group snapping selfies by the grave of Rudolph Valentino, then another meandering toward a mausoleum that housed the earthly remains of Judy Garland. Leopold and Isabel were headed for the southeastern end of the cemetery and one of the newer celebrity interments: the grave of Johnny Ramone. His life-sized, guitar-wielding monument was unmissable, and Leopold had suggested Emmet meet him there because it was one of the few landmarks he was certain Emmet would know, even with his memory revised back to age fourteen.

Leopold quickly checked the sky: no spying crows in sight.

In the distance he could see the wall that marked the border between Hollywood Forever and the Paramount Pictures backlot, a block-wide metropolis of soundstages and prop workshops whose tall, curving roofs gazed down upon a million graves. He'd always thought it the height of LA weirdness that such an insubstantial border separated this self-contained city of make-believe—the place where they'd shot *CSI* and *Star Trek*—from the final resting place of the people who'd made them. As if the studio might one day reboot *The Ten Commandments* and resurrect Cecil B. DeMille to pop next door and direct a few scenes.

Leopold pulled out his phone and checked for new texts, but there were none. He'd been struggling to compartmentalize his anxiety about Emmet all morning, but they were so close now that he could no longer rein it in. They jogged around a grove of cypress trees and an enormous crypt, and then, despite pleas from Isabel to be cool and not attract attention, Leopold broke into a full-on run.

There, lounging in the grass beside the bronze statue of Johnny Ramone and his guitar, was Emmet. He wore one of their old, home-made paladin costumes, black boots and a green army coat with a bandolier of fake Aether vials strapped across his chest. He was munching from a greasy bag of Astroburger, a slightly concerning absence in his expression as he studied the clouds.

Leopold shouted his name.

Emmet snapped out of it, surprised—then visibly annoyed. "Jesus, what took you so long?" He dropped the Astroburger bag and hopped to his feet. "I've watched, like, three funerals already."

"Hey, are you okay? How are you?"

"What? I'm fine—"

"You didn't talk to anybody, did you?" Leopold had grabbed him by the shoulders and was peering into his eyes. "Who's the president? What year is it?"

Emmet shook him off uncomfortably. "Why are you being weird? And where's your costume, Mister Berry? This whole video project was your—"

Emmet stopped midsentence.

"Uh, hi," he said over Leopold's shoulder. Then, to Leopold in a whisper: "Larry. *Girl.*"

Isabel raised her eyebrows at Leopold. *Mister Berry?* she mouthed, stifling a laugh.

Leopold grimaced. "Isabel, this is my old friend Emmet. Emmet, this is my new friend Isabel."

"Hey." She lifted a hand. "I've heard a lot about you."

"What've you heard?" Emmet said, looking both confused and suspicious. "Wait—how do you two know each other?"

"We, uh—we met at school," Leopold improvised.

Emmet's eyes narrowed. "*Our* school?"

"Different school," Leopold said quickly. "Hal's school."

"Your stepbrother goes to our school, idiot."

"Right. That's what I meant. Same school." Leopold forced a casual smile, but he was starting to sweat. "Look, Emmet, we have to get going. Let's pack up your tripod."

"But you just got here!" Emmet shouted. "We have a full day of shooting ahead of us!"

"I know, I'm sorry, something important came up—"

"Excuse us a sec," Emmet said to Isabel, then pulled Leopold around to the other side of Johnny Ramone's grave. "Seriously, Larry, what the hell is going on? You come all the way over here just to cancel the shoot?" He frowned, looking Leopold up and down. "Wait a second, did you get taller?"

Leopold stalled. "No?"

Emmet's frown deepened, but he let it go. "Is this about her?" he said instead. "I mean, no offense, you're a handsome gentleman and everything, but your chances with a girl like that are insanely low. Forget it. I've already got this shot framed up—"

"Hey," Isabel said, coming into view. She looked wary. "Everything okay?"

"This is a private conversation," Emmet said irritably.

"Not when you're shouting," she pointed out. "Everyone in this graveyard can hear what you're saying. And you should know: Leopold is only trying to help you."

"*Leopold?*" Emmet barked a laugh. "Nobody calls him that. His name is Larry—"

"Emmet," Leopold hissed. "Let it go, man."

"Whatever." Emmet was studying Isabel unkindly. "Listen, Yoko, you're already in costume, so I guess we can pencil you into the script—"

"You can call me Isabel."

"—but it won't be a major part, so don't get your hopes up—"

"All right, that's enough." Leopold grabbed Emmet by the arm, half dragging him across the grass. "She's not wearing a costume."

Emmet broke away from Leopold angrily. "What the hell is your deal, man? I know an apprentice paladin's cloak when I see one. The props on her belt are a dead giveaway—and you can't just drag me out of here, all my gear is still on the ground."

"Fine. Grab your things, but we're leaving. I'll explain everything later, I promise. Right now you're just going to have to trust me."

Emmet dusted himself off, then shot Leopold a scouring glare. "This is massively uncool," he said. "At least tell me where we're going."

"To my place," Isabel cut in. She was already walking, Emmet's tripod gathered under her arm. "We're, um, going to watch a movie."

"Hey!" Emmet was pointing. "She's taking my stuff!"

Leopold had forgotten how much Emmet used to shout when he was younger. Drove his parents crazy.

"I'm just helping," Isabel called back to them. "Where'd you park your car?"

"What car?" Emmet scoffed. "We can't drive!" He turned to Leopold as they started after her, lowering his voice a little. "Who the hell is this girl? How old is she? And what's up with everyone today? God, my head is killing me," he said, rubbing his temples. Leopold scooped up Emmet's camera bag without slowing. "Everything has been so weird. My room is different. My phone's all different. You're hanging out with some hot girl who's probably going to rob us. Even my parents were acting weird today—my mom kept crying for no reason and my dad refused to let me leave the house. I had to sneak out, can you believe it? I took the bus here." Emmet paused, fixed Leopold with a funny look, and said, "You know, you really do look different. When did you start working out?"

"There's a metro stop a couple blocks from the cemetery!" Isabel shouted from up ahead.

"Hey," Leopold said. "I'm sorry you had such a bad day. We're going to fix this, I promise—"

But Emmet's eyes had gone glassy. A drop of blood leaked out of one nostril and blotched his costume.

Leopold tried not to panic. "Whoa—you okay? Your nose—"

"Ahh, crap," said Emmet, still walking as he pulled an old, bloodied tissue from his pocket. "This has been happening all day. I don't know what's wrong with me. Probably just the dry air . . ."

Emmet's faraway look had returned.

Everything was coming unraveled. Leopold wondered whether they'd even be able to guide him through a crosswalk without a full-blown freak-out. They'd just cleared a small hill when Leopold heard something that made him go cold.

"Larry! Emmet!"

Emmet frowned, then turned around. "What the . . . *Mom*?"

Dr. Laura Worthington was hiking toward them, small in the distance but fast approaching across the grass. But that wasn't the half of it—or even the worst of it.

Striding along beside her was Richter.

SIXTY

Leopold, Emmet, and Isabel came to a crashing halt, the three of them toppling together, then freezing in a parody of a police lineup. Leopold wondered if he was dreaming.

Then he heard his name, bellowed by his father.

"*Larry!* Don't you dare run away from me!"

That nails-on-a-chalkboard voice, somehow both nasal and baritone, was evidence enough: This was no dream. *I can't believe he used to scare me,* Leopold thought.

Isabel grabbed Leopold's arm. "That's your dad?"

He met her eyes, then stared down at her hand on him, surprised. "Yeah," he said quietly. "Hey, uh, you're cutting off my circulation."

"Sorry." She pulled away, then looked ahead. "I just—I swear I've seen him before."

Leopold frowned. "Really?"

"Yeah, I don't know— His face looks so familiar—"

"You probably saw him on a billboard," Leopold suggested. "That big one on Sunset?"

"Mom!" Emmet hollered, then waved. "Did you bring any snacks?"

"Stay right there, baby!" Dr. Worthington waved back from afar. "Don't move!"

"Okay, Mom! Love you!"

"Dude. Stop." Leopold yanked Emmet's arm down. "We need to get the fuck out of here."

Emmet reared back. "Whoa, Mister Berry, *language*. When did you start using the F-word?"

Leopold narrowed his eyes at his dad. "Yesterday."

Emmet started giggling. He looked high, and his nose was bleeding again. His head swung around as he took in the scenery, then wobbled upright. "Holy moly, your girlfriend has a limiknife!" he said, his words slurring a little. "Can I hold it?"

Leopold cast a sidelong glance at Isabel. "Take care of him, I'll be right back."

"Where are you going?" she said, sounding panicked. She was looking from him to Emmet, who was making half-hearted efforts to snatch the knife off her holster.

"I have to talk to the parents," Leopold said. "Convince them to give us some space."

"Then take this with you." She pressed something into his hand. "There's an easy trigger."

He felt the slide of cool metal, the warmth of her hand, a spark of heat in his belly. For a fraction of a second, he forgot what he was doing. He blinked, looking at her. "What is it?"

"My uncle calls it a bewilderlite. Theoretically, it'll make them forget everything that happened to them in the last half hour."

It was the size and shape of a small light bulb, but heavy, cast entirely in riveted gunmetal. Leopold raised his eyebrows. "Theoretically?"

"It hasn't been tested much." She had the decency to look sheepish. "Maybe try not to use it if you don't have to."

Leopold regarded the bewilderlite uncertainly, nodded at Isabel, then jogged toward the adults. He was halfway there when Richter turned to shout something over his shoulder.

Over the rise behind him, a pair of uniformed LAPD officers appeared.

Leopold came to a sudden halt and swore under his breath.

Richter hadn't only been in contact with the Worthingtons—he'd brought a couple of cops with him. Classic, asshole Richter. *Of course* his dad would turn this into a Teachable Moment. Richter had probably made a deal with the police to keep Leopold in a holding cell overnight, just to scare him.

The only option now was to backtrack and bolt, though he'd wanted to reassure Mrs. Worthington that Emmet was going to be okay. It seemed he wouldn't get the chance.

"Leopold!"

He spun around at the terrified pitch of Isabel's voice.

She was waving at him frantically. "RUN!"

≡ SIXTY-ONE

Leopold ran like hell, slowing just long enough to turn Emmet in the right direction. With Isabel grabbing one of Emmet's arms and Leopold the other, they broke into a mad dash. In his semi-dazed state, Emmet was pliable enough.

They'd had no choice but to abandon Emmet's equipment in a heap by Johnny Ramone's grave. At their backs was a chorus of shouts, Richter's loudest of all, while Emmet registered a steady litany of complaints re: the status of those snacks from his mom, the unfinished bag of Astroburger, and the wisdom of leaving his gear unattended in a graveyard. Leopold knew it would've been simpler to bewilder the adults with Norm's device, but his conscience was too heavy. He'd be lucky if he could get Emmet's head right again; if he used untested magic on Emmet's mom and messed up her brain, too, he'd never forgive himself.

Distantly, Leopold heard one of the officers swear, then grumble about being forced to run.

"This was supposed to be my day off," groaned the other one.

Leopold exchanged a look with Isabel. Clearly, Richter had recruited a pair of bargain-bin cops for the job.

Running three across was slow, but Leopold knew Hollywood Forever well enough to make a few clever, sudden turns that kept them ahead and mostly out of sight of their pursuers—all while answering Emmet's increasingly agitated questions with *Trust me, trust me, I know this is crazy, but please trust me.*

Finally, after rounding a blind of trees and surprising a goth couple making out on Boris Karloff's grave, Emmet whispered, "Okay, I do, okay, I trust you," in this sad, scared way, like he knew something big was wrong, and wrong with *him*, too—a moment of clarity that, combined with Emmet's worsening nosebleed, made Leopold feel like dying.

After that, they didn't need to coax Emmet along anymore. He was athletic and ran cross-country. Suddenly they were having trouble keeping up with him.

"Is his nose still bleeding?" Isabel asked, her words punctuated by chugging breaths.

"Yeah," Leopold said, lungs burning as he guided them through a weedy patch. They darted into a passage that squeezed between a long, white mausoleum and a high wall, past a section with the graves all in Cyrillic, then through a clique of strutting peacocks that honked in haughty annoyance. Despite their efforts to stay ahead, Richter and Dr. Worthington's shouts hounded them stubbornly. More distantly, and much more occasionally, one of the cops would blurt out a half-hearted *Stop, kids!*

So far, the teenagers had done a fair job of keeping out of the adults' line of sight, but it seemed there would be no evading them completely. Now, shouldering through a prickly boxwood hedge, Leopold faced a series of bad options. Hard to their left were a smattering of graves and a few big tombs in the shadow of the adjoining Paramount wall, which was unscalably high and topped with razor wire. To their right was a wide-open lawn where they'd quickly be spotted.

Far ahead was yet another unbreachable wall, but this one, at least, had an exit gate, beyond which lay Gower Street and the promise of escape.

That would have been the obvious choice, except the adults seemed to have reached this same conclusion.

Richter and Dr. Worthington appeared ahead of them now, crossing the broad stretch of lawn and, in the process, cutting off their only path to the gate. The two uninvested cops were still somewhere behind them. The adults were closing in from both sides.

"Over here!" Emmet cried, beelining for a row of fancy crypts.

"Emmet, wait—"

They dove after him, ducking behind a glassy tomb that looked like something out of *Architectural Digest: Eternity Edition*, while Emmet darted over to its next-door neighbor: a miniature Greek temple ringed by black columns and mildew-stained statuary. When they caught up with him, he was gazing through the bars of its heavy door. Inside, Leopold glimpsed a cramped stone room that held graves stacked like drawers in a file cabinet.

"Nice digs," Emmet said, his eyes wide with interest. "We should hide in here."

"Bad idea," Leopold said urgently. "Even if we managed to get the door open, all they'd have to do is look through the bars and they'd see us."

"No, they won't—this one's veiled," said Isabel, studying Emmet with mild amazement. Emmet was busy gathering a bouquet of dandelions from the overgrowth. "There's an enchantment on it."

"What kind of enchantment?" Leopold asked, throwing a look behind him. No sign yet that they'd been spotted.

"I don't know." Isabel reached up to run her hand over some runic inscriptions beside a carved winged skull. "I think this says it wants some kind of payment."

"*Payment?* Like, money?"

"I don't know," she said again, shaking her head. "I dropped out of the Lyceum a few months ago, never finished my Sunderunes seminar—"

"What?" Leopold turned, stunned, to stare at her. "Why would you drop out of the Lyceum?"

She almost laughed. "Why are you so upset?"

Emmet shoved between them, then pushed his freshly plucked dandelion bouquet through the bars. The flowers fell, without fanfare, onto the dusty interior floor. After a moment, the door returned a heavy *clunk*, groaning as some interior latch released.

Leopold and Isabel stilled, then turned in unison to study Emmet in fresh astonishment.

"How did you know to do that?" Leopold asked.

Emmet shrugged. "Everyone likes flowers."

Isabel, meanwhile, was struggling with the door. "Help, please!"

Leopold moved quickly, shouldering it open with a hard shove. Stone grinding on stone, the giant door swung inward. They stumbled into a cold, stale-smelling room.

Together, Leopold and Isabel pushed the door closed.

From outside, the crypt had looked no bigger than a garden shed. Inside, it was easily three times larger. The walls were a checkerboard of grave markers, all washed in pale yellow light filtered through a stained-glass ceiling. Occupying the middle of the floor was a dark marble obelisk, taller than Leopold and covered in Sunderunes and hieroglyphic pictographs.

It was all weirdly beautiful.

"Mister Berry," said Emmet, looking around in wonder. "There's something super wrong with me, isn't there?"

Leopold clasped his shoulder. "Nothing we can't fix, Mister Worthington."

Emmet nodded. His eyes, dull but darting, came to rest on the nearest grave slab. "Cool."

"*Larry!*"

"*Emmet!*"

The sudden shouts of their parents made everyone jump. They couldn't have been far from the crypt's door. Emmet spun toward the voices, about to shout back, but Leopold shook his head seriously— *not yet*—and Emmet looked confused, then sobered, then scared.

"We can't stay long," Leopold whispered to Isabel. "His mind keeps weaving in and out. It's making him unpredictable."

Isabel nodded grimly, and they led Emmet away from the door toward the black obelisk in the center of the floor. Emmet rested his back against the pillar and struggled to wipe blood from his chin.

"Oh, you're smearing it," Isabel said, digging a handkerchief from her seemingly bottomless cloak. "Let me help—"

Watching as she dabbed carefully at Emmet's face, Leopold felt something stir within him. He hardly knew Isabel and yet here she was, helping him—looking out for him and for Emmet, too—with a sincerity that was so rare in his experience he could hardly define it.

He'd make it up to her somehow.

Afterward, Emmet looked better, if still worryingly distant. Isabel, too, was flagging: Her cheeks had drained of color, and her hand was at her side again. She'd been hiding it well, but it was clear now she hadn't fully recovered from her earlier cast. She needed rest—and probably more of Norm's cooking. The Aether snacks they'd bought from the convenience store, he realized with dismay, had been left behind in the subway car.

Leopold urged Isabel to sit, then crouched beside her, at the ready in case Emmet decided to bolt for the door. For now, Emmet stood puzzling at the obelisk, passing his hand over its arcane inscriptions.

Isabel, meanwhile, had removed the black vial from its holster clasp again. She was sipping at it, wincing as the dark liquid passed her lips. Leopold noticed it was nearly empty.

"What can I do?" he asked. "Do you need to lie down?"

She shook her head. "I just need a little time. I'll be all right."

She let her head fall back against the stone while the solution did its work. He peered at the vial in her hand. The etched glass read *Ghost Ship Enceladus. Foremast. Pine.*

For reasons he couldn't explain, he committed the words to memory.

There were more shouts from outside, distant now, then static from a faraway police radio. The adults seemed to be losing their trail. When Leopold's eyes returned to Isabel, she was staring at him with somber urgency.

"Leopold," she said, quiet and intense.

"Yeah?"

"There's something I need to tell you. I wasn't sure I was going to. I mean, it's pretty serious, and we only just met." They shared a look, in it a charged and mutual acknowledgment: It didn't feel like they'd just met. "But if anything happens to me," she continued, "there's something I need you to know."

"Nothing's going to happen to you," he said sharply, his reaction so visceral it surprised him. "I told you—you can count on me. I've got your back."

She shook her head, smiling a little. "Like I said, I appreciate that. But we could get separated. Or one of us could get arrested. Or"—her eyes darted away briefly—"you never know. And then you'll have to figure things out on your own." She was looking at his shirt now, at the circular shape outlined beneath it.

"Isabel—"

"Richard and Maria Alvarez." She took a breath, almost trembling with the effort it had required to summon those words. "Those were my parents' names."

Leopold went still.

"They were alchemists," she said. "And scientists. And before they died, I think—I'm almost certain—they had something to do with creating that object on your chest."

He blinked, a chilling theory crystallizing in his mind. "The lab accident that killed them. You think it had something to do with this?" His hand rose to touch it, the movement unconscious.

She nodded.

"Isabel," he said quietly. "If that's true, I think there's a chance your parents might've known my mom."

She straightened then, her eyes sparking back to life. "What do you mean?"

"The Guide." His voice dropped to a whisper. "It belonged to my mother. She wanted me to find—"

And then the crypt filled with a sharp, echoing sound that took them both by surprise, because in that moment it was the last thing either of them expected to hear:

Emmet was laughing.

SIXTY-TWO

Isabel and Leopold leapt to their feet and scrambled around the obelisk. Emmet was pointing at something on the pillar and laughing his ass off, the sound so loud it reverberated off the walls.

"Emmet—you have to lower your voice—"

"Please, we need to be quiet—"

"Look at it," he was saying, still cackling. He nodded at the runic inscription. "It looks like a penis!"

Isabel cringed.

"He thinks he's fourteen," said Leopold by way of apology, then led Emmet away by the arm. "All right, Mister Worthington. Let's play the quiet game."

"The quiet game is for babies!"

"Hey!" Someone was banging at the door. "Who's in there?"

Leopold tensed. *Shit.* It was one of the cops.

"Just us!" Emmet called back. Leopold tried too late to clap a hand over his mouth, but Emmet shoved him away. "We're in here!"

Isabel shot Leopold a worried glance.

Emmet got that faraway look in his eyes again and turned back to gaze at the obelisk.

"Open the door, guys." The other cop now. "This isn't a game."

They both sounded more irritated than angry, but the jig was up either way: There would be no hiding from them now.

"Leopold," Isabel whispered. "Do you still have the bewilderlite?"

"Yeah," he said, patting himself down. "It was right..." He searched one pants pocket, then the other, but came up empty.

Her voice hollow, Isabel said, "You lost it?"

Leopold was shaking his head, searching the floor in a panic. "I swear I had it. I don't know what happened. It must've fallen out of my pocket while we were running—"

"I've got it," said Emmet, looking dazed but triumphant. He held up the bewilderlite, fumbling it between his fingers as if it were a toy. "I snatched it from Larry earlier."

"What? Emmet, give that back—"

"No way," he said, souring. "You two get all the cool props. *She* has a whole tool belt full of them. You can take the limiknife. I want this one."

"You can't use a limiknife in here," Isabel said, as if this should've been obvious. "Too many protective enchantments—too dangerous—"

"*Too dangerous,*" Emmet mocked in a whiny voice. He tucked the bewilderlite in his pocket. "Whatever, Mom."

"Larry!" Richter bellowed. "Get out here before I ship you off to military school!"

The pounding at the door had only grown louder. Leopold's dad was his usual belligerent self. Emmet's mom, on the other hand, sounded like she was barely keeping it together.

"Emmet, baby, *please*—there's no need to keep running—no one's going to hurt you—"

But the tremor in her voice said she wasn't so sure. Between bangs on the door, Leopold could hear Dr. Worthington assuring the cops that neither her son nor Larry were any threat, but then he heard the cops bandying about the words *breaking and entering*, and suddenly Leopold was wondering whether busting into a private crypt was some kind of felony.

His anxiety kicked into high gear.

Then he heard Emmet say, "Oh, *hello*," in this bemused sort of way, gathering up the fallen bouquet of dandelions before stalking toward the rear wall.

Leopold, concerned, started after him. "Emmet, wait, what are you—"

Without hesitating, Emmet arranged the limp bunch in a marble vase—a permanent fixture for displaying flowers—then grasped the base with both hands and twisted it forty-five degrees to the right.

A loud clank of gears issued from deep inside the stone wall, the sound such a shock it stopped Leopold in his tracks. A grave slab slid away to reveal a dark cavity the size of a small door.

Leopold and Isabel gaped at it.

"A secret passage in a wizard's tomb," Emmet whispered, quoting a line from the *Sunderworld* theme. "Cool Thursday."

"How did you do that?" Isabel asked him.

"I read the instructions." Emmet pointed behind him at the obelisk and its indecipherable carvings.

Isabel turned to look at them—then, with renewed fascination, at Emmet. "You can read Sunderunes? I can only make out half of it."

Emmet wasn't listening. "Holy Swedish meatballs," he breathed. He bent down, peering into the dark of the door he'd opened. "Is that what I think it is?"

Leopold crouched, Isabel scrambling to join them. Deep within the gloom was a large, cube-shaped appliance covered in flaking white paint, a round door built into the front.

"It's a tumbleport," said Leopold, his voice tinged with awe.

"Totally," said Emmet. "But some prehistoric model. Not like the one Max uses."

Nodding in agreement, Isabel asked, "Who's Max?"

"No one worth discussing," Leopold said flatly, then pulled open the tumbleport door. It produced a loud shriek and a flurry of rust from its hinge. He made a face as a musty stench wafted out at them.

"Oh my God, can we use it?" Emmet cried.

"Hell no." Isabel was already backing away, head shaking. "Rich people used to put these in family tombs—to make visiting the dead more convenient, I guess—but this one's gotta be eighty years old. It's almost definitely broken, and even if it's not, we have no idea where it—"

"Don't make us break down this door!" Richter bellowed from outside.

"Emmet!" Leopold cried. "*No!*"

Leopold, who'd looked away for only a moment, had turned back in time to catch a glimpse of his friend's feet disappearing into what looked like a void filled with stars.

Emmet had leapt into the open tumbleport.

There was no time to react: The door had already slammed shut, the machine thrumming loudly as it worked. There was a crescendo of sound and a strobing red light that flashed from a dozen cracks in its rusting body. Leopold could've sworn he heard the receding cry of Emmet going *wheeeee!*—and then the machine fell silent.

The lock tumblers clicked free. Leopold yanked open the tumbleport door. A cold blue mist billowed out, but the barrel itself was empty.

Leopold lost it.

He pounded on the machine. "Where are the goddamn buttons on this thing? How do we get him back? Come on, *come on—*"

Isabel's steady hands drew him back. "Leopold, stop—it doesn't work that way." Calm and focused, she kept a gentle pressure on his shoulder as she leaned around him, searching along the right side of the machine with her free hand. "It should be here somewhere," she was saying, "if I can just find the . . ."

She must have hit a button, because a moment later a small receipt buzzed from a narrow slot on top of the machine. She tore it off, quickly read it, then offered it to Leopold.

"This is where he went."

In blurry blue print, the receipt read:

Klovis Memorial Home, Manchester Ave., Inglewood, Ca.

"Inglewood." Leopold looked at her, cautiously hopeful. "That's just across town."

She was nodding. "Don't worry. We can go get him."

Relief flooded through Leopold in a disorienting wave, tempered just as quickly by a new worry. Only seconds after Isabel had taken the receipt from the machine, it spat out another, this one printed in red ink:

OUT OF ORDER

As if to put the matter beyond dispute, the door fell off its rusted hinge and hit the floor with a deafening clatter.

"Well, shit," Leopold said. Appraising the useless machine with renewed panic, he remembered Emmet's fragile state. "I just hope he made it—"

Leopold's pocket buzzed.

He pulled out his phone to find a text from Emmet.

THAT WAS AMAZING

Before Leopold could reply, Emmet sent another: U guys coming or what?

As a fresh wave of relief hit Leopold, he typed, Stupid machine broke! You okay??

Emmet returned a thumbs-up emoji, then: holy crap this place is like Wal-Mart for caskets haha what

Don't go anywhere, Leopold typed back. Be there ASAP.

Leopold showed Isabel his phone screen. They shared a quick smile, this brief respite interrupted by a swell of commotion from outside. The bangs and shouts at the crypt door were now too loud to be ignored.

They turned to face the exit, then each other.

"You ready?" Isabel said.

Leopold nodded. "There's no way out but through."

SIXTY-THREE

They stepped into bright sun.

"Put your hands up!" one of the cops shouted.

"Is this really necessary?" Leopold heard Dr. Worthington ask. "They're not criminals."

"They may have vandalized the crypt," the other cop was saying. "Breaking and entering is a serious crime, ma'am."

Leopold and Isabel raised their hands above their heads, Leopold's heart thudding as the scene came into focus. The cops were a short distance away in the grass, red-faced and sweating from exertion. Richter and Dr. Worthington stood behind them, crackling with nervous energy.

"Where's Emmet?" said Dr. Worthington, her voice taking on new urgency. "Where's my son?"

"Yeah, there were three of you. Where's the other one?" said the first cop.

Leopold's mild relief regarding Emmet gave way to sudden, crushing guilt.

"He never went inside with us," Leopold lied, mostly addressing Dr. Worthington. "He said he wanted to go home." Leopold nodded in the general direction of the Gower Street exit.

"I thought I heard his voice—"

"That was me," Leopold assured her. "Emmet's okay. He ran off ten minutes ago."

She raised a trembling hand to her face in tentative relief. One of the cops shone his flashlight through the crypt door. After a cursory examination of the interior, he grunted, "Yeah, it's empty," then asked Dr. Worthington whether she wanted to file a report.

She hadn't seemed to hear him. Her eyes, bright and angry, were focused on Leopold, and her voice broke when she said, "Larry, I'm so disappointed in you."

Leopold took it like a punch to the gut.

"Join the club," muttered Richter. "Kid's been a disappointment since the day he was born."

Dr. Worthington stiffened, then flashed a hard glare at Richter. "You're one to talk."

Richter looked stunned as she hitched up her purse and stormed off, but in her wake, he found his voice. "Now, officers," he said, addressing the cops in his Reasonable Man of Authority tone. "I realize my son has put you through a lot today, and while I appreciate all you've done, I'd prefer to handle the matter privately from here."

The cop with the flashlight shook his head and slouched over to join his partner. "Sorry, not possible. Things have escalated."

"Could be charges," the other one agreed, pulling out a notepad. "We'll have to call it in, see what the sergeant says."

"Sure. You do that," Richter replied, nodding as if it had been his idea. "Just tell him it's Richter Berry. He'll know who I am."

As the cops rolled their eyes and one unclipped a walkie-talkie from his belt, Leopold wished, more than ever, that Emmet hadn't taken the bewilderlite. Then Isabel hissed his name, tense and frightened, and when he saw her face, he knew things were about to get worse. He followed her gaze to a stand of nearby cypress trees.

Two men were striding out of the shadows.

"Stand down, fellas, we've got jurisdiction here!" the taller of them called across the expanse of grass.

The one who'd spoken wore a blue Sunder police uniform and had a shaved head shaped like a bullet. The other, Leopold realized with a dull shock, was Samuels—the detective they'd narrowly escaped in the Cash & Dash parking lot.

Not surprisingly, Samuels looked *pissed*.

"Jurisdiction, my ass," the cop holding the notepad answered with a swagger. "What division you with?"

"Hollywood," answered Samuels, he and Bullet-head quickly crossing the open ground.

"Bullshit. I worked Hollywood eight years—"

The Sunder detectives were pulling out their focusers. "Got our badges right here," Samuels said.

Leopold, meanwhile, had been racking his brain for an escape route and searching around frantically for anything that could be useful as a weapon.

His eyes met Isabel's.

In the brief distraction created by the detectives' sudden arrival, she'd lowered her arms and was starting to dip a hand into her cloak. They exchanged a look of shared understanding, then an almost imperceptible nod.

Notepad cop was now fumbling for his gun while the other barked into his radio. "We have a situation! Unknown individuals, possible weapon—"

There was a sharp crackle as the detectives' focusers brightened.

Twin bolts of blinding blue hit the slack cops, enveloping them in a tornado of incandescent particles. They juddered backward like malfunctioning windup toys, then collapsed.

"You!" Samuels boomed, stepping over the fallen cops with his partner. Richter had melted out of sight. "You're wanted on multiple violations of Sunder law! Code 806, illegal reentry into a veiled zone following official banishment. Code 507-A, exposing Sunder secrets to slacks. Code 653, suspected involvement in a magical explosion. And you!" His head snapped toward Isabel. "Code 1707, suspected possession of unregulated magical devices. And code 180, aiding and abetting a fugitive!"

Leopold gritted his teeth. He didn't particularly care if he had a rap sheet in Sunder, but Isabel had to live there. Despite her assurances to the contrary, it was clear he'd gotten her into seriously deep shit.

"We're authorized to bring you in using force if necessary," Bullethead was saying, the grin on Samuels's face telling them he'd enjoy nothing more.

The slack cops, meanwhile, writhed on the ground like sleepers in the grip of a nightmare. Leopold glimpsed Richter peeking out from behind a crypt in the distance. He hadn't fled—perhaps the sight of strange men threatening his son had activated some deeply held protective instinct—but finally, as the detectives raised their focusers at Leopold and Isabel, Richter turned and ran. The flicker of shame Leopold felt at the sight surprised him; he hadn't realized his opinion of his father could sink any lower.

Samuels ordered Leopold and Isabel to lie down face-first in the grass.

The two of them had been exchanging quick, tense glances ever since the Sunder police had appeared, but now Isabel gave Leopold the signal he'd been waiting for: a single, firm nod as she whipped a hand from her cloak, drew back her arm, and flung what looked like a small, blackened apple at the detectives.

Leopold sprang into motion, he and Isabel breaking into a run and sprinting around the rear of the crypt. A loud pop came from behind them, followed by violent coughing and cries of anger. Leopold looked back to see the crypt vanish in a cloud of whirling black dust.

"Befogger!" Isabel explained as they ran. "It's meant for use on slacks, so probably won't slow them down long—"

As if to illustrate her point, a bright blue spell-bolt shot past them and buried itself in the ground nearby, kicking up a fan of earth. "We just have to reach the Gower gate," Leopold said, his adrenaline surging as they curved into a new section of tombs. "Then we find that Metro station—"

"To Inglewood," Isabel readily agreed. "And Emmet."

Leopold felt such a swell of affection for her then, he wondered if it was the adrenaline, messing with his head.

A squadron of pigeons scattered before them. Picnickers on a blanket dove for cover behind a bush, one letting out a delayed scream as Leopold and Isabel ran by. Leopold felt the beginnings of relief, nursing a delicate hope that perhaps the befogger had been enough—

He and Isabel ducked reflexively as another cast streaked by, missing them by no more than a few feet. Leopold looked back to see the detectives chugging after them with grim determination, far behind but gaining. The befogger had bought them a small head start and covered the detectives in soot, but that seemed to be the extent of their injuries. More concerning, Isabel was beginning to flag, her breaths labored and her cheeks flushed.

Leopold hooked an arm through her elbow and pulled her along faster; she looked at him sharply, then gave a nod of thanks. He guided them to the left, away from any semblance of a path—and, Leopold hoped, out of the detectives' sight. They were coming into a section of comparatively humble crypts, and as the monuments shrank in size, so did the cover they would provide.

They shouldered through a gap in some hedges. "What else can we throw at them?" Leopold asked, holding back some branches for Isabel before they resumed running.

Isabel rummaged in her cloak, muttering with dissatisfaction as she dismissed several objects as useless against sparks. Finally, she pulled out a pair of cracked dice the color of strong tea.

"Take these," she said between gasps for breath. "They're curse deflectors. They won't work perfectly—the cops' magic is too strong—but it should screw up their aim a little."

Isabel brought the dice to her lips and seemed to whisper something before passing them to Leopold. As he shoved them into his pocket, he noted that they were covered now in frost. Isabel went back to rummaging, and they passed a small reflecting pond, startling an old man feeding ducks.

"My dazzler! Forgot I had this!" Isabel handed him a large glass eyeball. "It's already activated, so don't hang on to it long—"

Another bolt split the air beside them, this one so close it singed Leopold's arm, then hit a marble angel and knocked off a chunk of its wing. Angrily, Leopold turned and chucked the glass eye behind them.

"Don't look!" Isabel cried, turning him forward just as a series of brilliant white flashes lit up the tombstones and trees around them.

There was another scream from an unseen cluster of slacks, over which Leopold was pretty sure he heard Samuels shout, *You little shits!*

He and Isabel broke through more shrubs and came into a rolling expanse of low graves. Beyond it, screened by a line of towering palms, was the Gower gate. They ran by a clutch of tourists in socks and sandals, one turning to ask, "They shootin' a movie or some-thing?" just as another bolt whipped past and sent them scattering in terror.

The cast left a comet's tail of sparks scintillating overhead, then slammed into the line of palms. A man selling flowers screamed and ran as their frizzy tops burst into flame. Leopold's mind went briefly to the raccoon, the flaming sycamore tree, the unrecognizable life he'd been living just a few days ago. This startling reverie was broken by the staccato chop of a helicopter and a loudspeaker booming, "Clear the area! Police action in progress!"

The side of the chopper read LAPD.

Nearby, three slack cops were herding a tour group to safety. "Two officers down!" a voice crackled over one of their radios. "Unknown weapon!"

All hell was breaking loose.

"Just a little farther," Leopold encouraged Isabel, who was doing her best to keep pace. "Almost there—"

They passed beneath the palms and through a gentle curtain of fire, shredded, flaming fronds raining down surreally, then came to a halt on the other side. The gate just ahead of them—their only exit—was now blocked by LAPD patrol cars. Cops were standing guard nearby, hands at their holsters. Leopold suppressed a clawing panic that threatened, briefly, to paralyze him.

"Now what?" Isabel gasped. She was struggling for breath, ex-hausted from back-to-back sprints on top of her previous casts. Leo-pold worried he'd never be able to get her the help she needed if they couldn't even escape the cemetery—and now the only way out had been barricaded. There were no other gates nearby, no doors at all.

Which meant they would have to make their own exit.

"Isabel," he said. "Do you still have that limiknife?"

"Yeah," she replied. "Why?"

"I think I'm going to need it."

She hesitated for a beat, then nodded.

"Follow me," he said, steeling himself.

They ran along the line of flaming trees, away from the gate massing with cops and into a narrow lane crowded on both sides with tombs and monuments. Leopold needed to find an alternate path to the Gower wall, which was tantalizingly close but blocked by a hulking mausoleum that seemed to go on forever. After another sprint—or as close to a sprint as Isabel could muster—they reached the end of the mausoleum, then darted down a root-gnarled path that wove through a maze of leaning graves. Leopold spotted the wall over the tops of some tombs—they were no more than a stone's throw from it now—when they came to a gravedigger's shed, rakes and shovels leaned against the corrugated structure, and staggered to a halt.

They'd hit a dead end.

Leopold swore and turned them around again—only to find Bullet-head stepping out of a literal hole in the air, which zipped closed behind him as he raised his focuser.

"Hands up," the detective said, his measured tone belied by a voice that trembled with barely restrained rage. He nodded at Isabel. "Don't even think about touching that belt."

She and Leopold backed against the rakes and shovels, arms rising. There was nowhere left to run.

"You chose an appropriate place to dig your own graves," Bullet-head said as he stalked toward them. He was caked in soot, his face lacerated with angry red scratches, his uniform partially burned. "Assaulting an officer—multiple times, with illegal devices—not to mention exposing who knows how many slacks to our magic. You might've been able to wriggle out of the charges we had you on before, but now . . ."

He stopped a few feet away, a cruel smile expanding.

"Me and Samuels are gonna make sure they put you away for a long, long time. Consider it my personal mission. You know what they do to teenage criminals in Salton State?"

Leopold's voice was surprisingly steady when he said, "Go to hell."

Isabel offered up an additional, enthusiastic *fuck you*.

Bullet-head laughed ruefully, turning his gaze to Isabel. "You know what, you're right—I *should* start with you." He gestured to his face. "Your little toys gave me some fresh scars today. But don't worry," he said, adjusting his focuser. "Mine won't leave a mark. They'll just hurt like hell."

Leopold didn't realize he'd grabbed one of the nearby shovels until he was swinging it. Metal clanged as it connected with the cop's jaw, the crack of bone doubling with the crack and flash of his focuser.

Teeth and blood flew. Bullet-head went down. It all seemed to unfold in slow motion.

Only when Isabel screamed did Leopold realize he'd been injured. He looked down to see blood darkening his left arm, then dropped the shovel, going numb with shock.

Suddenly Isabel was shouting, asking if he was okay, could he still run. Leopold must have nodded. Pain shot through his arm as Isabel pulled him into a stumbling, lopsided dash back down the rutted path, the agony so profound it tunneled his vision. Whatever spell the detective had hit him with was gradually disconnecting his mind from his legs, so that he almost seemed to float through the blurring world. They rounded one corner, then another, Leopold only dimly aware of where they were going. Vaguely, he clocked Samuels in the periphery—then saw Isabel throw something egg-shaped at him that hatched in midair. In a flash, a squadron of screeching black birds were attacking Samuels, pecking and clawing as he screamed *Backup, we need backup* and thrashed at the birds with flailing arms.

Somehow, they reached the wall.

Leopold sagged against it and sank to the ground while Isabel dug frantically in her cloak.

"Don't go to sleep," she said, hands shaking as she worked something out of the holster at her waist. "Just hang on—You're going to be fine—"

She was uncorking the vial of black liquid.

"No," he gasped, his words slurring, "you need that—"

He cried out as she shook its last drops onto his wounded arm. The agony suddenly intensified, black spots blooming before him, and then the pain halved—and halved again. After a moment, it had diminished such that he could sit up.

"You shouldn't have," he managed. "I—"

"Would've been in a coma in another minute." She looked him over, eyes narrowed with concern. "You need a doctor, but that should hold you for now."

"Thank you." He nodded, feeling both his strength and urgency return in equal measure.

Isabel slumped against the wall beside him. He could see that this last push had brought her to the brink; now she looked obliterated. He had to get her out of here. Leopold reached for her belt and drew the limiknife carefully from its sheath. When Isabel made no protest, he knew she was suffering even more than she let on.

He took a breath and studied the blade, which shone in the flat noonday sun.

It made infinitely more sense for Isabel to be the one to wield it:

She was practically an artist with the limiknife, while Leopold barely qualified as an amateur. But Isabel was badly weakened, her Aether reserves tapped. He'd have to rise to the occasion—for Isabel's sake, and for Emmet's.

Gripping the knife in his good hand, Leopold staggered upright and plunged it into the smooth concrete wall.

It sank quickly to the hilt.

Clenching his jaw with the effort, he dragged it slowly downward until, faintly, a gleam of light shone through from the other side. Aether and concrete dust puffed from the lengthening gap as scenes from Gower Street began to appear through a thick, cottony webbing: passing traffic, the odd pedestrian, the bold neon letters of the Astroburger sign.

After a minute, the air sparkled with Aether and the hole was nearly large enough to wriggle through.

"LARRY BERRY!"

Leopold froze, then spun around. At the end of the alley of tombs stood the two detectives: bloody, angry, eyes afire.

There was no warning before twin bolts slammed the wall near Leopold. The force of the blast launched him sideways into a crypt. His skull connected with stone and he fell to the ground. Somehow, he clung to consciousness, lifting his pounding head to look for Isabel—who was getting to her feet, seemingly unhurt.

The two men laughed as they adjusted their focusers.

Leopold tried to get his legs under him, then to stand. He was rewarded with an agonizing jolt of pain that unfocused his vision—until he saw something that snapped everything into laser-sharp clarity.

Isabel.

Torn butcher paper fell away from her hands. She'd unwrapped the mystery package Jae had given her at the Cash & Dash; now she gripped a small, plastic circle. It looked like a toy you'd win from a claw machine on the Santa Monica Pier.

Leopold knew better.

Crappy though it might've been, a focuser was a focuser—and he'd promised Norm he wouldn't let her cast.

"Isabel, *don't*—" he cried.

A thunderclap rattled the tombs.

Two blue bolts tore through the air toward Isabel. A ball of green fire answered, rocketing out of her small focuser, the force of it throwing her back against the wall.

Isabel's cast blackened the grass beneath it as it flew, then collided with the detectives' bolts in midair, creating a burst of light and a small shockwave that knocked both men to the ground.

Leopold was stunned. Even with a cheap plastic focuser, Isabel was truly powerful.

Dazed and spent, all color drained from her face, she slid down the wall. Not only had she cast another spell, she'd used the last of her healing liquid on *him*. Leopold tried to rise, to reach her, but his spinning head and trembling legs betrayed him as he nearly blacked out, sinking back into the puddle of blood that spread steadily beneath him.

There was another violent rumble. He looked up at the sound.

The bolts were returning.

The detectives' casts had overwhelmed Isabel's and somehow combined with it, and now the gathered force of all three was speeding back in her direction: two blue bolts and one green, woven together and writhing like a knot of electric eels, throwing off sparks as they went.

Isabel's eyes widened in horror.

One bolt probably wouldn't have been lethal. The effects of two would've been terrifying. The collective power of three, however, seemed likely to kill.

And this braided power was heading straight for her.

All else dimmed. Suddenly there was only Isabel, only the sound of blood pumping in Leopold's ears. He watched Isabel try to move, but it was clear she had nothing left; in fact, it seemed a miracle she could keep her chin up long enough to face death head-on as it approached. She looked almost regal then, her cloak pooled around her like a dark green shadow, her black hair sparkling with Aether dust.

Leopold knew he was a nobody. He wasn't a channeler. He wasn't chosen. No one had ever chosen him for anything, and somehow he'd allowed this to define him. He realized then, with a sobering rush of clarity, that he'd been waiting his whole life for permission to be somebody. To do something important.

He was done waiting.

It was strange, how this simple decision seemed to inject fire into his veins. Where before he couldn't move, suddenly he was standing. And then he was running.

"Leopold!" Isabel screamed. *"NO—"*

He launched himself at her, pushing her out of the way just as a green flare filled his peripheral vision and a sudden, searing pain exploded through his sternum. Leopold cried out, fists clenching as he lifted his head toward the fire.

The bolt had struck him dead center in the chest.

He was blinded, then consumed by a heat so furious it felt like he wasn't merely on fire—he'd *become* fire. And just as he was certain this strange agony was the last sensation he'd ever experience, he realized the heat was emanating from within him. The object on his chest had absorbed the bolt with a mighty, excruciating burn—and then, in a flash, the heat was gone.

He felt as if he'd been hollowed out.

Leopold collapsed, his knees hitting dirt as Isabel struggled to her feet, the world darkening as he fell, with a dull thud, onto his side. He blinked desperately through a smear of black, blood seeping from his lips, his body consumed by pain—but when, finally, he saw her standing, he felt nothing but relief.

Leopold Berry might've been a disappointment to the world, but he'd never again be a disappointment to himself.

≡ EPILOGUE

Leopold awoke in fragments, his body a heavy, alien thing made of stone. He ached everywhere, but his awareness of the pain seemed to occupy some distant chamber of his mind. He heard the familiar metronomic beep of health monitors. Shoes tapping a hard floor. Presences, felt more than seen, hovering around him. Muttering voices that faded in and out, traces of a vanishing dream. He strained to decipher more than snippets—

hell of a mess

take weeks to fix everything

never seen the boss so excited

—but their words kept slipping away.

His eyes split open to gauzy layers of sterile white: rough white sheets pulled up to his armpits, a white curtain screening much of the room from view, a nurse in white blinking down at him through a thick lens. Then a soft glow of pinkish dusklight, rays whispering through an otherwise darkened window as hazy figures passed back and forth.

Leopold slid a trembling hand to his chest beneath the sheets. The cold metal ring occupied the same space it always did. Further inspection revealed a bandage wrapping his left bicep and a plastic IV dripping some dark but gently shimmering solution into his vein.

Somewhat belatedly, it occurred to Leopold that he had survived. That he was in a hospital—a hospital in Sunder, apparently—and the force of the braided bolt had not, in fact, torn a hole through him.

Instead, somehow—

Was it possible the object had saved his life?

The room faded out. When he woke again, he found he could turn his head slightly, enough to discover the source of the muttering voices. Below a muted TV bolted into a corner, a frizzy-haired man stood talking to a compact woman. He felt some slight relief at the familiar faces. One was Norm, pacing a narrow path in a D.A.R.E. T-shirt and fleece pajama pants. The other was Executive Ramirez.

Gradually, their words became clearer.

"A Sunder PD unit brought them in," Executive Ramirez was saying. "Mister Berry and Miss Alvarez put up quite a fight against two of our officers, they tell me, and caused a huge amount of trouble—which is why they had to call in an entire squad. Nothing the Department couldn't handle, of course," she added briskly, "though we're still in the process of cleaning it up—memory revising all the slacks who witnessed the incident—the crowds, a number of LAPD officers—"

Leopold's eyes fell closed, though he kept listening.

"The kids aren't being charged, are they?" Norm asked apprehensively. "After what those cops did—I mean, talk about excessive force—"

"That remains to be seen. For now, Miss Alvarez and Mister Berry are under observation. Fortunately, once the object on Mister Berry's chest was discovered, the matter was referred directly to me. He put on quite a show, I hear. Our officers were gobsmacked. They say they've never seen anything like it. From what I've heard and from what you've been able to tell me, this object will be of great interest to the Department."

"Sure, yeah." Norm sounded uneasy. "I would've reached out sooner, you know, but we only just discovered it—"

"It's all right. I'm sure you had no idea of its importance."

"Uh." Leopold could almost hear Norm swallowing his pride. "Right."

There was a brief, awkward silence.

"Oh, hey," said Norm, snapping his fingers. "What about Leopold's compadre?"

"We've contacted our best memory specialists. They should be able to clear up Mister Worthington's faulty revision by tomorrow morning at the latest. Now, if you'll excuse me, I'm late for a press conference."

Her heels clicked past the bed and out of the room. A moment later, Leopold heard Norm's husky rasp beside him, then felt a heavy hand on his arm.

"Hey, Lunchtray," said Norm. "I saw you move a minute ago. You awake?"

Leopold forced his eyes open. Norm was looking down at him with a crinkly grin.

"Hi," Leopold croaked.

Norm's smile expanded. "How're you feeling?"

"Like shit."

"Totally understandable under the present circumstances."

"Where am I?" Leopold asked, his voice shaky.

"Cedars. Sundered wing. Been here about thirty-six hours."

Leopold tried to move and regretted it immediately. "Why am I not in jail?" he asked. "Or dead?"

"Those are two really good questions, little dude." Norm's eyes hardened a little. "That's what I'm trying to figure out, too."

Leopold felt a twinge of fear in response, but he only nodded. "Where's Emmet?"

"Right over there," said Norm, gesturing to the opposite corner. After a painful turn of his head, Leopold was overwhelmed with relief to discover Emmet on a hard sofa, knees drawn up and head buried in a book, still wearing his homemade paladin costume. It was a sight so unexpected and welcome that Leopold surprised himself by laughing out loud, the action making him wince.

Emmet looked up at the sound, blinking owlishly. "Oh, hey, Larry," he said casually, then went back to his reading. He took a pencil from behind his ear, scribbled something in the book, and let out a triumphant little *yes!* before tossing it aside. Immediately he reached down to grab another from a pile on the floor. There must've been twenty or thirty, surrounded by a sea of scribbled-on papers.

Leopold felt his relief waning.

Emmet was muttering to himself as he flipped the new book open and readied his pencil, an intense, hyper-focused expression on his face. Leopold hadn't expected Emmet's condition to miraculously improve on its own, but he seemed to be acting even weirder than before.

"He's been like this since they brought him in yesterday," Norm explained, answering Leopold's unspoken question. "He's been asking for puzzles—it's all he wants to do—so we got him a ton of puzzle books. He hardly stops to eat."

"Since who brought him in?" Leopold asked sharply.

"The cops. Isabel refused to leave the cemetery until Sunder PD promised to go get him. She knew exactly where to find him—some funeral home in Inglewood."

Leopold's chest tightened as he pictured Isabel, physically ill and hardly able to stand, arguing with a gang of angry cops about the safety of a kid she'd only just met.

She was like no one Leopold had ever known before.

"Cops brought him here so we could keep an eye on him," Norm was saying. "Until the revisionists come to fix him up. They're sending their top people this time, so says Ramirez, instead of the idiots who botched the job in the first place."

Finally, Leopold exhaled.

The fact that the very organization responsible for breaking Emmet's brain was now tasked with its repair was a worry he didn't have the capacity to grapple with at the moment. But at least there was hope.

"Where's Isabel?" he asked. "Is she okay?"

Norm shifted his weight. "She's down the hall in another room, asleep. Got some recovering to do herself. Casting all those spells did a number on her—but she was lucky." He sighed. "She'll be all right."

"Thank God," Leopold said quietly.

"You should get more sleep, too, little dude. Doctor said that's the best thing for you. That and, you know, a shitload of healing spells." He rolled his eyes a little. "I've been trying to get them to let me bring you some of my homemade Aether bread, but they have idiotic rules here."

Then he patted Leopold's arm, flashed another craggy smile, and excused himself to go check on Isabel. Emmet was still lost in his puzzle books, *hmm*ing into their pages as he chewed his pencil. The muted TV was showing an infomercial for some kind of potion blender, its two familiar-looking hosts yammering silently as they poured broken glass and green liquid into its jar.

Leopold didn't want to sleep. His mind was restless. He wanted to sit up, to think. To untangle, perhaps, some of the ever-accumulating mysteries that dogged him. After a minute of minor agony he managed to ladder his back up against the pillows, but the effort exhausted him to such an extent that, within another minute, he found he could no longer keep his eyes open.

Gradually, he slipped into twilight.

He didn't know how long he'd been asleep when a strange, slightly painful sensation tugged him fully awake. He opened his eyes to find that the sheet had fallen away from his shoulders, exposing the object on his chest. Weirder: Emmet was leaning over him, actively messing with it.

"What the hell?" Leopold said sharply, trying to move out of reach. "Emmet, what are you—"

"Stop squirming." Emmet's eyes were locked on the object. "I'm doing a puzzle."

"It's not a puzzle— *Ow!* Cut it out—"

"Wait, I've almost got it—just one more click—"

With a sudden, painful twinge, the object detached from Leopold's chest. Emmet held it up with a victorious smile. "*Cool!* You got any more of these?"

Leopold gaped at him. "How'd you do that?"

"Well," Emmet started to explain, but then he sucked in a breath and winced—"Ah, it's *hot*"—then bobbled the object and dropped it.

Leopold's hands shot out to catch it.

The object spun as it fell, tumbling in what seemed to Leopold like slow motion. It flashed brightly, then appeared to shrink in midair.

What landed in Leopold's hands was not the same object that had occupied his chest for the past few days. Now a tenth of its former size, it could no longer be confused for a focuser. It had no glass anymore, no lens, no aperture markings around the circumference of its golden rim.

It had come to rest in his open palm, against the ridge of his old, moon-shaped scars.

"Whoa, it's a ring," Emmet said in a hushed voice.

Leopold felt as if he'd floated free of his body. As if he were watching himself, and the whole strange scene, from above.

He tipped the ring into what weak light shone from the ceiling. Inset into the interior of the gold band was a small green gemstone. The moment it changed shape, Leopold had guessed instinctively what it was—but now he knew beyond a doubt. This was the prize his mother had so desperately wanted him to find. The powerful, mysterious object forged from ancient, arcane magic. The thing that had, in all likelihood, saved his life.

It was his father's wedding ring.